Oth

Linda Nagata

Mythic Island Press LLC
www.MythicIslandPress.com

PACIFIC STORM

LINDA NAGATA

Mythic Island Press LLC
Kula, Hawaii

Pacific Storm

Copyright © 2020 by Linda Nagata

First edition: October 2020

ISBN 978-1-937197-33-9

Cover art by Bukovero.com
Cover art copyright © 2020 by Mythic Island Press LLC

Mythic Island Press LLC
P.O. Box 1293
Kula, HI 96790-1293
MythicIslandPress.com

PACIFIC STORM

chapter

1

IT WAS EARLY December, two-fifteen AM, and the chill of KCA Security's operations center had sunk into Ava Arnett's bones. She stood at the observation window, forty-nine stories above the beach, hands resting in the pockets of a quilted vest—non-regulation, but an essential defense against the room's unchanging climate.

Adapt or die—or find an excuse to get outside again.

Beyond the glass, the night air stewed, sticky and warm, unseasonable weather even for Honolulu—because a monster was on the way. The heavy, humid air, its exhalation.

Behind Ava, a chair creaked in the near-dark. Fingers pattered a faint arrhythmic beat against a computer screen, and the dispatcher softly murmured to an officer on patrol, "Stay strong, Sugar. We're not at the hard part yet. You know it's gonna be crazy-town, the next few days."

An unwanted burst of adrenaline—signature of lurking anxiety—sent Ava's heart into a flurry of shallow beats. Without turning around, she murmured, "*That* is the understatement of the year."

Out of habit, she conjured a scene in her head: A brief dancing flame, a lit cigarette, its dry feel between her lips and the burning taste of tobacco smoke—a drug that both soothed and sharpened the mind. Ava had never smoked in her life, but the mental exercise stymied the rise of real memories she did not wish to revisit and, like the action heroes in century-old movies, it let her bleed off her anxieties in a long, soft exhale of imagined smoke.

With Hurricane Huko churning ever closer, faithfully following its predicted path, everyone needed some means of coping—especially when the memory of round one remained so raw.

Just nine years ago Hurricane Nolo had come up out of the south. The Category 5 storm had hit the island of Oʻahu like a slow-motion bomb, decimating Honolulu. Its 215 mile-per-hour winds had shredded tens of thousands of family homes and stripped the city's towers, tearing away their glass facings and purging their interiors. The storm surge had washed away coastal neighborhoods, redistributed toxic chemicals, and caused the collapse of highways and underground utility tunnels. But the massive rainfall was worse. As the storm churned north across the island, ridge-top neighborhoods had their foundations washed out from under them, and the densely populated valleys were swept with landslides and apocalyptic floods. Even now, much of the city remained abandoned, inhabited only by ghosts.

But not Waikīkī.

Half a trillion dollars of Chinese capital had gone into reimagining the famous coastline and in restoring it as an economic engine of tourism. Ava's worried gaze wandered protectively over the result: an expanded shore, built on reclaimed land, fortified against the rising sea level, and designed to be resilient in storms. So different from before and yet still beautiful, still capable of rousing her sense of wonder.

All along the former oceanfront, hotels that had survived Nolo had been refurbished, others had been newly built, but they no longer stood at the ocean's edge. Instead, they faced an earthwork reaching eighteen feet above sea level. Grassed over, planted with tropical vegetation, its wide, flat surface served as an esplanade marking the inland edge of Kahanamoku Coastal Park. Footlights illuminated the path in gold and red holiday colors.

Beyond the esplanade, clusters of coconut palms shaded a long, inland beach—a sheltered strip of sand that embraced a chain of artificial lagoons, their waters black and glassy at this hour, undisturbed by swimmers, and reflecting the gleaming lights of the hotel towers.

An embankment of tall dunes stood beyond the lagoons, their slopes stabilized by waist-high, salt-tolerant grasses, silvered by moonlight and nodding in imitation of ocean waves under the stroke of a restless night breeze. Softly lit tiled paths wound between the dunes, and out, to a wide, reconstructed beach, and the open ocean beyond. Ava watched two night surfers, tiny with distance, making their way back to the hotels with boards tucked under their arms.

Sealed as she was within thick glass walls, she could not hear the surf, but the foaming lines of breakers were bright with both reflected moonlight and a white glow generated by the pummeled carcasses of bioluminescent jellyfish.

Equally luminous, but more colorful—pink, green, blue, yellow—sea serpents up to six feet long fed on the doomed jellies, their limbless bodies gliding in sinuous threads just beneath the ocean's surface. By design, the engineered creatures ignored the pod of twenty or so surfers sitting their boards beyond the break. Most of the surfers wore rash guards made to glow like the sea serpents. As a new swell rolled in, three moved to catch the wave.

Farther out, appearing and disappearing between the swells, a tiny but intense green beacon marked the position of DeCoite's patrol boat.

Officer DeCoite, unhappy with his current assignment, insisted on sharing with Ava his heartfelt concerns over his future fertility. His gruff voice reiterated his main point through her earbud: "It's not just debris out of the Pacific garbage patch, Ava. It is *ra-di-o-ac-tive*." Each syllable pronounced separately to ensure she grasped the true hazard of his situation.

Ocean currents occasionally carried debris from the Mischief Reef incident into Hawaiian waters. KCA Security's ocean patrol existed in part as a last line of defense to ensure none of it ever washed ashore.

"You wearing your hazmat suit?" Ava asked, conscious of the faint pressure of her tactile mic. It lay firmly against her cheek, a thin transparent wand curving from earbud to chin, monitoring the muscular activity of speech, its software mapping that to her audible words.

"You know it," DeCoite affirmed.

"So you're good."

Ava held the rank of shift captain in Kahanamoku Coastal Authority's limited hierarchy. Duties rotated among the four KCA patrol officers she supervised on the nightshift. DeCoite had been in the boat when a buoy alarm went off. So he'd caught the assignment—roping the debris, preventing it from being carried any closer to shore.

"If I gotta wait here any longer," he groused, "I am never going to be a father again."

"The navy is responding, Doug. Current ETA, fourteen minutes." She could see the silhouette of a patrol ship to the west, either the *Makani* or the *Ho'olua*, on its way from Pearl Harbor. "And anyway, you got three kids already."

"Need more than that," he growled, "to make up for what we lost . . . what we're about to lose."

A tightness in her chest. Another flurry of heartbeats. "No, brother. We're ready this time."

She had meant to sound confident, but she wasn't good at faking it.

Hurricane Huko had popped up out of season, spawned from summer's lingering heat just two days before, but winding up rapidly toward Category 5 status. Its predicted track had it taking a turn to the north, with a high probability of a second direct strike against O'ahu's already-shattered southern shore.

In the sky out over the ocean, a new light came into sight every few minutes. Another passenger jet, come to evacuate the tourist district and to spirit away the handful of island residents who had the money for a last-minute ticket out. Ava's ex had called from Spokane, begging her to get on a plane, "for the girls' sake."

"Not possible," she'd told him. "If I step out on my duty, I won't have a job when I get back." That was true—and a pointed reminder that the money she transferred to him every week kept him, their two daughters, and his new wife in better circumstances than he could afford with universal basic income alone.

An alarm pulsed, soft at first, but louder with each successive beat.

Ava turned to look down past a railing into the operations center's circular well, where screens displayed a curated selection of videos gathered from the park's omnipresent security cameras. At this hour, half the desks were empty. Staff consisted of only Joni, the dispatcher, two communications specialists, and a solitary researcher who sat transfixed, her youthful face illuminated by the subdued light of her screen as she announced, "EP4 at the Ala Wai gate."

Joni whistled softly.

"*Another one?*" Ava asked in disbelief.

"This is what?" one of the specialists demanded. "The third EP4 in nine days?"

"Number three," Ava confirmed—and all on her watch.

"He just stepped aboard a streetcar," Tammy, the researcher, reported. "And the streetcar is underway. No transit officer at this hour. He's alone. Status is red, on the prowl."

Ava grabbed the rails of a rapid access ladder and slid down into the well, the situation feeling weirdly routine.

Tammy continued to recite details: "Name of Expected Perpetrator is Robert Bell. Age forty-three. Island resident. Former real estate agent. Now basic income only. No current occupation. Estranged from family. Accusations lodged against him include sexual assault, battery, cruelty to animals. No convictions, but a minus twelve social rating in his assigned village."

No doubt Robert had been a nasty piece of work even before Nolo blew his life out from under him.

Ava shed her non-regulation vest, dropping it on her chair at the captain's desk while scrutinizing Robert Bell onscreen. A live feed from one of the streetcar's surveillance cameras showed him standing on the running board, one large hand clenched around a pole as the car rolled silently east past Fort DeRussy Park. A tall man, six two, a little overweight, graying hair neatly trimmed.

He'd come dressed in the local standard—aloha shirt, khaki shorts, and leather sandals. Nothing overt in his appearance to suggest a violent nature. Just hints: a slow twitch in his lips, and a sense of tension around eyes obscured by the lens glow of his rimless smart glasses.

"Have we seen him before?" Ava asked. "Maybe as an EP2 or 3?"

Like the FBI, Homeland Security, the US military, and hundreds of local law enforcement agencies including the Honolulu Police Department, KCA Security used the AI-driven HADAFA system to identify Expected Perpetrators. The acronym stood for Human Algorithmic Decryption And Forward Analysis. HADAFA kept a profile on everyone. It used a subject's background, medical history, behavioral quirks, media preferences, social media activity, location data, Chinese social rating, and any other information it could scrape from the cloud to interpret behavior and predict a propensity to commit a crime—both in the immediate future, and over the long term. The baseline EP tag wasn't uncommon. But EP4? That was rare.

Ava knew the names of every EP4 who had ever entered the park, and Robert Bell was not among them—though maybe he'd graduated. A propensity for violence could increase over time.

"We have not seen Mr. Bell before," Tammy reported. "First time in our jurisdiction—but it looks like he knows where he's going."

Just like the other two . . .

Both prior EP4s had quickly closed in on their intended victims: melancholy women lingering in dark, unsurveilled areas among the dunes as if they knew someone would come, as if they'd made an appointment with fate.

Not on my watch.

Ava's officers had moved in quickly, confronting the EPs before they could carry out an assault.

But no crime meant no arrest, no interrogation, no clue what was driving this unsettling new game.

Ava opened a cubby, retrieving her duty belt.

"Joni, I want you to give everyone a heads-up," she instructed the dispatcher. "When he gets off the streetcar, have our two closest officers move in." A moment of hesitation, of reconsideration. "Have them move in, but do not intercept. I want them to stay out of sight. Take no action unless the crime is imminent. I'll be on-scene in a couple of minutes."

"Yes, ma'am," Joni said, a doubtful note in her crisp voice. But she repeated the instructions.

Ava strapped on her duty belt—a lime-green engineering marvel that held a two-round shockgun, four additional rounds, a folding knife, zipties, flashlight, disposable gloves, spray paint, do-not-cross tape, a canister of red smoke, and another of disinfectant. The belt's color suggested fire trucks and heroic first responders. That was the theory. And it made a bold contrast to KCA Security's all-black uniform.

The lightweight uniform was designed for sun protection in hot and humid oceanside conditions. It consisted of a long-sleeve athletic shirt with name, badge, and rank insignia embedded in the textile weave, knee-length cargo shorts, and high-top athletic shoes made of a fine mesh that resisted sand but drained water. All of it black—even the thin rim of the smart glasses she'd pushed up on her head so that they held her short golden-brown hair away from her face—because black stood out among the light colors and bright tropicals most tourists wore.

Ava liked the way the uniform provided camouflage at night.

She spoke to the specialists. "Forward me a list of potential victims in the path of this freak, especially anyone who's disappeared into an unsurveilled area."

"You got it, Ava."

She strode across the well to the open elevator door, where a four-foot-tall artificial Christmas tree stood sentinel, placed there by dayshift only a day before. The soft, steady glow of its LED lights ignited sparks of guilt in her mind. She'd be working through the holidays this year and wouldn't get to see her daughters. But she'd sent their gifts.

Stepping aboard the elevator, Ava pulled her smart glasses

down over her eyes, activating them. "DeCoite," she said as the doors closed. The comms system registered the name, automatically linking her to the officer.

"Yes, ma'am?"

"Notify me when the navy takes over."

"Oh, you'll be able to tell, Ava. I'll be glowing green as a sea serpent by then."

2

KAHANAMOKU COASTAL AUTHORITY'S security division occupied the forty-eighth and forty-ninth floors of the Pacific Heritage Sea Tower. During standard work hours, visitors could use the hotel's guest elevators to reach KCA's reception desk on the forty-eighth floor. But security personnel had the use of an express service elevator, out of sight of the public eye. It let Ava descend uninterrupted, at ear-popping speed, to KCA's second-floor ready room.

There, glass doors allowed a one-way view outside onto an authorized-personnel-only deck bordered in waist-high planters holding colorful low-growing lantana. A short gated bridge linked the deck to the public esplanade, where a trio of young men wandered by on the tiled path.

Ava eyed them through her smart glasses. HADAFA tagged them as harmless, but she studied them for an extra second anyway, compiling her own profile based on appearance and mannerisms. They were lithe and trim, but not in the taut, coiled, contained manner of young soldiers. No, these were civilians with money to spend, dressed for a night out in voluminous slacks and tight-fitting, subtly glittering tank-tops scaled like reptile skins. Faint lines of luminous paint shone in their hair. Chinese, she guessed. Possibly Korean. They swayed a bit as they ambled on the path, looking like they'd reached the end of their evening.

Harmless, Ava decided, agreeing with HADAFA's assessment.

She moved on to the locker labeled *Arnett*. A quick biometric scan, and it opened. She retrieved her helmet, strapped it on, then turned to the charging rack where nine small electric motor-cycles waited, green-lit. Taking the nearest, she mounted up and switched it on.

"Dispatch, give me an update."

Joni responded immediately: "The EP4 is still alone on the streetcar. Passing the Hotel Taipingyang as we speak."

At this hour, with few passengers to pick up, the streetcar could roll through most of its stops and make good time. Robert Bell had already penetrated deep into the district. Another minute, and he'd pass the Pacific Heritage Sea Tower.

Ava looked forward to meeting him.

She rolled the motorcycle, triggering the glass doors to open. The movement startled one of the glamour boys. He looked back as she exited into air thick with humidity and laden with the crisp scent of salt spray cast up by the roaring surf.

"Hey, cop!" he called out in a whiskey-roughened Chinese accent. "You take good care of this Chinese property, yeah? We have big plans for when we come back after the storm."

By interacting with her, he'd waived his right to privacy. HADAFA responded by whispering to her his identity in the gentle masculine voice she'd chosen for it: "Subject is Zhang Zhengying. Chinese passport, age twenty-eight, materials scientist with Shanghai Industrial Nanosystems, social rating +14."

A high-flying asshole, then. But he wasn't wrong.

After Hurricane Nolo, when the faltering US federal government had failed to release disaster aid, a Chinese consortium stepped in, providing permanent housing for tens of thousands of displaced residents, with mortgage payments not to exceed seventy-five percent of a household's universal basic income—the monthly federal stipend paid out to every legal American citizen. The only requirement: residents had to abide by a good-citizen agreement that enrolled them in the social rating system.

That was the first stage in an ongoing takeover. Stage two had come with the restoration of Waikīkī. And the completion of stage three was imminent. Despite bitter protest, the cabal of oligarchs known as the Venturist party—presently in power in Washington—had pushed a deal to cede the island in a ninety-nine year lease, in exchange for debt relief and the lifting of economic sanctions imposed against the United States.

Venturist propaganda made Ava seethe: *We have no choice but to cut our losses and focus on the heartland of real America!* Fuckers.

It was of course coincidence—and not divine judgment—that Hurricane Huko had spawned on the opening day of a conference meant to culminate in a signing ceremony that would ratify the handover treaty.

The gate opened for Ava. She crossed the little bridge, stopping just short of the esplanade. Silently, subtly, she mouthed a question: *Dispatch, where am I going?*

The subvocalized query generated faint neuromuscular signals that her tactile mic picked up and interpreted. A synthesized version of her voice echoed the question in her earbud.

Joni answered, "Stand by."

Got it, Ava acknowledged.

The mic activated when it picked up a trigger word or phrase. Ava could get away with thinking *Hurry the hell up*, confident the sentiment would not be relayed to the operations center.

Her impatient gaze tracked the trio of young men as they strolled off toward the Hotel Taipingyang. She wondered if Huko's looming presence would delay the signing ceremony. Some small part of her *wanted* to see the storm strip the value from the pending lease, because maybe then, the Chinese would back out of the deal in a last-minute move to cut *their* losses.

But that wasn't likely. Not for a people capable of thinking in the long term. And the hardship Huko could cause to everyone still left in and around the city was incalculable.

Joni checked back in. "Our EP4 is on the ground. Disembarked outside the Imperial."

"Got it," Ava said, speaking aloud this time.

On the east side of Waikīkī, the Kalakaua Avenue pedestrian mall had been re-routed to pass behind a string of new hotels—the Imperial Garden among them—a planning decision that had granted them the coveted lagoon-front status.

Ava rolled onto the esplanade with her headlight off. She could do nothing to stop the handover, but she could at least interfere with Robert Bell's night out.

She turned her motorcycle toward Diamond Head, opposite to the direction the young men had taken. On this stretch of coast, the points of the compass were rarely used to give directions. Instead, Diamond Head and Ewa substituted for east and west. Mauka meant toward the mountains, and makai toward the sea.

Ava moved out slowly along the empty path, determined to allow Robert Bell time to reveal his destination. Footlights lit the way with seasonal splashes of red and gold, while overhead, moonlight filtered through the canopies of trees—all regrown from stumps salvaged out of city neighborhoods abandoned after Nolo.

On her left—below the esplanade and just past the Pacific Heritage—lay the sprawling festival grounds, where the famous Duke Kahanamoku statue still stood. Post-Nolo, the statue had been recovered from the debris, refurbished and resurrected so the Duke, native Hawaiian ambassador of the sport of surfing, again welcomed visitors to Waikīkī. On Ava's right-hand side, at hundred-yard intervals, narrow pedestrian ramps angled down to the lagoons. Each ramp served as the start of a path that meandered through the dunes and out to the beach, occasionally intersecting. The paths were named for coastal plant species: Niu, Hala, Pōhuehue . . .

Joni said, "EP has skirted the Imperial. Now entering the public access alley."

From this, Ava surmised that Robert Bell did not mean to hunt on hotel grounds. Through the alley, he could access the coastal park without encountering any questions from hotel staff.

"Who's on scene?" Ava asked.

"Akasha's coming up from the beach. Mike's on foot, a few minutes behind you."

"Good."

Joni said, "Robert Bell is walking like he's late for a date. Crossing the esplanade now."

"Kīpūkai ramp?"

"Looks like. *Yes.* You better get up there."

Despite Joni's urging, Ava held back. She couldn't arrest Robert Bell because he *intended* to commit a crime. Even an EP had legal rights.

She mouthed the trigger phrase, *Formal request.* And then added: *Time?*

The system answered: "Two thirty-four AM."

A predator in search of elusive prey moves slowly, stealthily. But Robert Bell moved with a swift certainty that assured Ava he knew where he was going, and he knew when he had to be there. A two-thirty meet up? Let the victim arrive first . . .

Ava's own presence on-scene had to be precisely timed.

Now Tammy's voice spoke in Ava's earbud: "I think I've found the EP's target. A solitary female entered UA-34 fourteen minutes ago. She has not exited."

"Thanks, Tammy."

Ava slowed as she approached Kīpūkai ramp. Lingering in the shadow of an arbor draped in broad-leafed hao, she gazed past the lagoon below, to the dune path, looking for Robert Bell, but he was already out of sight.

She moved to follow, speeding down the ramp. At the bottom, she put one booted foot down, pivoting against it to make the hard turn toward Kīpūkai Bridge.

The susurration of the bike's tires shifted as she left the tiled path for the faux-wood planking of the low bridge. Below her, the dark lagoon rippled with the flirtations of a lone couple who reacted to her presence with a sharp gasp and nervous giggles.

A light breeze set palm fronds rattling as she left the bridge, creating a coarse white noise that swiftly transitioned into the sinistrous hiss and rustle of wind-stirred dune grass. In another hour, maintenance bots would emerge to noisily blow spilled sand off the path and reshape the slopes, erasing any evidence of footprints. Now though, she heard only the wind's hiss and the muffled roar of the surf—but in the winding, sound-channeling labyrinth of the dunes that was noise enough to cover even a shrill scream.

Joni spoke, tension in her voice as she said, "The EP has moved off the main path toward UA-34."

Got it.

UA—short for Unsurveilled Area—designated a pocket of privacy, demanded by popular opinion. Even so, "unsurveilled" was a conditional statement. Though no KCA ground cameras or low-flying drones were permitted in the UAs, eyes in the sky remained. Five hundred feet above the tallest antenna on the tallest coastal tower, an autonomous solar-powered surveillance plane flew a continuous patrol, returning to ground only when forced to by storm winds.

"Okay," Joni said. "Mr. Bell has stopped. He's holding a position behind the not-allowed sign. But you need to get in there, Ava, before she gets hurt."

"I'm on it. Is Akasha ready?"

The young officer had earned Ava's trust since her transfer to nightshift less than three months ago. She'd proven herself fearless and reliable, equally capable of persuading a grieving old gentleman to step back from a suicide leap, and of taking down a raging drunk twice her size.

Joni said, "Akasha just reached the intersection."

Ava rounded a curve and saw her, sitting astride a bike. At five-foot eight, Akasha had some height and the muscle to go with it. Her ancestry was mixed, but her round face reflected more of her Asian than her Hawaiian or her European heritage. She wore her long black hair wound tight in a service bun.

Ava rode up beside her, bringing her bike to a hard stop, letting the back tire fish-tail across the sandy path.

Lens-glow from Akasha's smart glasses hid her eyes, but the hard set of her mouth suggested an imminent retribution—an expression that had intimidated many would-be belligerents. "Looks like the target victim is another Chinese princess," she said to Ava.

"Yes, and I want an arrest this time."

"So we let it play out?"

"Just far enough that we can charge him with a crime," Ava said.

A quirked eyebrow. "You think someone's setting up these assaults."

Not a question.

Ava dropped the bike's kickstand and dismounted. "We need to time this perfectly. Let's go."

They loped down the path into the UA, their footfalls soft, stealthy, quieter than the tire noise their bikes would have made. Unsurveilled Areas were cul-de-sacs. One way in, one way out, with a little paved court, two palm-thatched gazebos, and no artificial lighting.

Silence enfolded them as the slopes cut off the wind and the surf's basso roar.

"He's moving again," Joni warned. "Going slow, but he's crossing the court, closing on the gazebo."

"We're right behind him."

Thirty feet in, the path hooked around a stabilizing wall that anchored the dune's sandy slope. Ava raised a hand, signaling Akasha to move into the waist-high grass. Stooped low, they resumed their advance.

Now Ava could see Robert Bell. Her smart glasses tagged him, and projected a blue glow around his tall, heavy-set figure. He stood near the center of the court, gazing up as if to admire the stars, pretending he didn't know anyone else was near. Then he looked down, looked at the gazebo, and moved slowly closer.

A woman's voice broke the silence. "Lokahi, is it you?" she asked doubtfully.

Robert Bell made his move with shocking speed. He darted into the gazebo. A light flashed under the thatched roof: a dropped phone, its display momentarily illuminating two figures. A clunk, as the device hit the gazebo's concrete floor. Darkness again. The woman grunted, gasped. A dull *smack!* and Robert Bell swore.

Akasha burst first out of the grass, yelling, "Down on the ground! Now!"

Ava came a step behind, flashlight out, the bright beam stabbing past the gazebo's side rail to reveal a dark-haired woman in a short silky dress, scrambling backwards on her ass, and Robert Bell in his shorts and aloha shirt, on his knees, one hand held against his bleeding mouth while he used the other to frantically gesture at a virtual screen Ava could not see.

A faint hum erupted from the dune grass surrounding the little court. Ava closed on the gazebo, with Akasha still ahead, now only two steps from the railing. The woman braced herself on her elbows and kicked out, striking Robert Bell in the nose with her flat-soled sandal. Blood erupted and he squeaked, rearing back. He grabbed at the gazebo's railing, used it to haul himself up. Then he spun around and staggered out the entryway just as Akasha vaulted in over the side rail.

The hum grew louder as Ava angled to intercept Robert Bell. "Down on the ground!" she ordered, her flashlight beam bobbing wildly as she pulled her shockgun from its holster.

The hum peaked. Then something punched a hole in reality, right in front of Ava. A doubled lightning blast of light and sound.

Next she knew, she was down. Cheek pressed against sandy concrete, sand in her mouth, head swimming, ears ringing, eyes dazzled. *Shit.*

She'd dropped the flashlight. Its beam stabbed across the court. Sparks of light danced in her eyes, impeding her vision, but from what she could see, Bell was not there—which meant he was behind her, readying to kick her skull in.

She rolled—and discovered her shockgun still gripped in her hand. Instinct guided her finger to the trigger, but Bell was not there. He must have run.

"Akasha," she called.

No answer.

Ava holstered the shockgun and forced herself to sit up. She spit sand from her mouth and tried again. "Akasha. Report!"

Past the ringing in her ears, she heard Joni making some incomprehensibly muffled demand.

Shit!

When Joni had reported that Robert Bell was lingering behind the not-allowed sign, Ava had assumed he was taking a moment to gather his courage or to confirm that his prey was alone and vulnerable.

Now she knew: He'd been releasing knock-outs instead. The flak-free chemical concussion grenades, carried on reusable micro-drones, were common in police work, but illegal in civilian hands. No doubt he'd pre-programmed them to crawl into position, where they'd be ready to take flight on command.

Ava holstered the shockgun and got to her feet, swaying a bit, relearning her balance as her vision cleared.

Joni's voice started to make sense again: "Ava. Report! You back with us, yet?"

"Confirm. I'm coming back together." She stooped to pick up the flashlight, then staggered toward the gazebo to check on Akasha and on the young woman who'd been expecting someone else, not Robert Bell. Guilt bit at her conscience. A crime had been committed and Ava now had grounds to make an arrest, but she'd let Robert Bell get too close. The woman could have been seriously hurt in just those few seconds when he'd had her alone.

Debrief later.

Right now, she needed to get Robert Bell in custody.

Wrenching her focus back to the present, she murmured to Joni, "Where's our perp?"

"Legging it back up the ramp to the esplanade. Mike's moving to intercept."

Inside the gazebo, Akasha gripped the railing, hauling herself to her feet. "That was an ambush," she growled.

"No, it was a backup plan."

The civilian sat on the gazebo's concrete floor, her back against a bench, teeth clenched, chest heaving. A trickle of blood stained the side of her face.

HADAFA whispered: "Subject is Ye Xiaoxiao. Chinese passport, age thirty, agricultural geneticist with Jinhua Agricultural Technologies, social rating +24."

Smart and competent, Ava concluded. Akasha could handle her. "Akasha, see to Ms. Ye—"

Akasha started to object. The young woman did too. "I am fine!" she insisted, her lightly accented voice low with fury. "You two go and get him! I will talk to you when the monster is in custody."

"We'll get him, ma'am," Ava assured her. "But we need to take care of you." She met Akasha's resentful gaze. "And that's your job."

Like it or not.

Akasha would rather run down Robert Bell than safeguard his victim, but it wasn't her choice.

Ava turned and took off, running hard, back to the main path, and her motorcycle.

chapter

3

No way Robert Bell was going to get away. He had to know that. Surveillance was ubiquitous throughout the Waikīkī District, and KCA Security had access to every camera and microphone along the Kalakaua pedestrian mall, in the streetcars, and in the hotel grounds and lobbies. All nearby hotels had been ordered to close their doors against him, and Joni had assigned a micro-drone to track him.

That tracker had audio capabilities, allowing one of the communications specialists to speak to Robert Bell. The stern monologue played in Ava's earbud as she raced her little motorcycle across the Kīpūkai Bridge and up the ramp to the esplanade: *Robert Bell, you have been identified. There is nowhere for you to go. You are ordered to stop. Stop now. Lie face down on the ground and you will not be hurt—*

Ava crossed the esplanade, then descended to the grounds of the Imperial, following the route Robert Bell had taken, the way marked with a translucent green guideline projected in her virtual display. Her path veered right, past a no-access sign, into a maintenance alley—where a refrigerated van blocked the way.

She braked hard, back wheel fishtailing. The two men working to unload the van looked up, wide-eyed, until they recognized her. Both were familiar faces.

"Eh, Ava, who was that guy?" one asked as she rolled forward, squeezing past the van. "What's going on?"

"Later!" she promised. And then she emerged onto the pedestrian mall.

Coconut palms, imported after Nolo from plantations in the south Pacific, grew in clusters of three all up and down the tiled mall. In between, closed kiosks decorated with holiday garlands alternated with picnic tables, or benches flanked by blooming hibiscus plants growing in concrete containers. The streetcar tracks ran down the mall's center, with stops every three hundred feet.

A glance up and down the mall showed a surprising number of people out, despite the late hour. Ava estimated fifteen bystanders, every one of them looking east.

She turned that way too and glimpsed the tracker drone's red flashing light, just before it disappeared mauka, up Paoakalani Avenue. A black-clad officer, tagged by HADAFA as Mike Ching, came running hard from the Diamond Head end of the strip, rounding the corner seconds behind the drone. More chatter from the communications specialist, warning Robert Bell he had nowhere to go.

Truth, that.

Ava set off again, to the sarcastic cheers of a cluster of American tourists watching from a nearby picnic table.

She sped down the center of the mall, riding between the streetcar tracks. Just before she reached Paoakalani, the communications specialist went silent. Ava smiled to herself, thinking Mike must have gotten him.

She turned up the avenue, to find a posse of hotel staff in matching aloha shirts standing guard at the side entrance of the Kahakai Suites. Across the street, on the Diamond Head corner, a huge drop cloth printed with an idyllic scene of swimming dolphins hid the broken face of a still-shuttered hotel.

Beyond those two buildings, the street ended in the ghost fence: a chain-link barrier fifteen feet high, woven with polyethylene bamboo slats to hide what lay beyond.

Ava had expected to see Robert Bell on the ground, with Mike Ching applying cuffs as the tracker drone recorded the arrest. But the stub of a street was empty.

"Dispatch, give me a direction," Ava demanded.

"End of the street and to the right," Joni said. "There's a gate in the fence behind the construction yard. It unlocked for Mr. Bell."

"*What?*"

That was not possible. It *should not* have been possible. All of the district's security gates were networked, monitored, and controlled from the ops center. They did not unlock for random civilians.

"It's still unlocked," Joni added. "Mike's gone through."

The ghost fence divided the living from the dead.

Day and night, the makai side churned with the presence of thousands of visitors at play in a thriving tropical wonderland— an imitation of nature kinder than the real thing, and enhanced by booze, bright colors, luxury suites, imported palm trees, and shoals of carefully tended flowers. The soothing melody of a lone guitar might fill a quiet corner; a crowded bar might quake with thunderous electronic chords. Both suppressed ordinary conversation in favor of a dialog of touch and intimate proximity. And everywhere, the glamour of the beautiful, the wealthy, of glistening bodies wrapped in a heat that burned away caution, because the true lure of the district was the prospect of sex elevated above the ordinary by the amnesiac energy that had forged the place.

Visitors did not come to Waikīkī to be reminded of death and ruin, and of the time before.

But cross over to the mauka side of the fence and memory returned. No way to forget what had been, what had happened, what could happen again.

Ava reached the gate, pulled it open, and rode her bike through. The gate closed on its own behind her, a loud *ka-chunk* as the electronic lock engaged.

From the ghost fence to the flood walls of the Ala Wai canal, the lesser hotels and the apartment buildings crowding the backstreets of old Waikīkī had been deemed uninhabitable and forcefully evacuated in the months following Nolo. In the years since, a few intrepid residents had defied state edict and moved back. But for the most part, the buildings that still stood were ruined shells, doors and windows boarded up and marked with spray-painted red Xs that served as a shorthand declaring the premises had been searched and all bodies removed. Officially, the fence hid the ruins and kept out the curious. But rumor whispered its real purpose was to keep ten thousand restless ghosts from wandering into the new Waikīkī.

Maybe so, but Ava had never seen a phantom spirit among the ghost blocks and her duties brought her across the fence several times each year to deal with juvenile nuisance trespass, or elderly squatters whose time-shifted minds existed in the halcyon days of a different century.

More and more, the empty streets reminded her of images of Chernobyl taken years after a nuclear accident made the Russian town uninhabitable. There, a slow surge of wilderness had gradually dissolved the neat city blocks. In the tropical heat of Waikīkī, the process ran faster.

After Nolo, but before the decision to abandon the neighborhood, the ghost blocks had been cleaned up. The streets had been bulldozed of debris: fallen trees, furniture, shattered glass, broken asphalt, and thousands of ruined cars gathered up and hauled away. Then the unstable buildings had been cleared out and demolished, their concrete ruins dumped offshore to serve as fill in the foundation of the new shoreline.

Nature had been at work ever since. The shifting climate brought more heat and more humidity every year, but since Nolo, it had also brought an abundance of rainfall. In just nine years, a mixed assault-force of banyans, Alexander palms, and spindly orange-flowered tulip trees had come to fully occupy the vacant lots, with seedling armies spilling out into the streets and across the remaining rooftops. The banyans were the most intrepid. They sprouted from cracks and seams in the sides of the surviving buildings, sending out exploratory roots, like slow-motion tentacles seeking for the earth.

In daylight, the ghost blocks generated a ceaseless soundtrack composed of the coarse calls of raucous mynah birds arguing over territory, the cooing of libidinous doves, the startled flights of pigeon flocks, the cackling and crows of innumerable feral chickens, and the warbling and squawking of green parrots and lovebirds descendant from those liberated by Nolo.

Nights were quieter. Crickets buzzed and trilled, and mosquitos whined. Somewhere, a barn owl screeched, and Ava heard the distant din of cats fighting. For a time, feral dogs had been a hazard, but not anymore.

She switched on her bike's headlight. Its blue beam picked out Mike Ching, running hard. Farther out, a ruby-red point of light glinted between tree branches, marking the position of the tracker, and of Robert Bell, already at the Kuhio Avenue intersection.

Ava accelerated after them, weaving between bushes and bouncing over root-heaved asphalt. She steered well clear of each sinkhole and trench marking the line of the old sewer system, and she held her breath as she passed. Not because of the smell—there was none—but because of what had taken hold down there.

Robert Bell had faced these obstacles too, and he'd successfully negotiated each hazard while running full speed, in the dark. He had to be following a safe path projected by his smart glasses— and that implied he'd planned his escape, and that he believed he could get away.

Not possible, Ava thought. But then, the open gate had been an impossibility, too.

"Behind you, Mike!" she called.

He heard her and ducked aside into the brush. She zoomed past.

The stern voice of the communications specialist reverberated off the hollow shells of the buildings as he resumed his harangue: *There is nowhere for you to go, Mr. Bell. Give yourself up before you're hurt.*

Ava no longer found his argument convincing, and Robert Bell had never been persuaded at all.

She passed Kuhio Avenue, and a short block later, another street on the right. Then, past the vegetation, she saw Robert Bell at last. He'd made an impressive run, but now he stood spotlighted by the tracker in a cone of flashing red light, halfway up a short flight of stairs that led to the front entrance of an abandoned low-rise condominium. He stood bent at the waist, two hands clutching the stair rail, back and shoulders heaving as he fought to recover his breath.

Ava needed just seconds to close the gap.

She accelerated toward him. He heard the tire noise, looked up—and threw a mocking, triumphant grin in her direction. "I've got a ticket out of here!" he shouted, moving on to the top of the stairs. "You won't see me again."

This made no sense. Robert Bell had nowhere to go. Plywood sheets bearing the ubiquitous red Xs blocked the building's door and windows. He had no way to get inside.

But as Ava brought her bike to a skidding stop at the foot of the stairs, Robert Bell went down on hands and knees in front of the blocked-off entrance.

The communications specialist grew frantic: *Stop, Mr. Bell! Stop!*

Ava dropped the kickstand on her bike, looked up, and saw a dark hole open in the base of the plywood sheet. with Robert Bell already crawling through it. She bounded up the stairs under the ear-splitting boom of the specialist's voice—*Do not enter the building, Mr. Bell!*

Too late. Only his hairy legs and his feet in their leather sandals remained outside. He was quickly pulling those in when Ava grabbed his left ankle. For two seconds, it was a tug-of-war, her fingernails digging into his sweat-slicked skin. Then the specialist's voice shifted to a fearful tone: *Jesus, Ava! Get away from there. You're risking contamination.*

Fuck, he was right.

She rolled away from the sour smell emanating from the hole. Scrambling to her feet, she backed away.

Damn stupid, to let the heat of the chase burn away good judgment.

With the entrance clear, the buzzing tracker bobbed and dipped and then followed Bell inside. For a few seconds, the refracted glow of its red light pulsed from the hole. Then that too disappeared.

Unlike Chernobyl, the hidden hazard in the ghost blocks wasn't radiation. It was an engineered fungus that fed on the bodies of dead things in the moist darkness of sewers and utility tunnels, and in the shells of boarded-up buildings. The fungus's toxic spores had been given the recycled name *Angel Dust*.

Ava spoke to the communications specialist. "CS, give me the tracker feed on my tablet." She pulled the device from her breast pocket and flipped it open.

The screen lit with the red glow of the tracker's light. Steady now, no longer flashing. The point of view moved at speed down a stairwell. At the bottom, a semi-basement. The red light revealed a fine haze in the air obscuring a row of rusted heaps that might once have been laundry machines. There was a collapsed linoleum counter, a toppled vending machine, a fire extinguisher still in its wall brace, and Robert Bell, wailing in frustration as his fist hammered at the door of what Ava guessed to be a locked utility closet. He raged, "Let me out! Let me out!" But the closet did not open for him.

She looked around at the sound of running steps to see Mike Ching bounding up the stairs to join her, taking them three at a time, sweat gleaming on his youthful face and his broad surfer's shoulders rising and falling as he caught his breath.

"It's over," she told him. "He's gone inside."

"*No shit?*" Mike took off his smart glasses, using his sleeve to wipe the sweat from his dark eyes. "Does he have an exit on the other side?"

"No. He won't be coming out."

Even as she spoke, Robert Bell's wailing pleas foundered in a fit of coughing. The tracker hovered stationary near the low ceiling, looking down at him, its rotors stirring the dusty air.

Somewhere in that room—Ava hadn't seen it yet—there would be a small body. A rat. A feral cat. Unrecognizable now beneath a white velvety growth. In its reproductive phase, each tiny thread of the fungus would be crowned with a capsule that split when ripe, releasing into the air millions of toxic spores—the Angel Dust. Roaches and other crawling insects, brushing up against the settling dust, could carry it between buildings so that the fungus could crop up anywhere, at any time, in the dank enclosed spaces of the ghost blocks.

Bell had to know that, but he'd gone in anyway. *Why?* Had he believed this building to be clean? Maybe. But if so, he hadn't checked it out himself or he would have known there was no backdoor out of that basement.

The spores carried a nerve toxin. Inhaled into the lungs, they triggered breathing to shut down—swiftly, if the dose was high enough. But if not, if the infection went untreated, death came slowly, with wracking coughs that could spread the toxin even as a new fungal colony grew and bloomed inside the lung tissue.

Robert Bell had breathed in the concentrated dust of a fresh bloom. Ava watched on the tablet's screen as he collapsed to his knees.

Mike leaned in to look. "*Shit*," he whispered.

Bell's shoulders rose and fell in short spasmodic jerks. Then he looked up. He looked directly at the tracker, his mouth working. No sound came out, but Ava understood him anyway: *Help me. Help.*

Too late for that, and he knew it. He gritted his teeth, shook his head, as if he couldn't believe it had come to this. A spasmodic shudder ran through him, and then he pitched forward, pressing his forehead against the moldy concrete.

Mike walked away, but Ava kept watching.

Another minute passed before Bell's body relaxed, subsiding to the ground.

A faction in city government still hoped to someday rehabilitate the surviving buildings in the ghost blocks. Ava closed the tablet and slipped it back into her pocket. She wished that every one of these buildings would be torn down.

"Ava." She startled as DeCoite's voice spoke in her earbud. "Ava, you there?"

Was he still waiting for the navy to come?

"Confirm," she said. "What's your status?"

"Glowing green."

"DeCoite," she warned, in no mood for banter.

"The United States Navy has collected the hot stuff," he conceded. "I'm coming in."

chapter

4

AVA STEPPED OFF the elevator into the biting cold pervading KCA Headquarters. She'd left Mike Ching to wait for HPD's hazmat team, while she returned to the administrative suite, a floor below the operations center.

The sprawling room hosted a fleet of six desks and two large tables, all unoccupied at this hour. Ceiling lights were off, but light leaked from behind a room divider that walled off KCA Security's small lobby and its reception desk. Across the room, more light spilled from a hallway that curved out of sight as it followed the Sea Tower's oval foot print.

As Ava crossed the room, Akasha appeared at the mouth of the hallway. "I watched," she said, her voice low, and skeptical. "It was a weird scene. Strange currents there."

"Agreed." Ava joined her under the soft white light. "Robert Bell had to be following a mapped route, to move that quickly through the ghost blocks. And he believed he could get away."

Akasha cocked her head, chin up, lips pursed, eyes cold. A brawler's pugnacious pose. One hand rested on her holstered shockgun. "Not a map *he* charted or it wouldn't have dead-ended like that." A slight cold smile. "Joke's on him."

Ava exhaled a long breath, imagining tainted black smoke swirling into the hallway's cold clean air. She felt shaken by what had happened to Robert Bell. Not because he didn't deserve it, but because she didn't like what the manner of his death implied.

She echoed Bell's words, remembering his triumphant grin. "I've got a ticket out of here. You won't see me again."

Akasha snorted in cold amusement. "He got that right. I didn't know an unsigned strain of Angel Dust could put someone down that fast."

A strange thing to say. True, it was standard practice to embed signatures and copyright notices in the genomes of genetically modified, aka, CRISPRed lifeforms—but not if the product represented an unlicensed and ill-conceived liability.

"You know Angel Dust has never carried a signature."

The stuff was a mystery. No one knew how it got started—or anyway, no one would admit to knowing. Popular theory deemed it the failed product of a low-skill CRISPR hobbyist. A backroom-biohacker chasing a solution to the overwhelming stench of death that had hung over the city in the months after Nolo. In a twist of ironic justice, Ava imagined that hobbyist as the first victim of his own monstrous creation.

From Akasha, a moment of hesitation, followed by a slight, mocking smile. "Sure. We're *supposed* to believe Angel Dust was an accidental catastrophe."

Ava didn't miss the political undercurrent. A second theory on Angel Dust, devoid of evidence but popular with separatists, suggested it originated with the military. Was that what Akasha was implying?

Ava pushed her glasses up on top of her head, deactivating their sensors. "You know something different?" she asked, keeping her voice low.

Given that the Chinese had financed the island's recovery, a small but significant portion of the population looked forward to official Chinese oversight. After all, they reasoned, the handover treaty included a bill of rights . . .

But a strong and rapidly growing separatist element existed, too. The 2,500-mile water gap separating Hawai'i from the mainland United States had helped the island hold on to a unique culture—one forged from a fusion of diverse ethnic groups and shaped by the isolation and essential fragility of island life. People here valued community. They had to, because when things went south, they only had each other. The aftermath of Nolo had proven that.

No one counted on the federal government anymore. It had failed Hawai'i, just like it had failed Puerto Rico years before when that island had been devastated by hurricanes. But people resented China, too—the way they'd used charity as part of a carefully orchestrated play to take control of the ravaged island.

Easy to believe, under such circumstances, that Hawai'i would be better off as an independent nation. Given the travesty of the handover treaty, Ava found it hard to disagree. And she'd seen hints enough to suspect Akasha had traveled farther along that road.

As if to confirm it, the young officer said, "Don't you think, sooner or later, some radical is gonna rise up and use Angel Dust to make a play?"

Ava rejected this with a shake of her head. "No. That's not who we are. That's not a path we want to walk."

"*We* don't," Akasha agreed. "But some might."

Ava pondered this. Had Akasha heard something? Was the revolution more serious than she had thought?

No. Ava kept track of her officers. She checked their profiles every week. If Akasha had any real connections with a separatist group, HADAFA would have noted it—and Akasha would have lost her job.

Time to remind the young officer of her obligations—and end this dangerous conversation. "Akasha, if you've heard any whispers, any rumors—"

Akasha's eyes flared. "It's not like that."

"Or if you've got names—"

"*No.* Nothing like that. I'm just thinking what you're thinking, okay? Robert Bell was set up. Someone gave him a map that led him into that laundry room. Maybe they didn't know it was contaminated or maybe they *were* testing the dust. Either way, he was done. Because he had no way out."

Right. And who in this city was clever enough to run a setup like that?

———

Akasha had left Ye Xiaoxiao seated at a rectangular table in a windowless interview room, with a cup of green tea and a blanket around her shoulders. In an adjacent room, wall monitors showed the young woman from multiple angles as she waited with a composed expression.

"She looks calm," Ava observed.

"She's a tiger," Akasha answered with an admiring grin. "She'll be angry you didn't bring her Robert Bell's head."

"Let's hope she doesn't take mine."

Ava left Akasha to watch remotely, entering the interview room alone. Ye Xiaoxiao raised a manicured eyebrow. In excellent English, she asked, "You are Officer Arnette?"

"I am. Thank you for agreeing to stay."

A bruise darkened under Ye Xiaoxiao's left eye, and on her shoulder an abrasion glimmered with antibiotic sealant, but she sat straight and proud, her makeup nearly perfect. A beautiful woman, one clearly accustomed to authority.

Ava sat down across from her. Met her skeptical gaze. "I have just a few questions for you."

"*I* have a question for you," she responded, pushing her empty teacup aside and letting the blanket Akasha had given her fall away from her shoulders. "Have you arrested the criminal who pushed me to the ground?"

"I was not able to arrest Mr. Robert Bell. But he will never again be a threat. He met with an accident, and did not survive."

At this news, Ye Xiaoxiao leaned forward. "You are saying he's dead?"

"Yes. He is dead."

She leaned back again, lips turned in a hint of a smile. "You are very good at your job, Officer Arnette."

Sarcasm?

No, a compliment. Undeserved. Ava had not caused Robert Bell's death. "Tell me what happened out there," she urged.

"You were there. You saw what happened." For the first time, a quaver marred her voice. But the moment passed. "You saw what the monster tried to do to me." A scowl transformed her lovely face, giving her the appearance of a vengeful goddess. "You saw what I did to *him*."

Ava flashed on Robert Bell holding a hand to his split lip.

"Tell me anyway," she urged. "What inspired you to be out walking so late at night?"

Ye lifted her chin and, as if granting a favor to an annoying minion, she said, "I did not want to sleep. My flight to Shanghai leaves in—" She looked at her phone, lying face-up on the table and it reacted to her gaze by flashing the time and a queue of messages. "In six hours. Why should I sleep? This night, beautiful, before the great storm. No. Better to walk in the park. It is safe. The guidebook said so."

Ava felt a sting of guilt. She could have had Akasha intervene before Robert Bell entered the unsurveilled area. A murmured warning, and he would have aborted his hunt, just like the other two EP4s. Ye Xiaoxiao could have flown home without the memory of this assault.

But Ava had wanted cause to make an arrest. She'd wanted Robert Bell out of circulation, and she'd wanted the opportunity to question him. For that, she'd gambled this woman's safety—and she'd almost lost.

Pressing her lips together, she spoke a stock phrase, knowing that tonight, it was a lie, "We do all we can."

"You do not do enough," Ye Xiaoxiao snapped.

Ava did not try to deny it. Instead, keeping her expression carefully neutral, she asked, "Why did you go into the unsurveilled area?"

Ye *tsked* and rolled her eyes to the right. "Always, everywhere, electronic eyes are watching. But not there. It is . . ." Her brow wrinkled as she groped for the right word. "*Relaxing*. Yes. Soothing, not to be observed. Not to be on display at every moment."

"Did you tell him you'd be there?"

She drew back with a snarl of contempt. "Not *him*."

"You didn't know him."

"*No.* I would not talk to *him*."

"You expected someone else."

Beneath her makeup, a rosy flush. Her brows pinched. Anger glinted in her eyes. "*Yes.*" She pronounced the word with a hiss of contempt. "He sent a text. I answered. He was a beautiful man— and I enjoy such men." She glared at Ava, as if daring her to speak some criticism.

Ava had none. Ye Xiaoxiao possessed a bold and fiery spirit that she could only admire.

"You arranged to meet him?" Ava asked. "In the unsurveilled area?"

A contemptuous shrug.

"Did you?" Ava pressed.

"Yes, I thought he would come. But it seems I was not worthy of his time."

Ava's brows rose. Ye seemed more irate at being stood up than by being the target of Robert Bell's assault.

"Do you still have his text messages?" Ava asked.

Ye tapped at the glass face of her phone, then turned the device, showing Ava a sequence of flirtatious messages. The sender: Ben Kanaele. A familiar name. He worked as a late-shift bartender in the Sandalwood Lounge at the Hotel Taipingyang—and he *was* a beautiful man. Good humored and well-liked, too. What connection could Ben possibly have with Robert Bell?

Ava took out her tablet, subvoking a request to HADAFA to send an image of Ben. The AI provided a crisp, clear shot of him smiling from behind the bar where he worked. From the angle of the image, Ava knew it came from a surveillance camera.

She showed it to Ye, who confirmed, "That is him." Her dark eyes flashed. "You *will* speak to him," she said imperiously. "You will question his motive. I want to know why he toyed with me."

Ava nodded, stone-faced as she suppressed an astonished laugh. Given Ye Xiaoxiao's commanding persona, she strongly suspected Ben had simply lost his nerve.

Ava assigned Akasha the task of escorting Ms. Ye back to her hotel, while she walked to the end of the hall, where KCA Security Chief Ivan Ishikawa waited for her at the door of his glass-walled office. Ivan must have arrived while Ava was still in the interview room.

A big man, six feet tall, he had the muscular build of a veteran cop and the discipline of a good commanding officer. Even at 4:00 AM, the thick gray hair that topped his sun-bronzed face was neatly combed, and he wore a fresh-looking uniform, down to the green duty belt.

"You let this one get away from you," he said.

She started to speak, but hesitated when a text message popped up on her display: *New boss is here. Tread carefully.*

Saying nothing, she followed Ivan into the office to find the Chinese liaison, Shao Hua, seated in a guest chair in front of Ivan's desk. Rumor had it that after the handover, he would be appointed as the first governor to oversee the ninety-nine year lease.

A relatively young man, no more than forty years old, Shao Hua wore gray slacks and an aloha shirt featuring cranes and swirling clouds in subdued blue and gray hues. His thick hair sported a fashionable tousled look. And though his face was round and his features soft, Ava wasn't fooled. The truth of his personality lay in the sharp gaze that evaluated her from behind the clear lens of his smart glasses.

Without waiting for an invitation, she sat in the second guest chair while Ivan took his seat behind the desk. "So what happened?" he asked.

She addressed her answer to him. "We recently experienced two earlier incidents that developed exactly like this one—"

"But in this case, you allowed the assault to occur," Shao interrupted. "It is understandable. Present law forbids an arrest despite the certainty of an intended crime. But your actions must always take into account the reputation of Waikīkī. Even in the face of the oncoming storm, the bizarre nature of this incident is sure to make the news."

"Yes, sir," Ava said, aware that bad press was an unforgivable sin. She'd been hired to help ensure visitor safety, but like everyone who worked in the resort, her position came with the collateral duty of helping to preserve the illusion of Waikīkī as an idyllic paradise. Even now, as Hurricane Huko threatened landfall.

And it *was* an illusion.

Waikīkī had first earned its international reputation well over a hundred years ago, when the weather had been cooler and less humid, the trade winds had been constant, the natural beach had been wide, and the palm trees had not been imported. Since then, the average temperature had climbed by several degrees. Now, nearly every day was hot and heavy with humidity, and the cooling trade winds were almost forgotten. Air-conditioning and alluring advertising could make up for that, could make visitors believe they'd truly bought a ticket to paradise—but any crack in the façade could cause the illusion to fail.

Ava said, "You're right, sir, that this incident is likely to be a blip in the news cycle. But it's part of a series of attempted assaults—and if we're still here after Hurricane Huko, you'll want these incidents stopped. Tonight I was able to interview the victim. She's a cooperative witness who provided a lead that may help to reveal the connection between all three incidents."

Shao's expression remained fixed and stern. "You believe there is a connection, though these incidents each involve a different Expected Perpetrator."

"Yes, I do, because each followed an identical pattern—entering the coastal park and then immediately proceeding to an unsurveilled area where they knew a victim waited. I need to know where they got their information. Once we identify the source, we can stop these potential assaults before our reputation is permanently damaged."

Shao Hua observed dryly, "You do not have much time before the game pieces are shuffled by the oncoming storm."

"You're right, *sir*," Ava agreed in terse syllables that left an unspoken implication drifting in the air: *Get out of my way, mister, and let me get on with it.*

"I will expect your report," Shao said, standing up.

Ivan stood too, and came around the desk. "I'll walk you to the elevator."

They started to leave, but at the office door, Shao turned back. "Be assured, Officer Arnett, that we *will* still be here after the storm."

She leaned forward in her chair. "Then do you plan to ride it out, sir? I mean, if the hurricane does turn our way?" Would he stay here to oversee his pending fiefdom? Or would he flee?

His eyes narrowed, recognizing the challenge. "I will be leaving for Kona later today. Negotiations are underway to move the signing ceremony there, to avoid any delay, given the storm's predicted path. When I return in three days, it will be done."

She remained seated as the two men walked away down the hall, filled with bitterness, knowing her country had done this to itself. A self-righteous refusal to cooperate with global standards for carbon emissions had brought on the international sanctions and the embargoes that had ravaged an already fragile economy. Meanwhile, national debt compounded as successive environmental disasters far exceeded the country's resources.

Operating in the style of corporate raiders, the Venturists had demanded the sacrifice of assets to improve the country's cash position, backing their play with skilled propaganda aimed at convincing the mainland citizenry that Hawai'i wasn't "real America" anyway. Visitors had lately begun to revive the old, exclusionary phrase "back in the States" to refer to the mainland USA.

On a different level of psychological warfare, people feared conflict with China. The Mischief Reef incident had involved Britain, not the USA, but the radioactive debris drifting throughout the Pacific served as a stern warning. Appeasement was popular, though it was never called that.

She looked up as Ivan returned. "What the hell are we doing here, participating in this?" she asked him.

He took his seat behind the desk, looking grim. "It hasn't happened yet."

"You think there's a way the handover can be stopped?"

He leaned back, his gaze faraway. "I won't be surprised if the separatists give it a try. And that was bullshit, about moving the signing ceremony to Kona. The security apparatus is here. Propaganda too. Shao's just going to have to wait a few more days."

"We should all be separatists," Ava said softly.

This drew a long, searching look, before Ivan said, "I'll pretend

I didn't hear that. By the time you're back on-shift tonight, we'll be feeling the first effects of Huko. I want you to learn what you can before then. If the separatists are behind these serial incidents, I want to know it. And I want to know what else they have in mind."

As soon as Akasha returned, Ava sent her off again. "HPD is sending a crime scene unit to Robert Bell's residence. I want you to go out there too. His social rating was in the dumpster, so his neighbors are going to be happy to talk stink. See what you can turn up. Call me with anything significant."

"What about Kanaele?"

"Ivan's agreed to take over the end of my shift, while I go talk to Ben."

chapter

5

An Ewa-bound streetcar approached, its eave decorated with a holiday garland of LED lights made to look like luminous green fern leaves and glowing red poinsettia blossoms, bright in the winter darkness. Despite the hour, despite the season, the air remained warm, and thick with a humidity that used to belong only to the muggiest days of summer.

The car came to a silent stop. Ava stepped aboard, scanning the other riders: two families and a young couple. Out of habit, she stood on the running board, her elbow hooked around a pole, leaving the bench seats of the open-air car for additional passengers.

Several more, all burdened with carry-on luggage, boarded at the next stop. Their anxious chatter made it clear they'd cut their vacations short and were on their way to the airport, having made the smart decision to get out before the storm.

No one waited at the stop after that, so they rolled through it. But a crowd milled outside the Hotel Taipingyang—enough that the streetcar reached capacity.

Ava found herself sharing the running board with a grinning blond carrying a small backpack over his shoulder. His slender frame, along with the smell of cigarette smoke, clued her that he was European. When he spoke, his accent confirmed this guess. "So we get a police escort now?" he asked, an eyebrow raised. "Should we expect trouble?"

"Trouble in paradise?" she asked, mirroring his teasing expression. "No. This just saves me a walk."

She looked away, out to the disappointed faces of a group of evacuating tourists queued at the next stop as the fully loaded streetcar rolled past them.

Trouble would come. Not right away. But within twelve hours, if the hurricane continued on its predicted path, people would start to panic. Right now, those with the means and the will to do so could still buy a seat out. But the gamblers would wait, riding out their bets against the storm's predicted track until it was too late. When the airport closed, reality would set in. Ava had seen it all before.

The streetcar moved slowly but steadily down the center of the Kalakaua pedestrian mall. No one got off. Every couple of minutes an eastbound streetcar, wearing its own holiday garland, slipped quietly by, occupied by only a few uniformed resort staff heading in for the early shift.

Between Duke's Lane and Lewers Street, old Kalakaua Avenue had been re-routed, so that it curved to meet what used to be Kalia Road. The streetcar wound past Fort DeRussy Park and on to Ala Moana Boulevard, continuing west to the Ala Wai Canal Bridge.

The bridge marked the end of Waikīkī, and of the Kahanamoku Coastal Authority's jurisdiction. At its western end, a double line of movable steel bollards formed a barrier to keep general traffic from entering the pedestrian mall. The streetcar swerved, moving onto the single track that passed through the barrier. Then it swerved again as the track doubled on the other side. The route continued down the center of Ala Moana Boulevard, now with vehicular traffic on either side—a mix of autonomous taxis, delivery vans, and the rare private car. Makai of the boulevard stood the massive concrete fortification of the Ala Moana Seawall. The concrete labyrinth of the old shopping center sprawled on the mauka side, a ghost town now.

The streetcar picked up speed, hurrying on until it reached Harbor Station, alongside Aloha Tower—the end of the line. As the car came to a smooth stop, Ava jumped down from the running board, relieved to escape the reek of stale cigarette smoke.

A sculpted white-canvas roof soared over the station, aglow at this hour with artificial light. Three black-uniformed officers from the Honolulu Police Department directed the streetcar's worried passengers toward an escalator that would take them to the elevated train to the airport. Their luggage would be delivered by cargo van, already checked through to their final destinations.

Ava nodded to an older officer she'd known when she'd been with HPD. Then she headed outside to the taxi station. Her apartment was just across the street, in one of the few refurbished towers of old downtown, but she wasn't ready to go home yet. Tablet in hand, she submitted her identity and a destination to the taxi app.

The queue was short. In less than a minute, the app assigned her to a rideshare with a young mother and her two small children. Five and six years old, Ava guessed. Born since Nolo. They hugged their Fantastic Space Force backpacks, looking sleepy until they noticed Ava. Then their eyes went wide.

Ava smiled at them. "Good morning," she said, as their mom hoisted a large suitcase into the cargo area. As the back hatch closed, Mom herded the kids into the rear seat, admonishing them, "Seat belts on." When the kids were secure, she joined Ava up front. HADAFA identified her as Anuhea Golden, twenty-nine, no criminal record.

As the autonomous taxi pulled away from the curb, she evaluated Ava with narrowed eyes. "That's a Coastal Authority uniform, isn't it?"

"Yes, it is."

"I thought so, but I've never been to the strip." A slight, satisfied smile, as her gaze shifted to the road ahead. "Too late now."

Right.

Resentment was an indulgence that didn't cost anything—and Ava understood it. It had been hard in the early years to see so much foreign investment poured into the construction of a luxury resort when the island's people had lost everything. They'd been living in tents pitched in fields that cycled between dust bowls and bogs of sticky mud depending on the weather. The iron-rich soil had left a red stain on everything, and on everyone.

But none of that changed the fact that Waikīkī and the Kahanamoku Coastal Park functioned as an economic engine, bringing much-needed outside money to the island.

"Don't give up yet," Ava said coolly. "You might still have a chance to visit. The coastal park was engineered with Nolo in mind."

The artificial shoreline was a façade designed to persuade wealthy vacationers that paradise still existed. But it wasn't just decorative. The esplanade, the lagoons, the dunes, the beach, even the artificial reefs—all served as layers of protection against sea-level rise and the storm surge of hurricanes. And along the Ala Wai canal, mechanical flood walls had been installed to prevent an overflow of rainwater into Waikīkī. The refurbished hotels had been strengthened too, and outfitted with hurricane-rated window glass.

But would it be enough?

Ava closed her eyes, remembering the way the concrete fortress of the Honolulu Police Station had vibrated with the force of Nolo's killing wind, with the floodwater in the street outside already waist high.

"Do you live in Q-12?" the woman asked.

Ava caught her breath, drawn back from that dark place by the sharp question.

"I don't think I've seen you there." Unmistakable suspicion in her voice.

"I'm going to see someone," Ava said in a well-practiced soothing tone.

"It's not your jurisdiction." A quiet challenge, an unflinching gaze.

Was Anuhea Golden a separatist, despite her innocuous profile? Probably. And why not? A future under Chinese control was frightening, but the feckless and financially strapped federal government had left the island in ruins. With friends like these, secession looked good.

"You're right," Ava agreed. "It's not my jurisdiction. I'm just going to talk to someone."

Ava needed to hear Ben Kanaele's story, before *he* heard what had happened to Robert Bell.

A minute or two of silence slipped by as the taxi passed through a wasteland of empty lots and still-shattered office towers. As they neared the freeway, the woman turned to check on her kids in the back. Ava looked, too. They were already asleep.

"I'm taking them to stay with my parents," Anuhea said, gentle-voiced now, as if regretting her earlier hostility. "They live in a Chinese dome house in Q-12. We'll be safe there."

Ava nodded. "It's a good plan. The dome houses were designed for this."

"My husband will come after his shift." A slight frown as she looked at Ava. "He thinks Huko will do enough damage to convince the Chinese to walk away . . . but I think it'll take more than that. A lot more."

A simple declaration, yet Ava shivered, a sense of foreboding rising within her as goosebumps prickled her skin.

Stay focused!

She reached to turn down the air-conditioning. "Your husband sounds like an optimist . . . but I think *you're* right."

The taxi accelerated along a ramp to the rebuilt freeway, easily merging into a sparse flow before gliding across the concrete expanse to the girded autonomous-only lane. Once behind the safety of the low wall, its headlights switched off and it accelerated to eighty, speeding past old, unreclaimed neighborhoods trapped in the limbo of court battles over liability and ownership, with only the occasional LED light testifying to a sparse occupation.

As the taxi climbed to the island's central plain, the broken neighborhoods gave way to solar farms mixed with agricultural land. Here and there, small farm trucks, defined by the bright beams of their headlights, moved along narrow dirt roads between the fields.

Entrepreneur farmers had taken over abandoned agribusiness lands, supplementing their basic income with fruit and vegetable crops, fish and shrimp ponds, poultry farms, or electricity production. Islands of amber lights marked the two hundred-odd villages of Chinese-provided housing.

After a couple more minutes, the taxi ducked through a gap in the autonomous lane's girding wall, then slid across the empty freeway to an off-ramp. From there, it was a short ride to Village Q-12—in total, a sixteen-minute commute from Harbor Station.

Five shift workers in airport uniforms waited at the taxi stop. They greeted Anuhea and her children by name, gave Ava a suspicious look-over, and then climbed into the cab, which carried them swiftly away.

Dawn glowed in the eastern sky as Ava waved goodbye to the kids. They scampered off to their grandparents' home, leaving Anuhea to contend with the suitcase. "Take care," Ava told her.

Anuhea nodded. "You too." Narrowed eyes and a teasing smile. "And keep your rich tourists out of trouble." She followed after her children, who had already disappeared down a side street.

Ava walked toward the opposite end of the village, following a guideline projected by her smart glasses.

The villages were all laid out in a similar way, each with five hundred homes, set out in precise rows, and sharing the same design: small, single-story, and with a covered front porch. The setting harkened back to plantation days a century gone, when immigrant laborers were housed in regimented "camps." But the old single-wall wood construction used in those days had been left to history.

Round "Chinese dome homes" populated the new villages. Built to survive, their vertical walls and domed roofs comprised a single monolithic concrete form. Firmly anchored to a concrete base, they were predicted to endure the winds of a Cat 5 hurricane with little to no damage. And on the high central plain, away from both mountains and streams, the homes would be safe from catastrophic landslides and floods.

Every village had its own water tank, and a multi-staged green sewage-treatment system. Photovoltaic panels tiled all the roofs. With shared battery storage and backup generators, each village was energy independent.

In another echo of plantation days, the generous yards were mostly devoted to food production. Vegetable and taro gardens vied for space with young breadfruit trees, mangos, lychee, papaya, a range of citrus, and ubiquitous chicken coops. The severe food shortages following Nolo had taught a harsh lesson. *Never again*, was the mantra, and most homes stocked packaged food to last a year.

The houses had gone up almost overnight, constructed in coordination with the state government. The carbon debt incurred by the concrete construction was being offset by reforestation projects in the foothills of the island's two mountain ranges.

As Ava made her way to Ben Kanaele's home, she suffered the suspicious gazes of village residents heading toward the taxi station, and others taking down Christmas decorations ahead of the storm. But no one questioned her, and the barking dogs all stayed in their yards.

After a few blocks, her smart glasses highlighted a house half hidden behind a front yard dominated by banana trees. She followed the walkway toward the front door. Before she reached it, the door opened. A young man—beautiful, but not Ben—looked out at her with a doubtful expression. Maybe a little worried.

Well, who wouldn't be worried, if a cop out of her district showed up at the door?

HADAFA highlighted the young man and whispered. *Keoki Jones. Age twenty-four. Village maintenance apprentice. Social rating +8.*

A nice kid, going nowhere.

"Good morning," Ava called softly, as she walked up two steps to the concrete lanai furnished with a little table and two white plastic chairs. "My apologies for the early hour, but I need to talk to Ben."

"Ben's asleep." Keoki Jones stood in the partly opened door, blocking her view inside. "And anyway, you work for the Chinese. Don't you?"

His tone made it an accusation. She kept her hands loose at her sides, her expression carefully neutral as she corrected him. "I work for the Coastal Authority. Now go wake up Ben. With the storm incoming, I need to do follow-up on an investigation while I still can."

Keoki Jones still held out, arguing with a soft pidgin inflection. "You know he works nights. He got home not even three hours ago—"

"I know where he works," she interrupted, dropping the soft approach. "I know his schedule. And if you want him to have a job after this storm, then you will wake him up and let him know he needs to talk to me."

Not a threat she would normally make or typically be able to carry out, but a word to Shao Hua about a non-cooperative potential witness would surely get results. Keoki Jones must have sensed her resolve because his resistance collapsed.

"Try wait," he murmured and withdrew, closing the door behind him.

Ava put on a stern expression and stared into the lens of the security camera until, less than two minutes later, the door opened to reveal Ben, tousled and red-eyed, dressed only in shorts, the hard, rectangular outline of a phone in his right pocket. He stepped outside and closed the door behind him. "Officer Arnett," he said, clearly confused. "What's up? What's gone wrong?"

She gestured at the chairs. "Can we sit? Talk for a couple of minutes?"

"Sure." He sank into the nearest chair, watching her pensively.

She sat down too, let him endure a few seconds of silence, and then told him, "Your name came up in an investigation. Do you remember meeting a woman, a Chinese national, named Ye Xiaoxiao?"

A nervous side eye toward the door. "I meet a lot of Chinese women."

"Do you make dates with them?"

That brought him fully awake. He straightened up, his red-rimmed eyes widening. "*No.* Hell no. I flirt with them, sure. They like it and they leave bigger tips. But the hotel I work for doesn't allow fraternizing. I could be fired. So whoever told you—"

Ava held up a hand, interrupting his denial. "She gave you her number. You texted her."

"I didn't."

"I saw the messages, Ben."

"I didn't text her!"

His hand dropped against the outline of the phone in his pocket, but his worried gaze watched her.

"Texting isn't a crime, Ben. I just need to know."

"But I *didn't*."

"Let's look at your phone."

He pulled it out. The device recognized him and the screen brightened. He stared at it for a few seconds before murmuring, "Text message history." The screen refreshed. Ava could not see what it displayed, but she saw the slight widening of his eyes.

"*Shit*," he whispered. "Someone must have been fucking with my phone . . . but that's bullshit. It's not possible." He looked up at Ava. "I swear, I did not send these messages. Hell—" He held the phone out to her. "You can look at the timestamps. I was still working the bar when those messages went out."

Ava took the phone. Scrolled. Saw the same sequence of messages Ye Xiaoxiao had shown her.

"My phone goes into a locker during work hours. I can't get to it until I clock out. Ask my boss. He'll tell you."

"Can *he* get to it?" Ava asked.

Ben shrugged. "I don't know. But it doesn't matter. My phone won't unlock for anyone else."

Ava scrolled further through his message history, studying his contacts, using her smart glasses to record what she saw. Queries, hellos, alerts. HADAFA identified them all as being from his circle of friends. Then it flagged a second cluster of flirtatious messages. Ava recognized the name of the recipient as the young Chinese woman who had been the target of the second EP4. She scrolled faster, looking for the date the first EP4 had entered the park. *There*. A third set of messages, setting up a late night romantic encounter.

She looked up at Ben. Despite the evidence on his phone, HADAFA did not flag him as a potential perpetrator.

"Someone's fucking with your phone," she agreed. "Any ideas?"

He shook his head frantically. "*No*. Who *could* do that?"

Good question. Who could send messages from a phone without touching it?

She turned the phone over. The brand was Chinese. Maybe a surveillance backdoor coded into the OS?

"What's this all about, anyway?" Ben asked. "Don't tell me something happened to that woman."

"Someone set her up. Sent her out into the dunes. She thought she was meeting you."

"Jesus, is she all right?"

"Do you have any idea who would want—"

"*No.*" A forceful denial, followed immediately by a look of reconsideration.

"What is it, Ben?"

"You gotta understand, I hear all kinds of shit and bullshit standing behind that bar. A couple times I heard guys, tourists, talking about some dark-side social media called The Predator Network. Sick stuff, where guys could post locations of vulnerable women. I thought it was probably a joke."

"It probably was, to them."

Just another one-step-removed thrill: call a SWAT team in on an innocent household; goad a social media mob into attack over the least transgression; set a woman up for third-party rape. A troll's game, its reward a sick sense of power.

Ava handed Ben his phone. "You might want to get a new number, *and* a new device," she advised.

By the time Ava returned to the Pacific Heritage Sea Tower, the sun had risen, its fierce glare darkening her smart glasses and casting long shadows between the towers. Just like at the streetcar's prior stops, a small crowd pushed forward: anxious and angry tourists laden with backpacks and small suitcases, all determined to board, even though the streetcar was Diamond Head-bound.

A transit official had been assigned to ride the car. He held up a hand, palm out, and in a kindly voice, he advised them, "You can get on now, but you'll have to get off at the end of the line and queue up again."

"At least we'll get a car that way," a large middle-aged man declared. "While we were waiting on the other side, three of 'em, completely empty, rolled past without stopping."

The official nodded, his polite expression holding steady. "We're distributing cars along the line, to minimize wait times for everyone. An empty car will be at this stop in . . ." He turned his forearm to check the screen of his bracelet. "Eight and a half minutes. There's no need to worry. We'll get everyone out."

Ava had listened to him recite this explanation, with different wait times, each time the streetcar had stopped on the way in. She admired his patience.

"No panic so far?" she'd asked him, after the first stop.

"Not yet. But give it time."

Once again, he succeeded in convincing the disgruntled to move to the Ewa-bound track. "Take care," Ava called to him as she stepped down.

The official nodded. "We'll get through this."

As Ava entered the hotel grounds, she passed more departing vacationers with carry-on luggage in tow. Her uniform earned her their curious stares, and polite nods. Avoiding the lobby, she walked through the grounds to the esplanade and KCA Security's restricted entrance.

The gate recognized her and opened. She crossed the ramp to the deck. The ready room's glass doors slid aside and she entered. No one was there. Day shift had already started, and all but three motorcycles had been checked out.

Later today, Ivan would put out a call for all hands to report to work. Ava needed to sleep before then, but she had two tasks to complete first.

Ivan must have been tracking her, because he was waiting when the elevator doors opened. "How'd your interview go?"

"Curiouser and curiouser," she answered. "Ben denies sending any texts. Claims no one could have sent them. I need to make a phone call to his supervisor, to confirm that."

"My office," he said.

Lights were on in the administrative area, with three desks

already occupied, their inhabitants staring at screens with sincere expressions as they engaged in video calls, their soft murmurs clearly intended to soothe the nervous:

The airlines are cooperating...

Assure them there's still plenty of time to get out ...

If you need an officer on scene, use the emergency line ...

The system spliced in a white background behind each agent and muted extraneous noise, screening all office activities from the caller.

Ava resisted the delicious scent of coffee as she walked with Ivan across the room, knowing that if she drank any now, sleep would be impossible. They entered his office. He closed the door.

HADAFA had already retrieved the supervisor's personal phone number. It put the call through—voice only—and woke him up.

"Sure," he said on speaker, agreeing with Ben's story. "Corporate regs. Employee devices get secured behind a time lock. To open a unit early, supervisor and employee have to be present—and you know how it's been. The strip's packed. Protestors, journalists, diplomats, on top of the usual throng of tourists. We've been too damn busy for days to let anyone off early."

Ava thanked him and ended the call.

"So you're thinking Ben Kanaele is not our man," Ivan said.

Ava leaned back in her chair. "Probably not, but he *is* involved. Not knowingly, maybe. But something's there." She stood. "I'm going to have HADAFA go over security video from his bar—"

She broke off at a soft knock on the office door. Turned to see Akasha through the glass. Ava crooked two fingers signaling her to come in. "What have you got?"

A slight flush warmed Akasha's dark skin, testifying to the rising heat outside. "Confirmation of Robert Bell's social profile. Dude was not popular. I talked to most of his neighbors. No one was upset to learn he wasn't coming home again. One woman was ready to throw a party, but most were just relieved. Like his record said, he was a creep, a troublemaker, a misogynist—and no one would admit to knowing what he did for fun. If he had any friends, they were online. CSU is still going over his house, but they aren't optimistic. All his gear is highly encrypted, probably inaccessible."

Ava nodded. "We'll need to focus on Ben Kanaele instead—"

"But not today," Ivan interrupted. "I'm putting the case on hold. We'll take it up again on the other side. Right now, I want both of you to go home. Get some sleep—because you're going to have a twenty-four hour shift when you come back."

6

THAT DREAM AGAIN ...

The roar of wind before anyone was ready for it, raging past the towers and howling through the streets ... and then a tornado. Spun off the outer rain bands of Nolo, it danced over the city, tapping its long black tail against the rooftops of neighborhood homes, obliterating another each time it touched down.

Get in the house! Get inside!

For once, her daughters didn't argue. They retreated in terror, into the false security of a doomed home.

Then came the rain, a deluge worthy of the Biblical flood. In minutes, every street became a running stream, and the streams that normally drained the city ran wild. They crested their concrete banks and swept through the old wood-frame houses that crowded close on either side—and they swept little children away.

Why didn't we go to a shelter?

The dream shifted. Ava sat hunched, trembling as she watched the feed from an extant video camera running on battery power and communicating by wifi, every lightning strike a burst of static.

The police chief had ordered all officers into shelter when the windspeed topped a hundred miles an hour. He should have ordered all the cameras off. Warm tears coursed down her cheeks as three little heads disappeared under the flood. She prayed, *Oh please, oh please,* but those lost children did not surface again.

Across the room, Miguel slammed his palms against his desk and shoved his chair back, shouting, "I'm not going to sit here and watch this. I'm going out! Who's with me?"

Kayla wanted to know, "What have you got?"

Ava and Tyree raced each other to his desk to see.

As Miguel stepped away from his screen, the three of them leaned in.

It was a live feed from yet another submerged street. Muddy water swirled past the windows of parked cars, carrying with it plastic traffic cones, broken tree limbs, sections of metal roofs and sidings, and filthy islands of brown foam that the wind picked up and shredded.

It took Ava a few seconds to spot the little girls. The oldest maybe seven, the youngest five, both with long blonde sodden hair. Half submerged in the rushing water, they clung with desperate fingers to the smooth bark of a wind-stripped rainbow shower tree, while the unrelenting rain continued to pour down on them.

Ava recognized the location. Kayla did too: "That's just two blocks from here!"

Both little girls turned their heads as if they'd heard Kayla's frantic shout—and Ava found herself looking into the accusing eyes of her own daughters. "No," she whispered. "No, no, no, oh God, please *no*."

Then Kaden was there, gently shaking her shoulder. "Come on, Ava. Come out of it." His voice soft but stern. "Let it go."

She scrambled to sit up amid a tangle of sheets, eyes wide, heart pounding, breathing hard, her cheeks wet with tears.

"*Jesus*," she whispered. And, "*Thank you, thank you.*" Because the dream was a lie. Her children had not been swept away. They'd survived Nolo. They lived in Spokane now, safe with their dad and his current wife.

But in the dream, those two doomed children always wore her daughters' faces.

Ava *had* gone out into the storm. She and Miguel and Kayla and Tyree. Brave heroes, defying orders, resolved to save another woman's children—only they hadn't. Ava had looked into a little girl's wide brown eyes, terror stricken as the violent current swept her past just out of Ava's reach. And in the end, only she had made it back to the police station.

Kaden knew the story, but he wasn't one to coddle. He opened her apartment's blackout curtains, revealing blue sky and the golden light of afternoon beyond the floor-to-ceiling windows. Then he disappeared behind the shoji that screened her bed from the rest of her little studio apartment, giving her time alone to compose herself.

Ava lay back, eyes squeezed shut, chiding herself: *be grateful for the dream*. It served as a recurring reminder of the cost of relying too heavily on her own flawed judgment. These days, she operated in tandem with HADAFA, relying on the data and analyses it provided to affirm her decisions and her actions.

She drew a slow breath in, then let it go in a long exhale, ejecting tension and remorse in an imagined black cloud of toxic smoke.

Again.

Again.

Again.

Oh, to hell with it. She grabbed her tablet. Checked Huko's status. As predicted, the daylight hours had pumped the storm with heat energy, bringing it to Category 5 status—sustained winds exceeding 160 miles per hour. Its path was still expected to turn north. Once that happened, all bets would be settled.

Next, she checked her messages, confirming no urgent demand for her to come immediately into work. Only then did she roll out of bed, slipping into the bathroom for a quick shower.

She had the apartment as a fringe benefit of her job. Despite the building's proximity to the shoreline—it stood almost across the street from Honolulu Harbor—it had taken less damage than most, allowing it to be fully refurbished only two years after Nolo. The units had been designated for law enforcement, first responders, and staff at the nearby Queen's Medical Center. Ava had still been living in a tent city at that point, newly divorced and on her own. She'd been ecstatic to get an assignment in the building. Ever since, the little three hundred-square-foot cubby had been home.

She dressed in a light, tropical-print tank-top, and a loose little skirt, comfortable to wear, then used an eyebrow pencil to quickly fill in brows that insisted on thinning more with each passing year. It was the only makeup she usually bothered with. Shocking, really, how much a carefully shaded browline contributed to the impression of self-assurance in a woman. That done, she joined Kaden in the kitchen.

"Hey," she said softly. "Didn't think I'd see you this early." It still surprised her that he'd come into her life at all.

From his post by the microwave, he greeted her with his characteristic crooked smile—only the right side of his pale lips turning up.

Enjoy it while it lasts.

She went to him. He stood just two inches taller than her, his buzzcut blond hair fading to gray over a face still smooth and pale despite years at sea. Kaden Robicheaux, US Navy, commander of the nuclear-armed fast-attack submarine *Denali.* Dressed in civilian-casual at the moment: a collared shirt and khaki slacks.

Two months ago, they'd been strangers seated next to each other at a large wedding reception, allies out of necessity, since neither had known anyone there except the bride and the groom. They'd snuck out early and gone for drinks—and he'd invited her to attend a demonstration event, already scheduled for the next day. "It'll be just a few hours at sea. You'll be riding along with two Congressional reps from the defense appropriations subcommittee. We'll deploy the midget sub for them, use it to send a few commandos to shore. Convince them we're spending our funds wisely. Then we'll head back to port."

It had been an exciting day, and Kaden had been irresistible—her first serious crush since her divorce.

Since then, *Denali* had been out on only a few brief training runs, and in between, they'd kept each other company.

Now they shared a hug, a deep kiss, her body warming against his.

"Missed you," he murmured.

For the past two days, he'd been filling out a dress uniform along with other ranking military officers, their attendance—though not their opinions—required at the ongoing ratification conference. The officers had been instructed on which speeches to attend and which to avoid. They'd been assigned to sit together. Cameras captured them politely applauding the administration's policy positions. It was an exercise in visual propaganda, implying support for the handover treaty from the nation's decorated military leaders—when most of them would rather be cheering the fiery opposition speeches, or the ongoing mass protests in Washington, DC.

Local protests had peaked a year before, when the state voted overwhelmingly to reject the treaty. But the president and his Venturist party doled out favors and pushed the deal through Congress anyway. So why protest the inevitable? It would only get you a negative social rating—and once that happened, it got hard to make a living.

Kaden told her, "Navy brass finally persuaded the president that Huko really does constitute a threat to what's left of our fleet. We got released from conference attendance so we can prepare for departure. Surface ships start leaving Pearl in the next few hours. Submarine fleet goes tomorrow morning. I wanted to see you again, before."

Ah, so this was goodbye.

A hollow melancholy had been building in Ava these past few days, though she strove not to acknowledge it. She had known from the start it would end like this. He would not be here past the handover, and once gone, the fleet would not be coming back. Any of the remaining docks and decaying facilities that survived Huko would be demolished during the transition period.

She forced a little smile, and spoke the truth, "I don't regret anything." Their time together had been fun, and exciting. A secret affair, kept separate from the rest of her life because she didn't want to deal with other people's expectations or share the time she had with him. She had hoped for a few more weeks, had imagined spending New Year's Eve together, but Huko had decided otherwise.

Kaden hugged her tighter, kissed her again. "I want you to leave too."

Ava pulled back, puzzled. "What do you mean?"

"Military families are being evacuated—"

"I'm not family."

"I don't care. I mean, I *do* care. I care about you. And you're former military. I can call in favors and get you a seat on a military transport. Tonight. Get you out of here. Ava, at least think about it."

She shrugged. A non-answer. "My roots are here, Kaden. I belong here. My parents are buried here. You know that."

How could she leave? How could she abandon the homeland where her family had lived for generations? Sure, a lot of people had made the decision to go. Some had moved to the outer islands, but many more had left the state . . . Ava's now-ex-husband among them.

"I'm needed here," she added, despising the hint of doubt she heard in her voice. "Please, let's not argue."

He retreated physically, turning away as the microwave finished its run. "I brought food," he said. "I knew your fridge would be empty."

"Thank you."

Silence followed until dinner was on the table. Baked salmon and a fancy rice pilaf with a generous serving of lightly cooked vegetables. "Good," she said, tasting the fish. Then, as a peace offering, she added softly, "I'm going to miss you."

His lips parted to speak. She saw it coming. He meant to ask her again to evacuate. But he caught himself, pressing his lips together as his blue eyes held hers in a frosty gaze.

She decided to talk around the tension. "I chatted with Shao Hua early this morning."

His brows drew together.

"We had an incident in the park. Our presumptive future-governor stopped by to express his concern." She smiled, showing her teeth. "I asked him if he planned to stay on for Huko."

A glint of humor in Kaden's cold eyes. "You didn't."

"I did." Her smile faded. "He said he was trying to get the signing ceremony moved to the Big Island, out of Huko's predicted path." She quirked her lips. "Which is ironic, given the coastal park was designed by *Chinese* engineers specifically to protect the strip from another hurricane. So maybe he doesn't trust Chinese engineering? Either that, or Conrad's goons have been too intense for him."

"Six bodyguards," Kaden said. "That's all Dan Conrad's had with him. He's given a few spontaneous press conferences in the lobby, but otherwise, he's saved the rhetoric for his scheduled speaking times."

Ava responded to this news with a dismissive hiss. "Trust me, he's just waiting for the right moment to put on a headline performance that'll erode the president's support—and augment his own."

Kaden went quiet, pensive.

"What?" Ava asked.

He shook his head. Forced a flinty smile. "You don't like it that you agree with him."

She put down her fork. Leaned back. Crossed her arms. "On this *one* point our views happen to coincide."

The treaty *was* a shameful concession—an act of infamy, in Conrad's words. She wasn't going to argue with that.

"The enemy of my enemy," Kaden suggested, quoting the old proverb.

"Nope." Ava shook her head. "Conrad is not now, and never will be, a friend of mine. And with all his talk of American sovereignty, he doesn't give a damn about this island beyond its propaganda value."

Unfortunately for the future of the nation, the Venturist party was equally contemptible, with their policy of spinning off the surviving assets of the American people. To his credit, Dan Conrad recognized that and he opposed it.

But as the leader of the opposition Cornerstone party, Conrad endlessly prophesied a day when America must rise up and reclaim its status as the world's leader—*a phoenix rising from the ashes!*

Ava could not abide that kind of militaristic shit.

Neither did she harbor fond feelings for Chinese colonial rule . . . but at least they weren't willfully stupid. Not so far, anyway.

"We need to do better," she said quietly. "We need more people like you in office. People who know what it means to serve their country, their *world*, instead of serving themselves."

For several seconds, Kaden just looked at her, and as he did, his gaze softened. "You done eating?" he asked, glancing at her empty plate.

"I am."

"Good. Let's go to bed."

A flush of warmth rushed through her, followed by a clutch of fear. Or was it regret, knowing this might be the last time? *Deal with it.* They'd both come into this, knowing it couldn't last.

She set her napkin on the table, burying her angst behind a coy smile. "*That* is a fine idea."

The curtains stayed open, the fierce late-afternoon sun contending against the heavily tinted glass to gloss their pale skin in a golden aura. Youth's raw beauty lay behind them, but in their forties both remained strong, with athletes' bodies, leanly muscled, and endowed with the knowledge of long experience. Lips teasing against cheek and neck and breast. Fingers stroking the smooth warmth of an inner thigh. The lightest pressure across a throat accompanying a slow hard thrust that only gradually quickened into something fierce and irretrievable until Ava arched back against the pillows in a maelstrom of pleasure, eyes only half open, basking in the possessive intensity of Kaden's gaze as he followed her over the cliff with a harsh gasp that sounded like pain.

Silence then. Slow, deep breathing. And after a few seconds, soft reassuring kisses. So warm in her little studio apartment, the air conditioning unable to counter the relentless sun.

"Time to move to a cooler climate," Kaden murmured. "You'll like it in Bremerton."

"*Hmmm,*" she sighed. A non-answer.

"You'll be closer to your daughters."

"I see my daughters every Sunday."

"On a video screen."

She closed her eyes, allowing the conversation time to expire. It had been the topic of distant daughters that first drew them together. They each had two, left to the care of a former spouse. That first night at the wedding reception Kaden had shown her pictures of his girls, the oldest in college studying engineering, the younger an officer in her high school ROTC. His pride in both had been plain to see. Ava liked to think he was a good father, that it was possible to be a good parent even if duty demanded your absence for months at a time.

Somewhere in the apartment an alarm began to gently pulse. Kaden groaned. "Is that you or me?"

"Me," Ava guessed. "My alarm to wake up."

She rolled out of bed and walked naked into the bathroom, where she'd left her smart glasses. Silencing the alarm, she got in the shower for the second time. Kaden joined her a few seconds later. Maybe that was not the best idea. The sun was at the horizon, melting into a tumultuous sea by the time they finally dressed.

"I had to go into the ghost blocks this morning," Ava said as she hustled to put away the dishes before leaving. She knew Kaden had seen a documentary exploring the abandoned neighborhood, both its hazards and the thriving ecosystem that existed there. "We had a security breach. An open gate—a deliberate escape route for our latest EP4."

"He planned ahead?"

"Someone did."

Trusting Kaden to be discreet, she told him about the laundry room in the semi-basement and the way Robert Bell had pounded in desperate frustration on the locker door. "He thought there'd be a way out."

"Not too bright, then."

"Maybe not." She wiped the kitchen counter clean. "I think it's a game. A sick kind of game controlled by someone out of sight, a puppet master manipulating both predators and prey for the jollies."

"No idea who?"

"None," she said, hanging up a dish towel. "But I'm hoping cyber-forensics will yield a lead. Whoever hacked that gate open might have left an electronic trail." Ava hesitated. Mostly, she tried not to ask Kaden sensitive questions, but this time, she resolved to plunge ahead. He was a navy commander, after all, and would know if he was free to answer or not. "One of my officers said something odd about Angel Dust. Left me wondering if there's a weaponized version."

Kaden grunted. "I think the separatists are right, and Angel Dust *is* the weaponized version, knocked loose by Nolo. I never bought the popular story, that its origin was an accident."

chapter

7

BRILLIANT PINK AND gold post-sunset colors had briefly gilded a fleet of low clouds hanging over the city, but by the time Ava's eastbound streetcar approached the Ala Wai Bridge, dusk had repainted them a charcoal gray.

Out of habit, she rode standing up on the streetcar's running board, even though the car was empty except for an exhausted transit officer who sat nodding off on the front bench.

No one wanted to get into Waikīkī. Everyone wanted out. Evidence of that was visible across the street. In the two hundred-foot span of sidewalk between the Atkinson Drive taxi station and the bridge, at least a hundred fifty people had gathered, all seeking the fastest way to the airport, prodded to action by the news that Huko looked to be making its long-predicted northern turn.

On Ala Moana Boulevard, a line of taxis waited to take their part in the exodus. As soon as the streetcar passed, they would be free to enter the little roundabout that preceded the bridge, picking up passengers on their way out.

Ava's gaze drifted ahead as the streetcar crossed the roundabout. No one waited at the eastbound stop, so after the car slid through the traffic barrier, it kept going, climbing the low arch of the bridge and then descending into Waikīkī.

The transit officer snapped awake, threw an apologetic glance at Ava, and took up his post at the front of the car. He should have slept a little longer, though, because no one boarded at any of the eastbound stops. All the activity continued to be concentrated on the westbound side.

As she rolled past, Ava estimated the number of people waiting, keeping a running tally in her head. HADAFA could have given her an exact figure, but whatever that turned out to be, she worried that too many people had stayed too long. No way could all of them score a seat on an outbound jet tonight.

But Ava had a seat, if she wanted one. Kaden had assured her of that. "It'll be there, if you change your mind."

No, love. I'm where I belong.

They had said their farewells amid the desperate good order of Harbor Station, alongside a snaking line of anxious travelers, tourists as well as fleeing residents, all waiting for a turn to board the commuter train to the airport.

A navy car had taken Kaden away to Pearl Harbor, to oversee preparations for *Denali*'s departure, while Ava had boarded the streetcar. She did not expect their paths to cross again.

Melancholy clung to her. The puzzle of the EP4s and the questions surrounding Robert Bell's demise seemed faded and trivial in the face of this new existence she must negotiate going forward.

Get over it.

It was only a two-month affair.

She signaled a stop at the Pacific Heritage Sea Tower.

"Take care," the transit officer told her.

"You too, friend," she responded, waving goodbye.

Quiet reigned in the administrative suite. Though Ava had come in hours ahead of the official start of her shift, the office staff had already gone—though Ivan was still there. She waved to him in his glass-walled office. He saw her and nodded, before returning to his conversation with Isaiah Mahoi, captain of the evening shift.

She went down the hall, claiming one of two desks in the research room. The desk wakened at her arrival, the keyboard brightening as it rose to a comfortable angle, the monitor shifting on its jointed mounting arm so that it hung in front of her at the proper height. "Welcome, Captain Arnett," HADAFA said in the gentle male voice it used when speaking to her.

Ava pushed her smart glasses up into her hair.

A lot of officers—both KCA Security and police—talked to HADAFA as if it was another member of the team. Not Ava. As much as she relied on the system, she liked to maintain a distinction between human and AI. "Subject is the Sandalwood Lounge," she said tersely.

"Affirmed. The Sandalwood Lounge is an establishment located on the roof of the Hotel Taipingyang—"

She raised a hand. HADAFA recognized the gesture and fell silent. Ava said, "Review security video from the Sandalwood Lounge over the past nine—no, *ten* days. Assemble a list of all patrons present during the shift of bartender Ben Kanaele. Assemble a second list of all patrons present on all three nights of November twenty-fifth, November twenty-ninth, and December second."

Ava wanted to know if the puppet master had been present in the bar, despite the potential breach of anonymity.

"Estimated wait time for this task is nine seconds."

The person who'd hacked Ben Kanaele's phone might never have set foot in the bar. They might be on the other side of the world, safely monitoring Ben's bar patrons through a surveillance device planted by an accomplice. But hotel security did frequent sweeps for such things, and anyway, what was the point of a thrill crime without a little personal risk?

"Task complete," HADAFA announced. "Displaying results."

Ben had provided drinks for several hundred individuals over the past ten days—but only nine of those names had visited the Sandalwood Lounge on all three of the nights when an EP4 had entered the coastal park.

Ava said, "For each individual on List 2, map their movements within the Sandalwood Lounge on each of the three nights, noting the amount of time spent at each location within the establishment."

She hadn't yet looked at their profiles, not wanting to bias herself.

"Task complete," HADAFA replied. "Displaying results."

Of the nine, seven had spent most of their time sitting at the bar. The other two occupied separate tables. One sat alone. The other had a different companion each night. Ava checked the socialite's profile first. Male, twenty-seven, a licensed sex worker. She slid him off the main list.

The solitary drinker, also male, was a former soldier freshly out of the army and freshly divorced. HADAFA cataloged his melancholy and cleared him of criminal tendencies, so Ava slid him off the main list too.

She thought for a moment, then said, "For the night of December second, create an equivalent activity map for Ye Xiaoxiao."

"Task complete."

The map showed that Ye had begun her evening seated with three other women at a small table, but after her companions departed, she'd relocated to the bar. Only two of the nine names from the short list were still in the Sandalwood Lounge at that time. One sat at the opposite end of the bar, and the other had moved to a nearby table.

Ava checked the bar-sitter's profile first. A thirty-nine year old interior designer from Osaka, in town to assist in the remodel of a new hotel scheduled to open in the summer. HADAFA cataloged her as another melancholy, no doubt homesick, and missing her three-year-old son.

Ava turned to the last prospect. The image that came up was that of a regal black-skinned woman, her hair super short and her makeup subtle. She could have been a runway model, but wasn't. HADAFA gave her occupation as *consultant*, without a specialty. And it gave her name as: *Lyric Jones, legal pseudonym*. Interesting.

Also interesting: The basic profile included no other information.

Legal pseudonyms were unusual, but not unknown. They could be granted for a spectrum of reasons, most commonly to escape massive online shaming and harassment. But given the limited information attached to the profile of Lyric Jones, Ava suspected another explanation: She was a federal agent, her history, relationships, and real name all classified.

Might as well test that theory.

"Expand this profile," Ava commanded. "Give me all you have on Lyric Jones."

A new window opened. It displayed security video of Lyric Jones walking into the Sandalwood Lounge dressed in a shimmery tank top and a tight black skirt that reached to just above her knees. She greeted Ben with a confident smile. Asked if he'd gone surfing that day. They traded a few more words, and then Lyric turned to the woman next to her, shepherding her into the conversation.

"Stop," Ava said. "Give me additional background information. Home address. Place of work. How long has she been in Honolulu?"

HADAFA answered, "Estimated wait time for this task—"

The screen blanked. It stayed dark for over seven seconds. Ava's gut clenched. She'd never seen the system go down before. Instinctive caution took over. She rolled her chair back a few inches and started to stand.

But then the screen refreshed—and she was no longer looking at her user account. At the top of the screen, her name had been replaced by one word: *Lyric.*

Now, row after row of profiles appeared, each with a thumbnail portrait and a brief text description that included the individual's name, age, and occupation. In the third row, a familiar face.

Name: Ava Arnett

Age: 42

Occupation: Kahanamoku Coastal Authority Security Officer, rank of Captain

All correct. But this profile included an additional field, one that should not have been linked to Ava's name:

Affiliation: Second-degree associations with Hōkū Ala, Sigrún

Ava shivered, her heart squirming with the shock of adrenaline. She rolled her chair a few more inches away.

The affiliation field was specific, meant for associations with terrorist or subversive groups. A second-degree association meant the subject had a close connection to a primary, someone known to be directly engaged with a listed group.

Ava had no such connections and her profile had always reflected that. So what had changed? What was she being accused of?

Sigrún was a mystery to her. She'd never heard of it before. But everyone knew of Hōkū Ala. The group had its roots in the enduring native-Hawaiian sovereignty movement. Its founders had recognized opportunity in the political vacuum after Hurricane Nolo. They'd made it their goal to serve the needs of people, first in the refugee camps, and now, in the village communities. Among their many activities, they arranged volunteer work parties, organized food distribution, arbitrated disputes, and acted as liaisons with government officials—winning hearts and minds while ceaselessly advocating for secession and an independent Hawai'i for all of the islands' people.

But secession remained illegal regardless of the handover treaty, and so Hōkū Ala was classed as a subversive organization. Intelligence reports regularly insisted the group's community activities doubled as a recruiting operation for an armed insurgency. And maybe there was truth to that, but Hōkū Ala was not the Taliban. At most, she guessed them to be capable of kickstarting a few massive demonstrations, and carrying out an occasional act of politically effective sabotage.

In any case, Ava didn't associate with Hōkū Ala or its members—not knowingly, anyway. She'd be fired if she did. She might have suspected Akasha of having an association, but none had ever appeared in her profile.

So what the hell am I looking at?

The answer came in an intuitive flash: *The truth.*

Ava knew HADAFA filtered some of what she saw. Lyric herself was an example of that. Anyone with a security clearance had a protected profile, allowing Ava only limited access to their history and habits. She'd checked Kaden's profile the day after she'd met him. HADAFA had let her learn his age, his hometown, his public record of promotions within the navy, but little else. Everything she knew about him—his children, his divorce, the officers he regarded as friends, the enlisted he most respected, and the hostility he felt toward the handover—she'd learned only because he'd chosen to reveal those things.

But it wasn't Kaden she suspected.

Softly, not really believing it would work, she said, "Display Akasha Li's profile."

The screen blanked, then refreshed again, and Ava was back in her own user account—except her activity had been rolled back. The last profile she'd been looking at had belonged to Lyric Jones. But the one now open onscreen was that of the interior designer from Osaka.

She cleared it with a hard swipe. Looked again at List 2. Nine names. That's how many there had been, but there were only eight now and Lyric Jones was not among them.

Anger flared. She glared into the camera at the top of the screen—HADAFA's eye—used to monitor her position, her expression, her level of satisfaction with the data provided to her.

"I know you're there," she murmured.

No answer, of course. The only sounds: the whispering white noise of air conditioning and a barely audible burr of male voices emanating from Ivan's office.

She straightened her shoulders, rolled her chair close again, and repeated her last command, "Display Akasha Li's profile."

The profile appeared even before she'd finished speaking. It did not include an affiliation field.

"Display my profile."

That affiliation field was hidden from her, too.

Ava sat back in her chair, thinking.

Whatever had just happened, it had not been by accident. The cause was not a fortuitous glitch in the system. *That* possibility was too absurd even to consider. No. She was being played, maybe by someone with the skills and backdoor access to compromise Ben Kanaele's phone.

Lyric Jones, legal pseudonym.

Ava guessed Lyric to be the agent's code name, and Jones an anonymous afterthought to fulfill a required last-name field.

But why would Lyric want to allow Ava that glimpse into her user account? Was it a benign gesture? A friendly warning that she should beware of those she might otherwise trust?

Or was it just another phase of the game Ava had been a witness to last night? Ben Kanaele, Ye Xiaoxiao, Robert Bell—they'd all been played, and now the turn was hers . . .

"Ava!"

She flinched at Ivan's call. Heard the tread of footsteps in the hallway.

"I'm here. Research room."

Again, she looked HADAFA in the eye. "Clear the screen and log me out."

"Done," the system replied in its genteel voice, as the display refreshed to a generic login screen.

Ivan appeared at the open door, with Isaiah Mahoi in tow.

"Yes, sir?" Ava said, leaving her chair to join them.

"You want to jump in early today?"

She hesitated, debating what, if anything, to tell Ivan about the glitch she'd just witnessed. A full explanation could throw a cloud of suspicion over Akasha, and they didn't need that now. Better to wait. Deal with it after the storm—if it even still mattered then.

"What have you got?" Ava asked.

Mahoi answered. "We found a John Doe."

"Really? HADAFA can't ID him?"

"Not in his current condition."

"Skeletal remains?" she asked, because even a badly decomposed body could be identified with a DNA swab.

"Nah, he's alive," Mahoi said. "God knows why. Limbaco hauled him out of the water, a mile offshore. A miracle he managed it without flipping the patrol boat. I don't know if you looked out the window on your way in, but the swells are huge. A warmup present from Huko."

"Yeah," she said in grim agreement. "So what *do* we know?"

"Found naked and semiconscious. Caucasian, possibly Hispanic. Approximately thirty. Face swollen and discolored. Limbaco thinks he had a close encounter with a railing before going overboard. Normally, I'd guess he'd fallen off a party boat. But the usual suspects stayed in harbor today—or they're hauling out on trailers if they can manage it." Mahoi leaned in. "I *could* send someone from my shift to do the interview, but—"

Ava raised an eyebrow. "You're a little busy?"

"Right."

"Sure. I'll take it." It would be time away to think, and right now, she needed that.

Only as the elevator door closed did Ava remember she hadn't had a chance yet to look into the possible existence of a social media dumpster called The Predator Network. Pulling her smart glasses down over her eyes, she started to query HADAFA—but doubt intruded. Unaccustomed and unwelcome, but there all the same. What if she lacked the necessary security clearance to access the full truth? Even if the system came up with an answer, how could she know it wasn't censored? That key facts hadn't been withheld?

What if her query brought down attention she didn't want?

Better, *safer*, to try a local expert—a friend at HPD who worked vice. But the call went to voice mail.

Shit.

"Hey Gina, if you've ever connected with something called The Predator Network, give me a call back. I'd like to know."

chapter

8

IN THE READY room, Ava glared at an absence of usable motor-cycles. Just two waited in the charging rack, both with red lights, still low on power. She crossed her arms, sourly contemplating the prospect of riding the westbound streetcar, packed with a hundred tourists, every one of them aggravated and on edge.

Then a better idea occurred to her. She smiled to herself. Why not hitch a ride?

Less than five minutes later she sat balanced on the back of a motorcycle, behind Officer Ikaika Mollenhauer as he sped west down the deserted expanse of Waikīkī Beach. A rooster tail of wet sand spewed high behind them and the air thrummed with the violence of the surf.

Harbingers of Huko, the storm waves began their break a quarter mile offshore, throwing up a fog of salt-laden air as they rumbled over an artificial reef built from the shattered concrete of demolished condominiums and fallen bridges. The waves rolled in, white water all the way to the shore, tumbling onto the beach and then flattening, gliding across the sand. One after another, they strived, but still failed, to reach the dunes. Ikaika nimbly dodged each one as he worked to keep the motorcycle running on the hard-packed wet sand.

Ava laughed in exhilaration, high on the wild energy of the waves, the pure joy of speed. Wind and salt spray blasted her face, her hair felt thick with it, and wet sand encrusted her high-top shoes.

Every now and then, this job had its perks.

All too soon, the low dark ridge of Komohana Point loomed before them. The artificial peninsula anchored the western end of the coastal park, extending a half mile out to sea. Storm waves shattered against it, exploding into fountains of white foam.

"Fun time's over," Ikaika warned. He slowed the bike, turning inland onto a concrete path that skirted the last of the dunes before climbing to meet the esplanade.

After that, they made their way to the Ala Wai Bridge, and then into Honolulu proper.

City traffic ran heavy. It felt as if every taxi in the autonomous fleet was on the road, along with most of the delivery trucks—half of them parked in no-parking lanes, though whether they were loading or unloading, Ava couldn't tell.

But even with the rush, it took only a few minutes to reach the Queen's Medical Center. Ava waved goodbye to Ikaika. She took a minute to brush the spattered sand off her legs and stomp her boots clean. Then she went inside.

An eight-inch-high ornamented Christmas tree decorated the reception desk. The receptionist behind it wore a festive woven-ribbon lei. Ava smiled, identified herself, and asked for the room number of her John Doe.

A few minutes later, Ava huddled in an eighth-floor hallway with Dr. Banerjee—a tiny woman who looked altogether too young to have an MD after her name. Even so, she wielded a brusque and polished businesslike manner that must have served to intimidate most of her patients.

"This is a strange case," Dr. Banerjee explained in a low, conspiratorial voice. "The patient was recovered from the ocean and his physical condition concurs with that history. He arrived dehydrated and suffering a mild hypothermia—of course we have treated both conditions—and he has significant fresh bruising on his face. Also, his blood tested positive for traces of a synthetic cathinone—a party drug—so it would not be illogical to assume he became incapacitated and fell overboard."

"But?" Ava asked.

"We have not been able to identify him, not by facial analysis or fingerprints—but he does have a chip."

Embedded identity chips were not unusual. Every branch of the military required them, and they were popular with civilians too.

"So you got a name from that?" Ava asked.

"No. As I said, this is a strange case. A scan of his chip produced nonsense. Encrypted data, I suspect. The only coherent string was a ten digit number."

"Oh," Ava said with a sinking feeling.

Dr. Banerjee went on, "I would ask him about it, but he's asleep. My staff is convinced it's a phone number."

"Yes. They're probably right."

Chips had just been coming into general use when Ava was in the army, but even then there had been a standing order that if a body was found with a scrambled chip and only one coherent number, they were to call it on a secure line. No explanation of why, but the absence of an explanation served just as well. John Doe was a spook. A spy. And the reality of that, along with the unreality and stress of recent events, caused Ava's adrenaline to surge again, kicking her heart into a thready beat and sending a quiet shiver up her spine.

What the hell had she fallen into?

Aloud, keeping her voice deliberately low and calm, she asked Dr. Banerjee, "Did you try calling the number yet?"

The doctor's eyes narrowed combatively, as if the question constituted veiled criticism. "Do you want me to?"

"No," Ava said. "That's on me."

Ava pushed open the room door. Inside, dim baseboard lighting picked out the shape of a single bed, a nightstand with two drawers beside it. Cloth rustled, followed by the anxious incoherent murmur of a troubled dreamer.

She slipped inside, her presence triggering the overhead lights to slowly brighten, revealing the John Doe. *Caucasian, possibly Hispanic*, Limbaco had said. Maybe. A tanned face with smooth, low-relief features. Tape across the compact nose, one eye socket swollen, and a darkening bruise running diagonally from right forehead to left cheek. A baton could have done that as easily as the rail of a boat.

He had black hair in a short military cut, and the stubble of a heavy beard. His sunken eyes visibly darted beneath closed lids thinned by the dehydration that followed hours in the ocean. The skin of his face and neck remained blotchy from the remembered cold, despite the thermal blanket that covered him to his shoulders.

Dr. Banerjee still had him hooked up to an IV line that disappeared beneath the blanket.

Every few seconds, slurred words slipped past his lips. Ava could make out only a fraction of his ramblings—*stay alive . . . has to know . . . now . . . stop it now*—and though she wasn't sure of even those, their suggestive nature sent her heart racing again.

She moved in along the wall, maintaining a wary distance from the bed and its restless occupant. His dreamlike murmurs had gone on for over a minute already, leading her to wonder: Was he really asleep? Or was he still caught in the effects of the drug he'd taken?

More broken phrases rising at intervals out of the incoherent baseline murmur: *'s real . . . 'ere in place . . . ready . . . es Sigrún.*

Ava froze. That name again, the same name she'd seen in her own profile's hidden field. Had she heard it right?

"HADAFA," she murmured, "what is Sigrún?"

"That information is not available at your security rating," the system answered in its gentle male voice.

She grimaced in frustration. But an absence of information *was* information. Easy to guess Sigrún was a subversive organization, likely with sensitive connections, and possibly violent, or with the potential for violence.

Her body flushed with an anxious heat as she recognized that every syllable she'd gleaned from the John Doe's drug-hazed speech suggested a terrorist action, one that was real, in place, ready *now*.

Or was she piecing together coincidence and misunderstandings to develop an entirely fictitious scenario?

An inner voice urged, *Call the number.*

Yes. Call it, and add one more data point to the puzzle.

HADAFA had already absorbed the hospital record. At Ava's instruction, it recovered the number from the scanned data and analyzed it, affirming it as a working number, one of a catalog of federal government phone numbers.

"Call it, then," she whispered.

Silence followed, a three-second interval. No sound of ringing before a woman's voice spoke out of the void. "Is he alive, Ava?"

Ava flinched at the use of her name, but recovered quickly. "Yes. Who is he?"

"Stand by. I'm accessing your current working files . . ."

Ava tensed, as if by physical effort she could hold off the intrusion. But HADAFA controlled access.

A soft, frustrated hiss from the nameless woman. "He's not talking yet."

Not coherently, Ava thought.

"You need to hold him, Ava. Protect him for me." The woman's voice, naggingly familiar. "It's a matter of national security."

Ava caught her breath as she recognized the voice of Lyric from the surveillance tape. "You," she whispered, the hair on the back of her neck standing up.

"Yes," Lyric confirmed.

"Something's going down, isn't it?"

"Why do ask that?"

"He's restless. Murmuring."

"What has he said?"

"*Not* without authorization," Ava warned.

A sharp *tsk*, and then, "*Sent.*"

In its familiar soothing voice, HADAFA announced, "New orders have been received."

"Source of orders," Ava demanded.

"Your security clearance does not allow you to access that information."

"Confirm legitimacy of orders, then. Am I obligated to obey?"

"Affirmative. The orders are legitimate. Compliance is required.

Orders read: You will answer questions posed to you by the individual you know as Lyric, whom you are currently conversing with. And you will guard and protect the person of Matthew Domanski, who is presently in the room with you. Database identification number: 67678311055."

A slow, shaking breath. Ava knew for sure she'd wandered well out of her depth. "All right," she whispered.

"What did he say to you?" Lyric asked.

"Not to me. He's just murmuring, talking in his sleep. Stuff like, 'It's real. They're in place. Sigrún.'" Ava hesitated. "Sigrún," she repeated. "You wanted me to see that name, didn't you? Why?"

"I'll hold off on that explanation for now. Let's see what turns up. Stay with Matt. Keep him safe. If anyone comes looking for him, *do not* allow them in that room. *Anyone*, no matter who they say they are."

"Where are you?"

"I'm close. And I'm watching."

Stone cold. A predator, on the trail of prey.

"You're expecting someone to come," Ava said. "You're using him as bait."

The call icon winked out.

"*Shit*," Ava whispered. She took off her smart glasses, folded them, slid them into a pants pocket. But she didn't feel like Lyric was gone.

What the actual fuck have I stumbled into?

She paced the room, while Matthew Domanski—doubtless a pseudonym—continued his restless murmuring. After a minute, she asked HADAFA for Matthew Domanski's profile. To her surprise, the system complied.

He was a twenty-eight-year-old naval officer recently assigned to the patrol ship *Makani*, based out of Pearl Harbor. Unmarried. Living in base housing. How the hell had he ended up in the water? Going by his bruised face, she guessed he'd had help with that.

She went to the room's intercom. Identified herself. Put the staff on notice that their nameless patient was under guard, visitors not allowed. Then she tapped her tactile mic to activate it: "Call Ivan." When he picked up, she told him, "I've got a situation here. Federal bullshit. Need to know."

"Damn it, not now."

"No choice, boss. I'm going to get Akasha in here, as back up."

Akasha was fearless, and though Ava hadn't known her long, she trusted her to have her back.

"How long is this going to take?" Ivan asked.

"I can't answer that. Not yet. But I'm in contact with a handler, and I'm hoping it'll wind down soon."

"See that it does."

"In the meantime, I want firearms authorization, for me and Akasha. Better safe than sorry."

"Don't make *me* sorry," Ivan grumbled. He ended the call.

Outside, the wind began to wail around the corner of the building.

Akasha arrived half an hour later, in uniform, with a pistol on her hip. Ava's call to her had been brief: "I need you for guard duty. Armed duty. Check out a weapon and come to Queen's. I'll fill you in when you get here."

Crossing her arms, Akasha eyed Matt Domanski, who had finally subsided into a quiet sleep. "Don't tell me," she said. "Let me guess. He's a navy officer who gets clumsy at night and managed to fall overboard from the *Makani* not long after the ship evacuated from Pearl Harbor."

Shock lanced through Ava at the accuracy of this assessment. Had Akasha talked to Ivan? That didn't seem likely. Primed for suspicion, her gaze flickered involuntarily to Akasha's pistol.

The young officer noticed. "Hey, I'm on your side," she said with a cool, teasing smile.

"Then how?"

"I came in behind three uniformed MAs." MAs—masters-at-arms—sailors responsible for policing duties. "They're downstairs at the reception desk. I listened for a minute. They heard we recovered a John Doe. They want to know if he's their missing man."

"Did they see you?"

"I don't think so. They were working the receptionist pretty hard when I slipped past—and I came up the stairs, not the elevator."

"All right. This is Matthew Domanski. He's a spook who came to us courtesy of evening shift. They pulled him out of the water. I took the case as a favor to Ivan, but now I've got orders from on high to hold him here, guard him, and keep him isolated."

"For how long?"

"I wasn't told. But I want you to stay here, while I go talk with our visitors."

Ava took the elevator down. The doors opened, allowing her a view across the lobby to the registration desk. The three sailors were still there, dressed in their khaki service uniforms, all men, and all with a master-at-arms badge glinting on their chests. One stood on the side, arms crossed, watching as the other two engaged in an arm-waving argument with a pair of husky hospital security guards. The receptionist had retreated, to stand nervously in the doorway of a back office.

As Ava stepped off the elevator, everyone turned to look at her. One of the arguing MAs, the shorter of the two, immediately broke off his debate and came to meet her. He wore a chief's rank insignia.

"We're told you're holding one of our men," he barked in a command voice that was not quite a shout, but was far too loud for a hospital lobby. HADAFA whispered his identity: "Noel Walters, age 31, stationed at Joint Base Pearl Harbor-Hickam."

"Am I?" Ava asked him, meeting him at the halfway point between elevator and registration desk. Chief Walters stood only an inch or so taller than her, but he was broad in the shoulders, with a weight lifter's arms. Her right hand shifted casually to the shockgun on her belt as she calculated that he probably had fifty pounds on her. "What makes you think so?"

Walters lowered the booming volume of his voice. "Word gets around. Look, I don't want trouble. Domanski's supposed to be a decent guy, an okay officer. But he's had some . . . personal stuff, lately. No reason to end a career over that."

Meaning this was a face-saving visit, off the record despite the uniforms.

"Who sent you here?" Ava asked with a thoughtful frown. "Not Domanski's captain. Surely *Makani* is still at sea."

"We look out for each other, you know?"

She held his gaze as her hand tightened on the shockgun. If it came to it—if Walters had been told to collect Domanski no matter what—she would have to take him down. She could do it. She didn't doubt that. But were the two security guards ready to handle the others?

Quietly, so only he could hear, she asked, "You're not here officially, are you? You're doing a favor for someone. What were you told? Pick this guy up, get him on a plane out of here? What were you promised in return?"

"You don't know what you're talking about."

"Let me do *you* a favor," she said. "Take your crew and go. Leave now, and I won't file a report on this incident. If anyone asks, I'll call it a misunderstanding. How does that sound to you?"

His gaze shifted uneasily, the muscles of his jaw tight with frustration. Then he asked, with honest curiosity, "Do you know what this is about?"

"No. But I *do* have official orders that tell me I'm going to hold on to this guy."

He weighed this. Maybe he weighed the value of his career, too. After a few seconds, he nodded. "Yeah, all right. This one's yours." He turned and strode for the door, signaling his two companions to follow.

Ava held her position, watching through the glass doors as they got into a white SUV with federal insignia, parked just outside in the drop-off zone.

One of the security guards strolled over to her, the older of the two. He stood tall, with powerful shoulders. His eyes small in a wide face. A broad nose, full lips, buzz-cut hair gray, and his complexion a deep dark brown that testified to years in the sun. He carried himself like he knew what he was doing. A retired cop, maybe. Or former military. HADAFA offered no details. It just identified him as Francis Hoapili, social rating +12.

"Those the visitors you were expecting?" he asked as the car pulled away.

Ava shrugged and told him, "There may be more."

The elevator required only a few seconds to ascend, but that was time enough for Ava to contend with an impenetrable tangle of questions. Her orders were clear: Guard Matt Domanski. Presumably, Lyric was his handler. But why had Lyric frequented Ben Kanaele's bar, presenting herself with a theatrical demeanor that insisted on notice? Why had she compromised Ben's phone? Or had someone else done that? Had Lyric been at the bar because she was on the case, investigating The Predator Network and she'd already worked out the connection to Ben?

Sure. Maybe. But why draw Ava into her web? And what did The Predator Network have to do with Matt Domanski, and with national security?

Oh.

Shit.

A disappointed sigh as the elevator doors opened. Had she misinterpreted Domanski's murmurings? Could this be just another navy sex scandal?

Akasha flashed a thumbs up when Ava returned to the room. "HADAFA let me link to a lobby camera. You de-escalated that nicely."

"Thanks." A glance assured her that Matthew Domanski remained quietly asleep. "Turn off your AR."

A flash of surprise, but Akasha complied without asking questions.

Ava took off her own smart glasses and used a fingernail to work the tiny slide that switched off the power. She slipped the glasses into a pocket. Privacy laws dictated there must be no fixed cameras or microphones in patient rooms so they ought to be secure here.

Fairly secure.

The window was double-paned, but Ava signaled Akasha to step away from it anyway.

"What's up?" Akasha whispered.

Ava answered in the same hushed tone, "I don't really know, but I want you prepared. We're in deep water, and Huko is not the only incoming storm."

Ava sent Akasha an image of Lyric Jones, captured from the Sandalwood Lounge security video. Then she filled her in on most of what she'd discovered: Lyric's presence in the bar on the three nights with EP4 incidents, the way HADAFA had briefly reset, giving her a glimpse into Lyric's account, and the phone call she'd made, answered by Lyric herself.

Ava did not reveal that she'd looked at her own profile while she'd had access to Lyric's account, and she didn't mention her supposed second-degree associations with Hōkū Ala and the mysterious Sigrún.

"I think part of Lyric's assignment is to track hidden relationships," Ava mused. "Who knows who, how many degrees apart persons-of-interest might be, and who's close enough to be corrupted. Showing me that must have been a little demonstration of her reach . . . maybe, to get me on her side."

"Aren't we all on the same side?" Akasha asked with faux innocence.

Ava smiled. "*Right.*" She turned to look at Matt, noting his IV bag was nearly empty. A nurse would come in soon. "Listen, I don't know if this is a sex scandal, a terrorist operation, or something altogether different. But he was talking in his sleep before, and it sounded like maybe something was going down." She met Akasha's gaze. "If you've heard anything at all about Hōkū Ala kicking off their rumored insurgency . . ."

Akasha drew back. "I don't know what this guy's been saying, but I know it's got nothing to do with Hōkū Ala. So don't go there, okay?"

Ava stared at her, stunned by the brazenness of this almost-admission. No pretense of denial. No hint of guilt. "Just like that?" she asked.

"Why?" Akasha's lip pushed out in that familiar, pugnacious glare. "You want me to lie?"

"You want me to let it go?" Ava countered. "Compartmentalize it?"

She'd learned to do that in the army. Focus on your own assignment. Don't think too hard about the shit going down in someone else's area of responsibility.

Akasha lowered her chin. Dropped into a light pidgin accent. "Come on, Ava. You know we stay on the same side. And we get enough to worry about tonight." She gestured at the hospital bed. "Whatevah this shit's about, it's not gonna be worse than Huko."

As if cued by these words, a civil defense siren burst into life, wailing from somewhere outside the grounds of the medical center. Ava flinched, as the rising and falling tone triggered an old reflex to grab for body armor and run for a bunker.

Deep breath.

Instead of body armor, Ava grabbed her smart glasses and logged back into the system. Immediately, an emergency alert popped into her field of view: an official hurricane warning, issued at last.

As predicted, Huko had turned sharply north. The eye wall was on track to reach O'ahu's southern shore in roughly twenty hours.

Three minutes later, the siren went silent, but Ava remained on edge, pacing the hospital room while Akasha walked the corridor outside.

Where was Lyric? She had to be working here in Honolulu. She'd been at the Sandalwood Lounge just last night. But more than an hour had passed since Ava had talked to her. Why hadn't she come for her agent? Or was she waiting to see who else would come for him?

Her words: *Let's see what turns up.*

"Let's not," Ava murmured aloud. She called Lyric's contact number again, but this time she got no answer.

Ivan called after that. The chief was not in a good mood. "Get back here now. I've put in a call to HPD to take over guard duty.

You can leave Akasha on watch until an officer gets there, but I need another supervisor on the floor, *now*. We've got panic breaking out all over."

"Can't," Ava said. "I've got orders, issued through HADAFA, that tell me I have to stay here."

"Bullshit. I haven't seen any orders."

"Hold on."

She spoke to HADAFA, requesting her documented orders to be forwarded to Ivan. The system hesitated: an anomalous one-second pause suggestive of a massive records search, ones and zeroes woven together in complex cross-references. Even with that hint, HADAFA's pronouncement caught her by surprise: "The referenced orders have been rescinded by a higher authority."

Holy shit. Had Lyric been taken down?

"Ivan—"

"Get back here now. We don't have time to babysit a drunk sailor."

"This is about more than a drunk sailor, Ivan."

"HPD can handle it. I need you here."

He ended the call.

Ava glared at the wall, lips pressed together. She wanted to stay. Instinct told her that whatever was going on with Matt Domanski and Lyric Jones, it was more critical than herding frightened tourists into hurricane shelters.

But she had her orders.

She stepped out into the hall.

"It's on you, now," she told Akasha. "Ivan wants me home, but you get to stay until HPD sends someone."

For the first time that night, a hint of worry in Akasha's eyes. "You think they can spare someone tonight?"

"We'll find out. But if you're still here when Matt wakes up, call me. I'll try to sneak back. And if he tries to leave, arrest him on terrorism charges."

AVA STEPPED OUT of the hospital into a gusting wind, no rain yet. Headlights approached around the driveway. Her ride was here, right on time. She met the autonomous taxi at the curb and slipped into the front seat. The dash screen confirmed her requested destination: Harbor Station.

It was 8:00 PM, and as the taxi turned left onto Punchbowl Street, Ava saw that the panicked rush of traffic she'd witnessed earlier had passed. People had gone home to their apartments or their assigned villages, or they'd checked into hurricane shelters. Most would not be going out again until after the storm. The exodus had left the street looking eerily empty under the amber glow of streetlights.

In less than a block, the taxi turned onto Beretania Street, passing between the illuminated lawn of the capitol grounds and the Eternal Flame memorial on the mauka side of the street. Past the memorial, lay the dark, empty lot where the governor's mansion used to be. As the taxi rolled by, Ava's earbud beeped an alert. "Call from Gina Alameda," the system announced.

Her friend in vice.

"Answer."

A second beep to let her know the call was live.

"Hey, Gina. Got something for me?"

"Not a lot, sister. You do know you're wading into nasty waters?"

"It's real, then?"

"I think so, but I've never gotten in."

Up ahead, two sets of red taillights. Both turned mauka on

Alakea Street. No other cars. No pedestrians. She was past the capitol grounds now.

Gina said, "I only know what I've read in reports. The Predator Network is supposed to be a honeypot for pervs. Manipulators, revengers, voyeurs—from all around the world. They post realtime locations of vulnerable targets."

The taxi turned makai onto Bishop Street. Buildings constructed like concrete fortresses ruled the first block. Then a city park, with neatly mowed lawns and immature landscaping—a green memorial to the historic buildings that had once stood there. There were a lot of parks in the city now.

A gust of wind came rushing up from the harbor. It thrashed the young shower trees so recently planted along the street, reminding Ava of the dream.

Focus!

Already, the lights and activity of Harbor Station were visible, just a few blocks away.

Gina was saying, "The Predator Network tracks men as well as women. And children too, of course. Creeps who crave physical interaction browse the list. If they go after something, they're supposed to go linked, share the—"

Between one word and the next, her voice cut out. Ava's glasses beeped a warning that she'd lost her network connection. Maybe the taxi had too, because it abandoned its programmed route. Braking hard, it turned left off Bishop Street and onto Merchant—and as it did, all the streetlights went out.

Storm damage? That was her first thought. Had the wind taken down a network tower already? No. The idea was ridiculous. The wind was no more than twenty-five at peak gusts. She also rejected the possibility of an isolated power outage, because the streetlights weren't on the grid. They ran on batteries charged by retractable solar panels.

A hack, then. An attack. A deliberate blackout.

Hand poised over the emergency stop button on the dash, she scanned her surroundings: the deserted street, the empty sidewalks. No traffic. Just one parked car, a bulky black SUV, ahead on the right. Twisting around, she checked her six. Nothing.

Wait . . . that parked car . . . did it have a federal license plate?

She looked ahead again, confirmed it, and glimpsed the silhouette of a figure inside. The taxi gradually slowed, as if preparing to stop. Ava helped it reach a decision by slamming the base of her palm against the emergency-stop button. To her relief, the taxi responded, cutting over to the curb and stopping some twelve feet behind the federal vehicle.

Was she going to have to face the MAs again?

The taxi's cabin light came on. She cursed it. Drawing her shockgun, she confirmed it was set to *projectile*. Then she checked the network. Still jammed.

Up ahead, a door on the parked car opened into the street. No cab lights there. She could just make out a male figure. Tall, muscular. Moving fast in her direction.

She bailed out through the right-hand door onto the sidewalk and bolted, back toward Bishop Street.

A high-pitched buzz erupted behind her. All too familiar. Needle drone. She'd used them in the army to secure fleeing targets. She'd been trained to defend against them, too.

In a split-second move, she ducked sideways behind a pillar— one of several fronting a series of shops, all dark now. Too damn bad she hadn't had a chance yet to check out a pistol. She pulled her shockgun instead, and knelt, knowing she had about a second and a half to get ready.

Holding the shockgun in two hands, she followed the drone's progress by the sound of its buzzing flight. When she judged it was about to round the pillar, she fired.

The wireless dart whispered out of the barrel, faster than the eye could follow. It struck one of the drone's propellers, sparking as it glanced off. The drone tumbled, and shattered against the street.

Soft footfalls warned that her human pursuer was only steps away. She had to assume he was armed. She stood, and at the first glint of motion, kicked out hard. Her foot struck against aluminum. A low-voiced curse. The green bead of a targeting laser appeared to wink—on, off, on. He'd been carrying a shockgun, too. It clattered to the sidewalk. A momentary distraction.

She stepped around the pillar and turned to fire. But he'd anticipated the move. He lunged at her in a diving tackle, taking her
down with his greater mass but rolling so he took the impact of
the concrete sidewalk in his shoulders, his body cushioning hers.

Even so, her head snapped back and cracked against his teeth.
It fucking hurt. It hurt him too. He grunted and his grip around
her body loosened. She still had her shockgun. Her thumb shifted
the selection lever to *contact*. Then she drove an elbow into his ribs
and twisted hard, breaking her gun arm free. Rolling to her knees,
she pivoted, concrete tearing at her bare skin.

He still held her left arm, a veil of black mesh hiding his face,
distorting his features, but she glimpsed blood oozing from his
lip. She shoved the gun against his chest and pulled the trigger,
sending a jolt of electricity into him. He gasped and jerked back,
writhing, as she scrambled to her feet.

He wouldn't be down for long.

She holstered her shockgun, grabbed a zip tie from her belt, and
moved in to cuff him. That was when she heard the tire noise of
another car approaching from Bishop Street. Rescue for her? Or
reinforcements for him?

She glanced over her shoulder. Another dark-colored SUV.

For him, she concluded, and abandoned her attempt to handcuff
him. As the vehicle skidded to a hard stop, she ran, racing past
the first SUV. She used the pillars and a series of concrete planter
boxes for meager shelter, and to confuse the line of fire.

Behind her, a car door slammed shut. She heard one set of footsteps in swift pursuit, and tire noise as the vehicle accelerated after
her. But no threats or shouted directions. Whoever they were, they
operated in silence.

She looked ahead to the end of the block. A bar on the corner,
still open, colorful holiday lights around its door and quiet music
spilling onto the sidewalk. Just beyond it, streetlights glowed on
Alakea. If she could make the corner, she might be able to get a
signal, call for backup—

Plink! Plink!

A hard metallic double tap against the dark glass of the shop window beside her. Shockgun darts. But no buzz of a needle drone. She was breathing too hard now to hear pursuing footsteps, or tire noise. Where the hell was the SUV anyway? It should have raced ahead, to cut her off at the corner of Alakea—except the hack didn't extend that far, did it? The streetlights on Alakea were working, and that meant the surveillance cameras were working too.

She made the corner. Glanced back to glimpse a dark figure climbing into the parked SUV, the other vehicle already reversing back to Bishop Street.

Rounding the corner, Ava ran until she reached the driveway of a parking garage. She ducked inside and waited, shockgun in hand, striving to push aside her disbelief at what had just happened, to lock it away. This was real. *Accept it.* And be ready when they came.

A minute passed.

As her breathing slowed, she noticed her network connection had returned. Video of the event would have already uploaded to HADAFA. HPD would be by soon, asking questions.

Shit.

She waited another minute, but her pursuers did not return. So she started jogging toward the lights of Harbor Station, calling Akasha as she did.

"You okay?" she panted when Akasha linked in.

"Yeah, of course. You've only been gone like three minutes."

"I just got jammed and jumped."

"Oh *shit.*"

"I'm okay. But I'm pretty damn sure it has something to do with Domanski, and I want you to take precautions. Detach his ID bracelet. Move him to another floor. Don't ask permission. Don't involve the staff. Don't discuss it with hospital security. Just do it."

"Affirmed."

"And if someone from HPD shows up, confirm their identity before you turn Matt over."

Ava meant to call Ivan next, but the post-adrenaline aftershock had set in. Her hands trembled. She didn't trust her voice to be steady—and that would be a liability when it came to convincing Ivan to let her work this case. Better to wait, and persuade him when they were face to face.

She stopped in at her apartment, taking five minutes to wash up and to clean and seal the abrasions on her knees. When she confronted Ivan, she had to look like she could handle herself.

Then she crossed the street to Harbor Station, wondering that she'd heard no wail of incoming sirens. Had her smart glasses failed to record video of the assault? She had two minutes to wait for the next eastbound streetcar, so she whispered, "HADAFA, replay video of my altercation on Merchant Street."

"Confirm location as Merchant Street, Honolulu?"

"Yes. A few minutes ago, on Merchant Street."

"There is no available record of an incident matching that description."

"No available record?"

"Correct."

Meaning there *was* a record, but it had been tagged with a security rating higher than anything she could access. Her hand closed into a fist. A game was being played around her on a level she couldn't see. Tempting to go back and look for the shockgun darts, hold them as evidence. Maybe her assailants had left fingerprints. And if they had? HADAFA would just tag them with an inaccessible security rating, right?

Shit.

She felt duped. Foolish. Set up and then betrayed by the system she'd come to rely on. How could she trust HADAFA, knowing its analyses might be based on a filtered selection of allowable facts? When reality might be tucked away behind an inaccessible security rating?

Doubt left her unmoored, wondering who to trust, *what* to trust.

The streetcar arrived, and she boarded. Looked around. This time, she shared the ride with a transit officer, two hotel staffers in aloha-shirt uniforms, and an entertainer dressed only in T-shirt and shorts, who carried her formal attire in a garment bag draped over one arm—all four of them glum, their worried expressions communicating they'd rather be anywhere else.

As they passed the abandoned hulk of Ala Moana Shopping Center, a westbound streetcar went by. From what Ava could see, it was only half full, and carrying resort workers, not tourists. She checked the Atkinson taxi station as they passed, and found it deserted, along with the westbound streetcar stop on the Ala Wai Bridge. So the panic to get out was over . . . or it had moved on, to the airport.

But not everyone had chosen to go.

Sounds of celebration reached them as the streetcar passed Fort DeRussy Park: pounding music and werewolf howls and whooping voices from the heart of the strip.

"What is going *on*?" the entertainer demanded, clearly offended. With no tourists riding the streetcar, she had no need to hide a dark scowl.

The transit officer shook her head, looking disgusted. "It's gotten crazy down there," she informed them. "Street party, in full swing, from the Taipingyang to the Pākīpika."

Ava soon saw this was no exaggeration. Starting at the Taipingyang, revelers filled the pedestrian mall, some with drinks in hand, others dancing, as music reverberated off the hotel towers. The mood: a weird boil of nihilistic joy.

Ava thought she understood it. The cautious souls had gone, departing on passenger jets or holing up in the concrete bunker of the airport terminal. That left the district in the hands of the romantic, the daring, the desperate—the idiots—all gathered in gregarious celebration of the coming death of a city.

The night was right for it.

A full moon rose behind thin scudding clouds that trailed veils of misty rain across the sky, decorating the night with a pale, red-tinged moonbow.

Delicate white fairy terns whirled in the gusty wind, diving amid strings of colorful, bobbing lanterns hung across the promenade, each one haloed by a haze of salt spray from the crashing breakers. The violent pounding of the waves could be felt in the bones as a constant, low vibration—or maybe that was the music generated by a live band. Ava recognized the sound as *Tequila Folly*. Despite the risk of rain, they'd set up in the festival grounds, playing out in the open, at the foot of the refurbished Duke Kahanamoku statue. Dunes rose behind them, and an ecstatic crowd boiled all around. No way did they have a permit, but Ivan must have decided to look the other way.

As Ava jumped down from the streetcar in front of the Pacific Heritage, the band concluded one happy dance tune and rolled right into another. All around her, and on the balconies above, revelers cheered their approval. They danced in sweaty ecstasy, some alone and others hip-locked with their partners, grinding out rhythms that made Ava hot with just a passing glance.

Some creative fool, throwing environmental considerations aside, had released into the crowd what looked like a hundred light-weight plastic balls, six feet in diameter, each glowing in a sequence of rainbow colors. They rolled and bounced among the dancers, or were volleyed overhead to be caught and tumbled by the wind, ricocheting off buildings and balconies and palm trees, or striking the lanterns and falling back against eager, upraised palms or unsuspecting heads.

Ava named it in her mind: *Disaster tourism.* Spawned by a philosophy that urged the individual to: Be present! Seek experiences! Take risks! And celebrate! All fun and games, right up until reality kicked in.

Had any of these people ever seen buildings torn open, infrastructure shattered, friends you trusted your life to swept away, and the bodies of drowned children drifting past in the muddy polluted waters of a killing flood?

Dance, she thought bitterly. *Dance! And stay to see it all. You should see it. Experience it. Every bitter drop. It's people like you who brought us to this—people with your greed for spectacle, who share a stubborn denial of any responsibility for the fallout from an ongoing global climate catastrophe that you continue to fuel through your own selfish choices.*

A pleasure-seeking suicide cult.

She punched a bright pink ball out of her way, sending it lofting over the crowd. Then, dodging among the revelers, she escaped to the shadows of the hotel grounds.

Ava called Akasha as she rode the elevator up to the administrative suite. "HPD show up yet?"

"No. It's quiet here, and I'm still alone."

"Let me know if anything happens."

"I will."

No one was in the administrative suite and Ivan's office was empty. A quick check with HADAFA told her he was out on the dunes. So she took the elevator back down to the ready room and checked out a bike from the rack. It was still red-lit, with only a sixty-percent charge, but that would serve her needs.

She followed a projected green guideline along a route plotted by HADAFA. It took her across the esplanade, and then to the lagoons. Here and there, people wandered the paths. Some couples, but most solitary. Few enough that she could ride fast. As she entered the dunes, the street-party noise faded, replaced by the low ceaseless roar of breaking waves.

She brought the bike to a stop when her guideline turned, climbing the side of a dune. Looking up, she discovered a startling concentration of humanity standing in silhouette at the dune's crest—like a primitive army putting in an ominous appearance in a Hollywood flick.

No way could she ride up there; she'd have to go on foot.

Parking the bike off the path, she secured her helmet to it, then climbed, following a zig-zagging path of crushed dune grass. The already humid air, laden with salt spray, felt heavy in her lungs.

Just as she reached the crest, a curling wave collapsed on itself, generating a sharp *boom!* like a rifle shot. Instinct dropped her into a crouch. *Incoming!*

"Damn it," she murmured to herself. "Get a grip."

Standing up again, she moved among the gathered storm watchers, their moonlit figures adorned with a constellation of green, gold, and red LED indicator lights as they used their electronic gear in what must surely be a futile attempt to capture the majesty of the ocean. White water everywhere for a half-mile offshore, and massive swells rising beyond that, their peaks glittering in moonlight.

She scanned the diffuse horizon, but nowhere could she make out the dark silhouette of a patrolling warship. They had all fled ahead of the storm.

Later tonight, the full moon would conjure a peak high tide, but already the storm waves rushed the full width of the beach, to chew at the dunes, slowly eroding them. Eventually, the buried seawall would be exposed. Not tonight. But by this time tomorrow? Surely.

She moved on, following a rope barrier, newly installed along the dune's crest. Up ahead, a soft gold glow highlighted Ivan's position. He wore the black uniform, with the duty belt around his hips. As she approached, he was warning two twenty-somethings to stay behind the barrier. "If you tumble down there and the sea takes you, you're on your own. No one is going after you."

The lifeguard buoy he carried over his shoulder stole some of the punch from this warning. But he had height, muscle, and an aura of authority that warned these young men, *Don't mess with me.* They wised up, apologized, and retreated behind the rope.

Ava stepped forward. He saw her and nodded. "We'll have to close the dunes in another couple of hours. We don't have the personnel to keep watch on the entire shoreline."

"We need to talk," she told him.

He watched the crowd, not her. "So talk."

She spoke in a low voice, trusting the noise of the surf to secure their conversation. "I can't prove it yet, but I know what the connection is between the influx of EP4's—and it's likely we've stumbled into an ongoing federal investigation. But all that's on the shelf tonight."

"Agreed. With this hurricane, we are in an all-hands-on-deck situation."

"It's more than that." As quickly as she could, Ava sketched for him what had happened that night, both at the hospital and in the street. She told him her fears. "Matthew Domanski knows something and there is a faction on this island who does not want that knowledge to get out. This is serious, Ivan. I think we're facing the possibility of a major terrorist incident—and Akasha is standing guard on her own. HPD hasn't come. They probably can't spare anyone—"

"I can't either, Ava."

"Authorize me to go back," she insisted. "As soon as we can get Domanski turned over to his handler, we'll be back here. Promise."

chapter

10

THE GUSTING WIND whooshed past the dull-green steel poles supporting the vibrating canvas of Harbor Station's roof. Maintenance crews had climbed to the top of the poles and were working to furl the canvas, winding it back onto mechanical rollers, one section at a time.

The crush of departure had passed here too, and the station had gone eerily quiet. Only two HPD officers remained. The one on the upper level stood alone beside a waiting train. The other, at the foot of the escalator, gently urged a tardy group of three Japanese visitors to hurry upstairs and board.

Ava eyed the officer. She'd summoned an autonomous taxi, now ninety seconds out, but given that her last ride had been hijacked, she would rather find an alternate mode of transportation. What were the odds she could bum a ride from the cop?

Doesn't hurt to ask.

She started to walk over, conscious of the weight of the Glock on her belt, and of the extra ammunition clips. But as she skirted the curb, a taxi—not hers—pulled in. Ava stopped to watch it, sensing something off. There was no queue at the taxi station and no one hurrying over to claim the ride. So why hadn't this taxi been assigned to her?

The vehicle's left front door opened, revealing an empty seat. After a few seconds, a woman leaned into view—black skin, hair close-cropped and tightly curled, her face as lovely as that of a runway model, despite the hard lines of her smart glasses. Even in such an awkward position her pose held a casual elegance. Ava did not need HADAFA's whisper to identify her.

Lyric Jones.

Abandoning her plan to hit up the cop for a ride, Ava stepped up to the taxi, bending low to scan its interior. No one else inside.

"Get in," Lyric said.

"What the hell is going on?"

"Matt's waking up. I'm hoping he'll be able to tell *me*."

"That order you sent me was rescinded."

Lyric raised a thin eyebrow. "*Please* get in. I may need backup and you're going there anyway."

If Ava didn't get in, she'd never get answers.

She slid into the open seat, a hand resting on her holstered shock-gun as she kept a wary eye on Lyric. "Talk fast," she urged. With the sparse traffic, it would take the taxi only a few minutes to reach the medical center. "What's your involvement with Robert Bell? What are you working on? And why did you show me my expanded profile?"

Lyric eyed her in turn, leaning against the armrest, her long legs stretched out under the dash. She wore a silky black, long-sleeve collared shirt, with black slacks, and black flat-soled shoes. Her feet shared the floor with an olive-drab cloth bag, like a military flight bag. She said, "You're a person of interest to me. A close associate of my primary target—and I want you on my side."

"Akasha is a good cop," Ava said defensively, incredulous that the young officer had drawn this level of attention.

"I'm not talking about Akasha Li. Right now, her documented association with Hōkū Ala is a peripheral concern."

Ava drew back, her gaze shifting to the street ahead. A passing shower had left the asphalt wet and gleaming with crisscrossed paths of light cast by the streetlights. "Sigrún then?" she asked, a slight tremor in her voice.

She tried to imagine who at KCA Security might be associated with a dissident group whose existence was so sensitive that a high-level security rating was required just to access its basic profile—and she couldn't come up with anyone.

Her stomach knotted, knowing she'd failed to read the people around her, even with HADAFA's aid. A failure that might endanger the civilians she was sworn to protect.

"Sigrún," Lyric confirmed, her inflection transforming the name into a curse. "A subversive nationalist organization, headed by Daniel Conrad, with deep roots in the military. Commander Kaden Robicheaux was recruited by Conrad, and is an active member."

A shockwave of anger and denial exploded across Ava's mind.

This is bullshit. Complete bullshit.

Her hand darted for the emergency stop button.

Lyric was faster. She caught Ava's wrist. "It's true."

"It's a lie. You're fucking with me, the way you fucked with Robert Bell." She yanked her wrist free. The medical center, less than a minute away.

Lyric said, "Robert Bell and all his friends were my side trick. My cover for the real game—the game we're both playing now. Have you figured out yet who your assailants were?"

"Friends of yours?" Ava guessed.

"No. Friends of your friend. The man who tackled you—did you notice he made sure he hit the ground first, saving you from a possible head injury?"

An hour had passed since the assault. Plenty of time for Lyric to review video of the incident—an incident for which no record existed, not at the level of reality Ava inhabited.

"They didn't want to hurt you," Lyric went on. "Just take you out of play. Keep you quiet, in case Matt had communicated some critical intelligence to you."

The taxi turned in at the medical center, rolled slowly up the driveway, then stopped just outside the hospital's lobby doors. The doors opened, and the security guard Ava had talked to before, Francis Hoapili, stepped outside to glare. Clearly, he expected trouble.

"Let's talk to Matt," Lyric said sternly. "Then you can tell me whose side you're on." She picked up the bag at her feet and opened the door.

"What are you carrying?" Ava demanded to know.

"Clothing. Gear. Weapons."

The first defense when faced with an intolerable future was denial: *It can't be true.*

But what did Ava know of truth?

She used to think she could recognize it, that she could assess a situation, know who could be relied on, and act accordingly. Then she had gone out into the storm with Kayla, Miguel, and Tyree, believing in them, sure they could handle the violence and the chaos of Nolo without panic taking over.

Ava had been wrong.

Since then, she'd come to rely on HADAFA, trusting the system to show her the shape of people's hearts, even though the conclusions she'd been allowed to see were half-truths based on incomplete data sets, crucial information absent if it intersected in some way with an area of national security.

Ava had known the system worked that way, even before tonight. Kaden's sparse profile had been proof. But she'd convinced herself it didn't matter. She'd trusted the system anyway, because she *wanted* to believe what it told her. She wanted to know the actions she took were right, based on fact, and not on bias or volatile emotion.

But Lyric had taken away the delusion of certainty, and in its absence, doubt spread like a virulent mold across Ava's mind. Doubt kept her from calling Kaden. It left her ashamed to call him, to question him. She *trusted* him. She didn't trust Lyric.

She got out of the taxi, her face locked in a neutral expression despite the heat in her cheeks.

Hoapili looked her over. His gaze lingered on her pistol, before sliding over to Lyric as she came around the front of the taxi, flight bag in hand. "You bringing more trouble?" he asked Ava.

"Have you had more trouble?"

Akasha hadn't reported anything.

"Officer Li indicated she was expecting trouble when I found her trying to move the John Doe to another room."

"Trying?"

The guard shrugged a huge round shoulder. "We moved him to the third floor to allow for the option of a fast exit from the building."

Even without HADAFA's guidance, Ava had guessed Hoa-pili to be former military. Now she felt sure. A small ironic proof that her own judgment was not entirely dormant. But *why* had HADAFA not included such a basic kernel of information in Hoapili's profile? Was it because the system had predicted Ava would try to recruit him as an ally if she knew the scope of his experience?

If so, good guess.

She nodded to Hoapili. "Thanks, brah. I appreciate it."

"We'll be exiting shortly," Lyric added.

Hoapili regarded her with deep suspicion. Ava's regard for the man grew. "Do me a favor," she said to him. She slipped off her smart glasses and held them out for an electronic handshake. "Call me if any more military types come to visit, uniformed or not."

Hoapili nodded, took his phone out of his pocket, and held it close to her glasses long enough for the devices to trade numbers. "I don't like this spook stuff, sister."

Ava nodded heartfelt agreement. "I don't either."

Akasha called, as they crossed the lobby. "He's awake. Agitated. Asking for a phone."

"Yeah? Good timing. Show him that picture of Lyric I sent you. Let me hear what he says."

A flash of white teeth as Lyric indulged in a cutting smile.

The volume of Akasha's voice dropped but Ava could still clearly hear her asking, "You know who this is?"

A male voice responded, low and hoarse. "Where is she? Is she here? I need to talk to her, *now!*"

Ava pressed her lips together, shaken again, because she knew now that at least part of Lyric's story was true. But how far did it go?

Could it go all the way to Kaden?

Please, no.

Denial was the first defense against an intolerable future ... but Ava was past that. Going forward, she would have to gather and weigh what facts she could, and pick through the half-truths Lyric offered, and somehow decide for herself what it all meant—and hope she didn't fuck it up along the way.

In a neutral voice she told Akasha, "We're downstairs. On our way up now."

Put on guard by the sound of an irate male voice, Ava acted with caution, easing open the door to Matt Domanski's hospital room, just enough to assess the situation. Akasha stood a few steps within, shoulders square and elbows bent, poised as if to guard the door against Domanski's early exit.

He sounded eager to leave.

"I have to get out of here! It's critical. Sigrún will know I'm here. And time is running out." The wild timbre of his voice suggested he'd emerged from drugged exhaustion into a state of dynamic paranoia. He sat on the edge of the bed, bare-chested, his skin flushed and mottled, facing off against the fiercely scowling Dr. Banerjee.

The diminutive physician gripped his sinewy shoulder with one hand, ignoring the reality that she did not have the mass to hold him down. With her other hand, she wielded a pen light in an effort to examine his eyes. "You will go when I say you're ready to go," she snapped. "Now, sit still! Let me finish my assessment."

Domanski was not persuaded. Jaw set, he seized Banerjee by the wrists. The pen light fell to the floor as he shoved her gently but irresistibly out of the way and stood, naked and unsteady, his hospital robe abandoned on the bed. "Don't make me hurt you," he warned.

Ava pushed the door open wide and came in, Lyric a step behind her.

"Settle down, Matt," Lyric ordered.

At the sound of her voice, his head whipped around. Frantic hope and manic desperation shared space in his wide-eyed gaze.

Dr. Banerjee gripped his arm. "You need rest," she declared, guiding him back to sit on the bed. "I'm keeping you overnight."

Akasha gave Lyric a dubious look, but flattened against the wall, allowing her to stride past.

"He won't be staying," Lyric announced. "He's going with me." She chucked the flight bag onto the foot of the bed. "Get dressed," she told Matt.

His gaze darted around the room. "I need to report. It's gotten away from us, Lyric. It's really happening. It's happening *now*."

"It can't be happening now," Lyric assured him. "Locations of the principals are known. There's time. Get a grip on yourself and get dressed."

Matt looked uncertain, but he reached for the flight bag, while Lyric turned to Dr. Banerjee. "Have your system identify me."

Banerjee looked like she wanted to spit, but she did as ordered, studying Lyric through the lens of her smart glasses. After several seconds, Banerjee's youthful brow wrinkled. Her lips pursed in distaste. "All right," she conceded—agreeing, but to what? To accept Lyric's authority?

Evidently.

Lyric told her, "You will leave the room, attend to your other patients, and not discuss this patient with anyone."

Banerjee went stone-faced with suppressed rage, but she nodded, and walked out the door.

Akasha turned to Ava. For once, the young officer looked uncertain. "I don't like this. It's way outside our job description." She jerked her chin toward the door. "I'm thinking we should step outside too."

"No, stay," Lyric countered. "Both of you. I said before, I might need backup."

Ava nodded reluctant agreement. "We're already in deep."

Akasha's lip curled. "You sure you trust her? I got a feeling she wants us here because we'll make handy fall guys, when this goes to shit."

Ava answered honestly. "You might be right. And no, I *don't* trust her."

Lyric defied trust. She had some still-undefined association with The Predator Network. Add to that Ben's hacked phone, the rescinded orders, her casual dismissal of Robert Bell, and that sly edit of reality causing her name—an essentially anonymous code-name—to vanish from a list of prime suspects.

Even Matt shouldn't trust her. Ava eyed him as he hurried to dress, zipping up brown slacks and then stooping to slip on a pair of dull-brown, flexible athletic shoes. She marveled at his quiet obedience, though Lyric had come late to collect him, after using him as bait when he lay helpless.

And Ava remained haunted by her teasing glimpse into Lyric's user account—an incident devised to coerce her cooperation, and entice her along a carefully charted path—much like Robert Bell, on his run through the ghost blocks.

Lyric was *not* to be trusted and Akasha was right—they both should go before their careers were ruined and their futures compromised. But it wasn't as simple as that, not for Ava, or for Akasha, who'd made herself vulnerable by a too close association with Hōkū Ala.

Ava spoke blunt truth to the young officer. "She knows who your friends are. But go if you want. I'll do all I can to protect you."

Shock softened Akasha's expression, but only for a moment. She drew herself up a little straighter. Defiant. "And you?"

"I need to know what's true . . . and what's a lie."

Akasha considered this. Then her shoulder twitched in a disdainful shrug. "Yeah, fuck. Like you said. We're already in deep. Too late to back out now."

Lyric nodded her satisfaction, then turned to Matt. "Talk," she ordered as he pulled on a long-sleeved knit shirt, light tan in color.

"It's not just theory anymore," he told her, a hoarse rasp in his voice. "They've put the pieces together. They're really going to do it—and they'll use the hurricane as cover, to sow confusion over the origin of the launch."

"The *launch?*" Ava interrupted, feeling her hackles rise. "What are you talking about?"

Matt shrugged on a lightweight tan utility vest, while Lyric turned to Ava. "You're here because I may need your help—"

"With Kaden."

A short nod. "Matt has been deep under cover as a member of Sigrún, recently assigned to a cell aboard *Makani*."

"I fucked up," Matt said, zipping up the vest. "I tried to get word out to you. They stopped me. And then they needed a story to tell. So they tried to shoot me up with this junk they called Glide Path. Wanted it to look like an overdose." He shook his head. "No way was I going out that easy. I *had* to get word to you, so I bailed."

"You went into the water on your own?" Ava asked, incredulous.

His handsome, muscular shoulders rolled. "We were less than five miles offshore. The sea though, it was rough, and they'd gotten some of the Glide Path into me. I started to think I wasn't going to make it ... but I had to get the chip to shore." He looked at Lyric with a righteous gaze. "I have video."

She nodded. "Let's see it."

"No way this is real," Akasha said. "A story like that? You should be dead. And you shouldn't have a chip. They would have taken it away."

"I didn't give them the chance," Matt growled as Lyric unfolded a tablet. She held it an inch away from his back, between his shoulder blades, the standard site of chip injection.

The tablet pinged. Lyric checked the screen, and smiled. "Got it."

"There are hours of video on there," Matt said. "Let me show you the critical part."

He took the tablet, slowly stroking its face. "Here's the segment I wanted to send."

Ava heard a male voice, soft and secretive: "We're on. We're going to do it." She squeezed in to see the screen. Caucasian male, dark hair lightened with gray, his features soft, his age probably early forties. "Daniel Conrad's made the decision. The timing's a gift from God."

A woman spoke from offscreen, her voice tinged with horror. "I can't believe it's real."

"It's necessary," the first speaker answered. "A necessary sacrifice. The first step to restoring our lost honor. The Chinese navy won't be idling off our shores much longer."

Another offscreen voice, this one familiar: "Is it still *Denali*?" That was Matt speaking, but less hoarse than he sounded now.

The woman objected: "It can't be. Robicheaux's in port."

Ava flinched at the name.

They're playing me. They have to be.

But Matt had been fished out of a stormy sea on the edge of death. This wasn't a game.

The first speaker: "The submarine fleet will put out to sea ahead of the hurricane. It's going to happen, Weaver. It needs to happen. Conrad's right about that. And the world will never be the same again."

The segment ended.

Belief and disbelief existed simultaneously in Ava's mind. "*What* needs to happen?" she demanded, suspecting she already knew.

Lyric smoothed a section of the blanket at the foot of the bed, and started tapping the soft surface, her lips parted in concentration as her fingers danced across a virtual keyboard that Ava could not see.

Preparing a preliminary report?

Matt used the time to continue his preparations. He took a small pistol from the flight bag, checked the load, then dropped it into a deep pocket on the front of his vest. Two extra magazines went in the opposite pocket.

After a minute, Lyric finished with a flourish that doubtless represented a hard tap against the *Send* icon.

Slipping off her smart glasses, she turned to Ava. "People used to speculate that Roosevelt let Pearl Harbor happen so he'd have an excuse to take the country into World War Two. In a neat geographic parallel, Sigrún wants a new attack on Pearl Harbor, one that will force the president into a confrontation with China.

"When *Denali* puts out to sea, it will linger near the coast. At the height of the hurricane, it will fire a single missile from underwater, programmed to detonate over Pearl Harbor. A false-flag operation. *Makani* will monitor. Its officers will synthesize signals intelligence, enough that the incident can be blamed on a rogue Chinese commander."

Lyric's lips quirked. Her shoulders moved in a slight dismissive shrug. "The intelligence community won't be fooled, but it won't matter. To keep the country together, the president cannot admit the attack came from within. So the propaganda will be intense. The claim will be made that elements in the Chinese military felt they were getting a bad deal—trading centuries of debt repayment for a real estate investment that would soon be hugely devalued by the storm. Better to have a limited war and teach America its proper place in the hierarchy of nations. No other interpretation will be tolerated. And of course, we will need to respond. Sigrún intends for it to be a brief cleansing war, one that will burn off weakness and corruption, and reestablish the American hegemony."

"That's fucking crazy," Ava said, and Akasha echoed her.

Lyric raised an eyebrow. "I agree. But it's been a long time since crazy and real were mutually exclusive."

"No. I don't get it. You know all this, so the president should know all this—and the conspiracy hasn't been stopped?"

"I'm doing all I can to stop it, but I still have to go through the chain of command."

Matt spoke grim words, "And somewhere in the chain of command, is Sigrún."

A chime, inaudible to anyone but Ava, announced an incoming call on her personal number. She allowed only a handful of preauthorized numbers to ring through. Her gaze flicked down.

The caller's name: Kaden Robicheaux.

11

SHOCK BOLTED THROUGH Ava at the sight of Kaden's name. She raised a hand, a gesture to excuse herself from the company of the others. Three steps toward the door, telling herself the timing of this call was coincidence—though she didn't believe that.

And so? What are you going to do? Turn against Kaden on the word of strangers?

No. Not yet.

She double-tapped her mic, shifting it to tactile mode as she answered the call. "*Where are you?*" Breathing out the words on a remnant of warm hope.

Kaden ignored her question. Brusquely, "I need to see you. Now. This storm is looking even worse than we thought."

Is it? All too easy to read a dark, unspoken meaning into those words.

She said aloud, "I'm working now."

His next words alarmed her: "I know where you are."

She had to remind herself: At his level of command, he had access to HADAFA too—a higher level of access than hers.

"I'll be there in two minutes," he continued.

She heard herself ask, "Are you alone?"

Only after the words were out was she conscious of the reason for the question. Lyric had asked her, *Do you know who your assailants were?*

Lyric wanted her to believe those goons had been sent by Kaden.

"Meet me outside," Kaden said, without answering her question. "I'm in a white government sedan."

He ended the call.

A timid inner voice whispered to Ava that she did not have to go downstairs, she did not have to meet him—but that was a lie. She needed to know the truth.

She pulled open the door, tossing an explanation over her shoulder as she walked out: "I have to talk to someone. Do not go anywhere until I get back."

Akasha bounded after her, catching the door before it swung closed. "Ava, what the fuck?" she demanded under her breath as a young man in scrubs pushed a cart past. "Where are you going?"

"Just downstairs. Stay here. Keep watch. I'll fill you in when I get back."

Ava opted for the stairs instead of the elevator. More time to think, less chance of running into someone, and she wouldn't be visible to everyone in the lobby when she nudged open the fire door downstairs.

The third-floor fire door chunked shut behind her. Concrete walls amplified the sound of her footsteps as she descended: a swift anxiety-inducing drumbeat—the austere soundtrack of an art-film thriller. She flashed on a scene: a chorus of soulless gunmen waiting for her in the lobby.

Stop it!

She grabbed the stair rail, pulled up sharply, overwhelmed by a sudden certainty that she'd wandered into Crazy Town.

"This is ridiculous," she whispered aloud. "All of it."

Stubborn refusal rose in her. She did not want to believe what Lyric had told her. She did not want to be seduced into cooperation. Played like a puppet to some end she could not see.

But what if, by refusing to cooperate, all hell broke loose?

She spoke in a nearly inaudible whisper, trusting her tactile mic to capture her meaning: "HADAFA, I need a psychological evaluation. Subject is me, Ava Arnette. What is my expected perpetrator rating in my current circumstances?"

That sweet male voice: "The system is designed to judge the behavior of individuals within a range of circumstances normalized for them. Your current circumstances exceed the calculable range. There is no rating."

No shit?

She really had wandered beyond the border of familiar reality. No illusion of certainty was going to ease the grip fear held on her heart.

"You're on your own, kid," she whispered aloud, resuming her descent, emerging into the lobby.

Outside, visible past the glass doors, a white sedan.

Lights from the portico did nothing to illuminate the interior of the sedan parked along the curb, in the shadows just beyond the sheltered drop-off zone. Ava approached cautiously, a hand resting on her firearm. But when the sedan's right-hand front door popped open, she froze.

A light came on inside. Kaden leaned out. He looked back at her. "It's just me." His voice terse, his face stony and unreadable— at least to her.

HADAFA, she subvocalized, *This is a personal conversation. Do not record.*

"Affirmed."

The easy agreement surprised her. She took it as a good sign. HADAFA could have rejected the request, if the system had suspicions about either one of them.

After a moment of hesitation, she added, *But monitor the conversation, and flag any suspected lies.*

The AI's gentle voice spoke in her earbud. "Warning: Subject is a protected entity under the General National Security Directive. Your security rating is insufficient to receive assessments involving classified information."

Understood. Flag what you can.

Willing her body to relax, she went to meet Kaden. He slid over in the front bench seat to make room for her and she slipped in beside him. He glanced at the abrasions on her knees. "Trouble tonight?"

She found herself reluctant to meet his gaze, so instead she looked out the front windshield, at a little strip of garden planted with dwarf palms, their fronds bobbing in the wind, rain water dripping from them to the bed of laua'e ferns below. "It's been a strange one, Kaden."

"It gets worse from here."

She flinched as he took her hand, grateful her sidearm was on her opposite side, out of his reach, and then ashamed of the thought.

He said, "Huko's gaining strength. It's going to be as bad as Nolo."

"We're better prepared this time." She hoped it was true.

"Ava, I want you to evacuate."

At last she turned to meet his gaze. "I can't do that, Kaden. I told you before. My life is here."

"It doesn't have to be. You can leave. Go to the mainland tonight. Be with your kids. Your real kids. Not those ghosts that keep haunting your dreams. Ava, you don't want to go through that hell again."

"You think it's that easy? You think I can just walk out on my duty, my responsibilities? Tonight of all nights?"

"And be a cop somewhere else? *Yes*."

"I'm a cop *here*, Kaden. I was born here, in this city, and I work for the people who live here, who stuck it out here, who want to make a future here."

"That's guilt talking, and you know it. You hate it here. The heat, the hopelessness, the isolation. You won't even let your kids visit you here! Why stay? Why stay and risk your life, just to be working for the Chinese?"

"I'm *not* working for the Chinese."

"You're going to be, if you survive Huko."

He had never talked to her like this before. "It's just too bad the president sold us off," she shot back.

"Yeah." He squeezed her hand, assuring her they were together, in this at least. But his gaze remained hard, determined. Mixed signals hinting at subterranean levels of meaning.

So she dug deeper, needing to uncover the truth, praying it was a truth she could live with. "What do you know about Sigrún?"

He drew back, lip curled.

"You're familiar with it, then." She watched him, waiting for HADAFA to flag a lie.

He said, "Of course. I didn't think you'd know about it. It's supposed to be a faction of ultra-nationalists, active within the military. All branches."

"Led by Daniel Conrad?"

"I've heard that."

"If Conrad's in, then Cornerstone's got to be behind it. What's their goal?"

"Why are you asking?"

Ava studied him, striving to see the monster in his eyes. But she could not. This was the Kaden Robicheaux she'd known these past two months. She said, "I've got evidence of an imminent terrorist operation, with Sigrún's name attached."

A frown of concern. "What kind of operation?"

She said it casually: "A nuclear strike."

"*What?* Where?"

Pointing straight up: "The plan is to blame China. Trigger a confrontation."

Kaden leaned back. Now it was his turn to stare straight ahead. "Has HADAFA confirmed it?"

"Not directly," she admitted.

He nodded. "I don't know what you've heard, Ava, but the only weapon of mass destruction aimed at this island is that hurricane." He hesitated, before adding with grim sincerity, "I don't want you to be here when it hits."

HADAFA did not flag a lie, and still, she found herself reading a double meaning into his words. What would it be like? To be in the midst of violent hurricane winds only to have them shattered by the airburst of a nuclear bomb. Ava had visited Nagasaki. She'd stood beside the monument at ground zero, looking up, the memory of the bomb haunting the blue sky above her.

She pretended to stretch her shoulders, drawing her right hand back so that it brushed the butt of her pistol. Pull the weapon. Keep it low. A gut shot first to disable him, to prevent him grabbing for the gun. Then a shot to the chest, one to the head, and it would be over. His part in it, at least. Maybe the whole scheme.

If there was a scheme.

Her hand slid away from the weapon. *No way.* No way could Kaden be involved in anything like that.

"It's too late," she said softly. "Even if I wanted to leave, the flights are full and the airport is going to close."

"Check your email," he said. "You're taken care of. I got you that seat on a military flight. It leaves in two and a half hours. Time enough to get to your apartment and pack. I'd drive you, but I have to get to Pearl."

He really wanted her to go. Because of the storm? Or because Matt's allegations were real?

A faint buzz in her ears, a momentary dizziness, consciousness flowing into alternate or impending realities.

What would it be like at ground zero? Hammered by the wind and torrents of rain, a crack of lightning, a glance up at the roiling clouds, glimpsing a dark shape arcing out of them, too fast to follow—and then light.

Ava swallowed past a hard lump in her throat, belief and disbelief circling one another. "It's all right. You don't need to drive me. I'll call a taxi."

"I'll do it." He tapped his phone. "Okay, one's on the way."

He leaned over to kiss her, pushing her smart glasses up into her hair as he did, his lips warm, soft against hers, and then feather kisses across her cheek. He pulled back, gazing at her for a few seconds more.

She returned his gaze and still she could not see the monster in his eyes.

Another kiss, as the taxi pulled alongside. "Oh," she said. "I should go."

He got out, walked around the car, hugged her. "I'll see you again, when it's over."

Last chance, she told herself. Heart pounding, she leaned in and whispered in his ear, "You're not part of it, are you, Kaden? You're not part of Sigrún?"

He jerked back, glared at her. "That's what you're thinking? You think that's possible?"

"It's been suggested."

"By who?"

"Just tell me it's not true."

"Of course it's not true. How could you even—"

She laid her fingers against his lips. "*Stop.* I have a duty to consider the evidence presented to me. You know that."

"It's not true, Ava. Someone's trying to get between us, to use you, against me."

She wanted to believe him.

"Go to your apartment," he urged. "Then go to Hickam."

She nodded. He kissed her forehead. She got into the taxi and he closed the door. As the taxi drove her away, she looked back. He stood watching. Then the taxi turned onto the street, and she couldn't see him anymore.

Ava faced forward, drew a deep cleansing breath, then reached to adjust her smart glasses only to discover she was not wearing them. Kaden had pushed them up into her hair, an inactive position, and there they were still, their external sensors asleep.

HADAFA had been denied the chance to evaluate the truth of his last answers. Belief and disbelief still endured together in her mind, both equally real.

The taxi advanced another block before she updated the route, instructing it to circle back to the hospital. Kaden might be tracking her. He might be tracking the taxi. If so, he would call again. He wanted her to leave the state.

She needed to make calls of her own. First, her new friend in hospital security.

"Eh, sistah," Hoapili said when he linked in.

"The white sedan that was out front, is it gone?"

"Yeah, left right after you. No visitors since. When you takin' your boy out?"

"I'll be back there in a few minutes. We should be leaving right after that."

"Gotcha."

Next, she called Ivan. It took him almost a minute to link, and when he did, his first words were, "Are you done over there?"

"No. I'm still working to confirm. I don't like it, Ivan. I want to call it bullshit. But I can't." Ava sketched the plot as she understood it.

A snort of horrified laughter from Ivan. "No way. Our own guys are not going to nuke Pearl Harbor. Wipe out their own shipmates? It won't happen."

She hadn't mentioned Kaden's name. She didn't intend to. Unless Ivan had seen it in her profile, he wouldn't know who Kaden was, any more than Akasha would, because Ava had not shared that part of her life.

"Their shipmates aren't in port," Ava reminded him. "The surface ships have already sailed ahead of the hurricane. The subs leave in the morning. The fleet won't be directly impacted . . . and they were going to lose the harbor in the handover anyway."

"*Fuck*," he whispered and she could tell he'd been hit by the surreal possibility that it was all real.

A flashing text on the periphery of her vision indicated another call. Her gaze shifted, taking in the name. Francis Hoapili.

Hold, she subvoked, and then returned her focus to Ivan.

"Talk to someone," she begged him. "I know you have connections with navy brass. Tell them what I've told you. Name names. And forward a picture of the woman, Lyric. See if you can confirm she's legit."

"Yeah," he said. "I'll call you back."

Ava shifted her gaze again to pick up Hoapili's call, but he hadn't stayed on hold.

The taxi turned into the hospital driveway. Ahead, there was now a tan-colored van parked under the portico. "Identify and log," Ava whispered, as the taxi pulled in behind it.

HADAFA sent a coded request to the van's transponder, then reported, "The vehicle self-identifies as owned by Bryan's Truck & Van, a vehicle rental company. VIN and visible license numbers are correct for vehicle make, model, and color."

If Ava had a case number, she could submit a request for the identity of the responsible party. But she didn't have a case number. She didn't even have any real evidence of a crime.

A voice mail came in while she was still in the taxi. Hoapili, sounding rumbly and tense: "Got a crew here, sistah. Five sailors, looking for their friend."

Matt had too damn many friends.

She called Akasha, who picked up instantly. "You left!" she accused, speaking under her breath. "I saw you on the security camera."

"No choice," Ava said. "But I'm back now, and we've got more trouble downstairs. Five, this time."

"Yeah, I saw 'em. Boy-gang. Military. You want me down there?"

"No. Stay quiet. Stay hidden. But be ready to move. And keep double-oh-seven in sight. I don't want that duo disappearing on us."

"You got it. And I talked to a nurse. I know a back way out."

"Thumbs up. Stay tuned."

As Ava entered the lobby she saw Hoapili standing on the side, hands on his hips and eyes narrowed, emanating irritation as he glared at a posse of young men hovering around the desk. Presumably they'd been talking with the receptionist, but if so, that conversation broke off when Ava came in. All of them turned to look in her direction.

To a man, they were lean and fit with neat military haircuts, but no uniforms. Three Caucasian and one Asian, the fifth a mix of both races. *Ah, shit.* She recognized that last one as Tyrone Ohta, one of Kaden's officers. His lower lip was cut and swollen as if—maybe—the back of her skull had cracked against it earlier that evening.

Ava felt sick, as the last of the scaffolding supporting her doubt began to give way. Just minutes ago, Kaden had denied any involvement with a how-could-you-believe-that intensity. But Ohta's presence transformed his denial into a lie.

What do you really believe, Kaden?

The voices on the video had spoken of restored honor, a necessary sacrifice . . . and the world will never be the same again.

Not long ago, Ava had watched a World War II documentary about the British assault on the city of Caen, in Normandy. For four years the German army had held the city. After D-Day, the British had been assigned to take it, but they could not, despite days of effort and extensive casualties. So they shifted strategy, deciding to bomb the city into ruins, to make a sacrifice of both it and the French civilians who still lived there—because sacrifice is called for, sometimes, on the path to a greater good.

Did Tyrone see it that way?

Did Kaden?

For decades, the death cult of right-wing politics had poisoned society, sowing discord and fighting every effort to mitigate climate change. Their leaders—the powerful few—had banked wealth, while pollution and pandemics indiscriminately cut short the lives of ordinary people. Hypocrisy, corruption, willful denial, cowardly decision-making, treason, and lies, lies, lies, had locked the country in a straitjacket of poverty and degradation.

Did the members of Sigrún really believe they could burn all that away with a glorious war? Did they imagine the Chinese would back down? That the sacrifice would be limited and the conflict controlled?

War never worked that way.

She drew herself up, spine straight. If there'd been a choice, she would have ducked back outside into the dark—but Ohta had locked eyes with her, recognized her—and by his expression she knew he had not expected to see her still there.

Conscious of the weight of her sidearm, she greeted him with a friendly but puzzled smile. "Why are you here, Tyrone?"

She watched him make a decision. His face went smooth, unreadable. He approached her. Met her halfway.

"Are you the cop in charge, Ava? The staff says Matt is under police guard and we can't see him. What's he supposed to have done?"

Play acting, just like her, pretending nothing was off.

"How do you know him?" she asked. "You're a submariner. I was told he fell off a surface ship."

"It's all one navy."

Ava allowed a tone of accusation into her voice: "Is it?"

"We got a call from *Makani*. They asked us to do them a favor. They want to keep Matt's case out of official channels. You know. The embarrassment."

"Embarrassment?" she echoed, incredulous—but also outnumbered, as Ohta's friends circled around. She glanced right, left, taking them in. None familiar to her . . . but surely they were Kaden's crew, too?

She said, "In case you haven't heard, there's a hurricane on the way and all of you should be at your duty stations, not here. This matter does not concern you."

Ohta's eyes flashed, frustration visible in the curl of his injured lip, in the vertical lines between his brows. He didn't know how to handle this turn of events, with a tough-looking security guard watching, and surveillance cameras recording every word.

Doubtless he'd been warned not to make a scene, not to draw the attention of civilian law enforcement.

Ava decided to help him out. "Go, Tyrone," she said, hoping he couldn't hear the hammer beat of her heart, that he wouldn't notice the sweat sheen on her cheeks. "You and all your friends. Get out of here, before you're found AWOL."

To her surprise, they did as ordered. Ohta signaled them to go, and they left without another word. Ava watched them get into the tan-colored van, with Ohta on his phone even before the door closed.

The van pulled away, but how long before they came back?

12

AVA TOOK THE elevator up, stepping off into a quiet third-floor hallway. The man staffing the nurses' desk looked relieved to see her. "There you are. Officer Li said you'd had some trouble out front."

"A little drama," she agreed. "Things quiet up here?"

"Depends on your definition. She arrested him, the John Doe. Checked him out of the hospital."

Ava spoke in a carefully neutral voice. "I didn't see them leave. You showed them a back way out?"

He pointed. "Down the hall, on the right. There's another set of stairs. When you get to ground level, take the staff-only door. Code to shut off the alarm is 9972." And then, as if an afterthought, "Officer Li said to call her, when you're free."

Nice to know. Why the hell hadn't Akasha just sent a message? Had Lyric told her not to risk it? Had they worried a message would be seen by the wrong eyes if Ava lost the confrontation downstairs?

She jogged down the hall, listening to Akasha's phone ring. The door to Matt's room stood open. Ava slowed, glanced inside. Empty. An untouched meal tray. An unmade bed.

She hurried on.

Four rings, and Akasha still had not picked up. Were they still on their way down? Matt had been unsteady on his feet. He'd be slow on the stairs. Was the stairwell blocking the signal?

Just as Ava reached the fire door, a flurry of gunshots broke out—*pow-pow-pow . . . pow*. The reports muffled by walls and the white noise of air-conditioning, but unmistakable.

Ava shoved the door open. From below, sounds of wind and a distant siren. Someone had killed the alarm and opened the exit door.

Two more gunshots, far louder, almost on top of each other, echoing in the stairwell.

The call went to voice mail. Ava dropped it and charged downstairs, making noise as she did, calling out, "It's me! It's Ava!" She didn't want to draw friendly fire. "What the fuck is going on?"

Two flights to go, when Lyric answered, her voice reverberant against the concrete walls. "Your friends are back, Ava! We've got black masks in the parking lot."

Tyrone Ohta and company. They must have gotten fresh orders.

"Right behind you," Ava warned as she descended the last flight of stairs.

The exit door hung open, twelve inches or so. Akasha crouched, peering out the gap, her service pistol in hand. "Twelve and two," she said.

Matt answered, "I see 'em."

He stood over her, holding his own pistol, showing no sign of weakness or disorientation. Rock steady, now, though less than fifteen minutes had passed since Ava had walked out of his hospital room. Matt had used the time well, equipping himself with smart glasses and a tactile mic. Around his hips, a large camouflage waist pack with bulging pockets.

Lyric lingered two steps behind them and out of the line of fire, a pistol in one hand, the now empty-looking cloth flight bag in the other. A faint illumination of data flickered across the lens of her smart glasses as she eyed Ava.

"Sit rep!" Ava demanded.

Lyric answered: "Three individuals arrived as we exited. They called for our surrender. We retreated under fire. They've blocked our taxi from coming in, but I've got an app cracking the security on their van. It'll be ours in another minute."

"And then we get the fuck out of here," Matt growled.

"No," Ava said. "No way." This case was careening toward a legal cliff. She had to stomp the brakes now before momentum carried them over. "We stay here. Wait for HPD. I've got Ivan working his navy contacts. If this is real, if Sigrún is real—*fuck*, if you're real—the navy will take over."

"Navy's not listening," Matt barked back at her.

"*Make* them listen. Jump the chain of command. Put it out in public. DM the goddamn president. No way can this succeed as a wildcat operation."

Dual sirens now, getting closer.

"Lyric?" Matt asked. "How's our ride?"

"Stand by."

"Stand down," Ava countered. She moved past Lyric. "Akasha, get that door closed."

"Van's ours," Lyric said. She caught Ava's shoulder, fingers squeezing, her gaze intense behind the lens of her smart glasses. "Maybe the chain of command will step up, but right now that's not happening."

Still crouched at the door, Akasha turned her head, shooting Ava a dark look. "You could have stopped this," she accused.

"*What?*"

"Eyes forward," Matt instructed. Akasha's head snapped back around. "On three," he told her. "One, two, three."

Staying low, he kicked the door wide. Akasha fired to the right; he sent a flurry of shots straight ahead. A scream of pain or rage and then a screech of tires. A van came into sight at speed, backing down a narrow lane. It was the same make and model as Tyrone Ohta's van—except this one was dark-blue.

Not the same.

The van reversed all the way to the exit door, rear cargo doors opening as it came.

Ohta had left in a tan-colored van.

"Identify and log," Ava whispered.

At the same time, Lyric barked, "Get inside!"

Akasha and Matt moved without hesitation, jumping into the van, clambering over the backseat. Lyric let go of Ava's shoulder and followed. Ava moved too. Herd instinct? A desire to protect Akasha? *Fuck it, just go, or you're going to be left behind.* She vaulted into the van.

HADAFA answered her query: "Vehicle self-identifies as owned by Bryan's Truck & Van. VIN and visible license numbers are correct for vehicle make, model, and color."

Ava crouched in the cargo space, arm hooked over the backseat to secure herself as the cargo doors closed and the van accelerated out of the lane, shooting past ancillary buildings in the medical center.

Same rental company, same make and model, but blue . . .

She looked out the rear windows, but saw no one—and saw no bodies. A dizzying sense of surreality washed over her as the van dashed through a parking area beneath a low-rise building, and skidded onto a side street.

She was being punked, wasn't she? Ah, it would be so easy to engage in that paranoid, self-centered fantasy! She was being punked. Royally punked. And even Akasha was part of it.

Absurd, she chided herself.

On the chance it would help, she shifted her smart glasses to stealth mode, switching off location data, GPS, and sensors that might be used to track her position. She messaged Akasha to do the same.

Even so, they were far from invisible. Cell tower check-ins would still yield general location along with their direction of movement, and the van's transponder might already be conversing with a police drone, but she did what she could.

The van slowed to legal speed as it turned onto Beretania Street. Out the back window, Ava saw two taxis a few blocks behind. Then a police car turned into sight, blue lights flashing—but it turned off at the side street they'd just left, while the van continued on through the capitol district.

Ava looked up front. "Were the surveillance cameras off for that little engagement?"

Matt had moved up to the middle seat. Akasha was in front behind the optional steering wheel, with Lyric in the seat beside her. At Ava's question, Lyric turned. "Yes. I tried to shut them down, but they were already off."

"I need to plug in a destination," Akasha said. "Where are we going?"

"Pearl," Lyric announced.

"To do what?" Ava wanted to know. "You think you can hack your way in past security? Hijack *Denali*?"

"Or prevent it from sailing?" Lyric asked. "Maybe. Maybe not. But I'm going to try."

The van turned mauka onto Nu'uanu Avenue. Akasha switched it to autonomous mode, then turned to glare at Ava from behind the lens of smart glasses that showed no glow of electronic activity. "Lyric told me why you're involved in this. It's because you've been fucking this guy, Kaden Robicheaux—"

"*Yes*," Ava snapped. Her gaze shifted to Lyric. "I've known Kaden two months. He's an honorable man. And yes, he has been my lover, and yes, Lyric thought she could use that against him."

"I thought I could," Lyric agreed. "But I was wrong. You had a chance to take him out—stop this whole thing—and you didn't do it. It's on you now, if that bomb goes off."

"*Fuck* you."

But wasn't it true?

If Lyric wasn't lying . . .

If Matt's video wasn't a deep fake . . .

If Kaden was not the man she had believed him to be . . .

Ava had asked Kaden for the truth and he had denied his involvement, but only after he'd pushed her smart glasses into her hair, putting them into sleep mode. He had done that so he could kiss her more easily . . . or he had done it to ensure she would not be using HADAFA to assess the truth of his denial.

"I may have made a mistake," Ava conceded, not knowing which of her actions was the mistaken one.

Matt spoke up. "It's hard to accept when the people you love and admire turn out to be the bad guys."

"Do you accept it now?" Akasha demanded. "Do you understand these assholes intend to burn *our* people for their own stupid political game?"

"That's the story Lyric is telling," Ava agreed as the van accelerated onto the Lunalilo Freeway.

Akasha said, "Don't pretend like you don't believe it. You have to believe it. With what's at stake, our only choice is to respond like it's real."

Ava's smart glasses chimed: Ivan calling. "Hold on." She linked Akasha in, then picked up, speaking before Ivan could: "Has the navy detained Kaden Robichaeux?"

"No, and they're not going to. I talked to a navy investigator. He couldn't tell me much—I don't have the security clearance—but you're being played, Ava. The navy has sent a special unit to the hospital to apprehend the woman, Lyric. She's considered dangerous. Do not approach. She's a double agent gaslighting for the Chinese, sowing doubt and dissension by starting rumors of domestic terrorism in the ranks. And they want the John Doe, too. He released malware on the *Makani*. When it goes down, you and Li need to stay out of the way."

Ivan didn't know about the gunfight.

Akasha stared at Ava, stunned, scared.

Thinking aloud, Ava said, "One of Kaden's men came to the hospital with four other sailors. He told me they were there as a favor to *Makani* . . ."

Could that have been true? Could Lyric have faked a message from *Makani*, asking for Kaden's help?

Gazing at Lyric, she tallied the score: The Predator Network, and at least three Chinese women set up for assault and possible rape; Robert Bell running on a mapped path to a gruesome death; Ben Kanaele's phone hacked; and Ava, drawn into a conspiracy that circled around a man she'd come to love and admire.

Lyric returned her questioning gaze with the calm of an innocent woman . . . or of a psychopath?

Had Lyric just hijacked a van being used by the navy's special unit?

"Are you still at Queen's?" Ivan asked. "Are you still with *her*? If you're in a position to do so, Ava, arrest her. And don't discuss with anyone! I'll relay to the navy. This is super-secret. You got it?"

"Confirmed," Ava said, her voice husky with tension. "I'll let you know when it's done."

She ended the call.

Lyric told her, "They know everything about you. They have your full psychological profile. They know what you'll react to, they can predict your behavior, and they know the best way to confuse you is with obvious lies."

"You know that, too," Ava said.

"Yes, but I'm telling you the truth when I say that they want to manipulate you into a weapon they can use against me."

Ava renewed eye contact with Akasha. A slight nod. She slipped her pistol from its holster.

Matt watched her closely, his eyes made visible by a slight illumination welling from the lens of his smart glasses. She had no doubt he had his weapon in hand. It might already be aimed at her, through the seats. Even so, he spoke gently: "It's real, Ava. I was part of Sigrún. I heard what I heard. And I didn't go into the water for nothing."

He had gone into a storm-tossed ocean. He should have died there. He almost did. He got very lucky, when Officer Limbaco pulled him out.

Ava's shoulders sagged. *Wait*, she urged herself. Work out the truth. There was still time. Don't risk a wrong move, because the cost would be unredeemable.

She slid her pistol back into its holster, feeling sick.

Nine years ago, she'd trusted her own judgment over the chain of command, and three fellow officers had drowned along with the children they'd imagined they could save. She'd sworn to never again defy the chain of command. An oath now broken. Who would die, this time, if she made the wrong decision?

Ava remained crouched in the van's cargo area. From that position she had a good view out the back, and a swift egress should she need to exit quickly. Traffic remained sparse. She counted only seven sets of headlights on the freeway behind them, and even fewer vehicles on the town-bound side.

The freeway's wet concrete absorbed the glow of streetlights and threw it back, changed into mesmerizing diamond glints.

Don't just sit, she chided herself. *Take action!*

Right.

She took the most direct action she could and called Kaden. The ring tone pulsed and pulsed and pulsed. The call went to voice mail. "I need to talk to you." Nothing more than that. She ended the call. Shifted her focus. *You're a cop, so investigate.*

She asked HADAFA for Kaden's profile. She had looked at it once, prior to their first date. Now she skimmed it again, to find it unchanged, the same bland, shallow bio she'd seen before. No hint of intrigue or malfeasance. Not at the level of her security clearance.

But there was one item that caught her attention. His oldest daughter, Astrid Robicheaux, age twenty years, was listed as next-of-kin. Ava had never been introduced to Kaden's daughters; he'd never talked to them in her presence. But Astrid's contact number was included in the record. Ava decided to call. Astrid might be willing to talk, and she surely knew more of her father's background and beliefs than appeared in Kaden's HADAFA profile.

Ava saved the number into her personal contact list and initiated the call—but she canceled it when a new message appeared in her field of view:

You are now logged out of
HADAFA

Akasha shouted, "Hey! What the fuck? I just got kicked out of HADAFA."

"Same," Ava told her.

A text message arrived from Gina Alameda in vice: *What the hell? A warrant just came in for you and Akasha.*

Ava relayed the news.

"We were defending ourselves at the hospital!" Akasha objected. "Protecting Matt. A person-of-interest. What the fuck were we supposed to do?"

"You did the right thing," Matt said in a reassuring voice.

"Ivan told us to arrest these two," Ava reminded her. "Warrants exist for them, too."

Super-secret warrants?

Akasha pulled her pistol. She aimed it at Lyric.

Ava wasn't going to let her go down alone. She drew her weapon, too.

But the van swerved, braking hard, a shift of momentum so sudden, Ava was thrown across the cargo compartment. Lancing pain in her upper arm. Her head cracked against glass. The shriek of skidding tires and a furious yelp from Akasha.

The van had come to a hard stop in the emergency lane on the right side of a section of elevated freeway. Akasha had been thrown against the optional steering wheel. Matt remained secure, braced between the seats. Lyric looked unruffled. She calmly released her safety belt. "Theft override function," she announced.

Ava gritted her teeth, cursing herself for her stupidity. She should have anticipated the override function. It was hard-coded and unhackable. Even Lyric couldn't get around it. Accessed through the manufacturer, it allowed law enforcement agencies to safely and temporarily brick a vehicle if suspected of being stolen or involved in a crime.

She unlatched the van's backdoors, kicked them open, and bailed out onto the rain-wet road, weapon in hand. A taxi sped past, and then another. More headlights on the way. Still distant, a wail of sirens.

Turning back, Ava aimed her weapon into the van. "No one move!"

Matt froze, part way over the back seat. Lyric stopped too, flight bag in hand. She'd been scrambling to the back of the van. It had stopped so close to the freeway's concrete wall, the front door wouldn't open; there wasn't even room on that side to squeeze out the window.

Akasha had scrambled out into the traffic lane, but she'd pivoted, holding her weapon in two hands, elbows bent, aimed inside.

"We can wait to be arrested and hope that what Ivan told us is true," Ava shouted at the young officer. "Or we can run with these two and see where it takes us. What do you want to do?"

Akasha's lips curled, her mouth worked, spilling a silent, *Fuck*.

"Run," she said aloud.

Ava lowered her weapon, stepped aside, and waved Matt ahead as a light rain began to fall. "Let's go."

The van had just completed the merge onto the elevated airport viaduct. To the east—Diamond Head side—the viaduct descended to Nimitz Highway. Ava pointed past a veil of falling raindrops glittering under bright streetlights. "That way. And run. It's probably a half mile to the bottom of the ramp."

Matt took off, with Akasha on his heels, but Lyric hesitated at the back of the van.

"Go *on*," Ava growled. No way was she going to let Lyric get behind her. For all she knew, her usefulness had expired and Lyric was only waiting for an opportunity to put a bullet in the back of her skull.

A quirk of a cold smile, and then Lyric was running too, her black street clothes and her flat-soled shoes performing well as athletic wear. She'd either abandoned her weapon or stashed it in the flight bag, which did not seem quite empty anymore.

Police sirens wailed out on Lunalilo Freeway, growing swiftly louder. More would be rushing in past the scattered bars and warehouses that still survived all along Nimitz—but maybe not right away. With the police stretched thin ahead of the hurricane, Ava bet that backup would be slow to arrive. She bet her freedom on it. Only when Lyric was a safe thirty feet ahead, did she holster her weapon and join the race to escape.

The broad ramp from Nimitz up to the viaduct had always passed in a flash whenever Ava had taken a taxi that way, or ridden in a patrol car. On foot, that same ramp felt like it had undergone an Alice-In-Wonderland transformation, growing immensely longer, or else she had shrunk to minuscule dimensions. Each all-out stride lopped off just a tiny percentage of the distance she needed to cover.

Blue lights and howling sirens raced in on the H-1 merge. Would the patrol cars make a turn against traffic to pursue?

But there was no traffic. A pull-over-and-stop signal must have been issued to every autonomous vehicle Ewa-bound on Nimitz because no one was coming up the ramp. But in the distance, refracted by rain, flashing blue lights marked the positions of two oncoming police cars. Ava saw them, and knew she did not have time to reach the bottom of the ramp.

She strove to fill her already heaving chest, intending to call out to Akasha, *Don't resist!* But Akasha had stopped running. She heaved herself over the side of the ramp and disappeared. Ava wanted to scream, knowing the jump from that point was too high. But Matt was gone from sight, too. Had he gone over first? Was there something below to land on?

Lyric remained in sight. She threw her shoulders back and slowed. Then she rolled over the ramp's low concrete wall. Ava saw it then: two heavy-gauge hooks fitted to the wall, rust stains running from them to the road bed.

Ava reached the hooks, and peered over. Hanging immediately below, she saw a narrow platform hemmed in with black netting. Lyric knelt on the platform as it swayed with her weight. She glanced up at Ava with a cool half smile. Then she crept out of sight beneath the ramp.

Ava looked around for surveillance cameras, but this wasn't the strip or the villages. If there had ever been security equipment here, she guessed it had been vandalized and not replaced.

Blue lights and screaming sirens both ahead and behind. Ava heaved herself over the wall, landing in a crouch, fingers clawing at the netting to keep her balance as the platform bobbed beneath her.

It was made of heavy steel, the kind of plate used to temporarily cover excavations in roadways. More chains shackled it to bolts drilled into the underside of the ramp. Beneath the ramp, a gap in the netting. Lyric slipped through it, disappearing below as police cars screamed past overhead.

Ava scrambled to the gap. She looked down, and saw to her shock that there were people below. Not just Akasha and Matt. A lot of people, at least a hundred, LED lanterns everywhere, shedding clean white light across a scene of organized chaos.

A settlement of tents and tiny homes on wheels occupied the gravel-covered ground under the soaring ramps of the freeway interchange. The tents were FEMA issue—the kind that should have been distributed after Nolo, but shipments had gone awry, disappeared, leaving people to devise their own emergency shelters.

Good to know at least one shipment had finally been found and put to use.

But now the tents were being taken down, the tiny homes hooked up to trucks and hauled away.

Akasha looked up, saw her, and waved at her to hurry.

Lyric was already halfway down a ladder that linked the platform to the ground. It was an emergency ladder, the kind that could be stashed in a box, ready for use as a fire escape, its steps linked together by chains. Ava bit her lip. She hated ladders. Especially dangling chain ladders. If even one link gave way, the whole thing might collapse.

You've been through worse.

She'd seen war. She'd endured Nolo.

Just do it.

She eased herself over the edge and started down, clutching hard at the chains.

13

A HEDGE OF mangrove, leaves bright green in the white lights, sheltered the settlement on two sides, separating it from Moanalua Stream and breaking up the wind that skipped in across Keʻehi Lagoon. In the resulting pocket of calm air, mosquitoes swarmed, so thick that as Ava descended the ladder they mobbed her, landing on her face and on her bare legs, their tiny feet tickling—but they did not bite. A rogue fragment of engineered DNA had contaminated their gene pool, changing their feeding behavior so that in the presence of human scent they could not extend their proboscis, a predicament that left them confused and easy to swat—but hardly worth the effort.

Several tiny bats swooped past as Ava neared the ground, feeding on the mosquito bounty. Carnivorous moths—another CRISPR creation—competed with them, their iridescent bodies darting through the air in tumbling, chaotic motion. Mosquitos had been allowed to live on because they fed other levels of the reconstructed ecosystem.

As Ava reached the ground, a bold female voice rang out. "Coastal cops? You kind of out of your territory, yeah?"

Ava turned to look. Akasha already had a hand up, palm out—a cautioning gesture—backed up by her stance: cocked head, raised chin, eyes narrowed in a combative expression. Mixed signals, entirely appropriate to the situation as a tall, heavyset woman approached.

Age and excess weight had worked together to shape soft pouches in the woman's dark brown face. Her long graying hair was wound into a tall bun like a pagoda on the top of her head. Gold crescent moons dangled from her ears, above strong shoulders damp with rain. She wore an olive-drab tank-top, brown cargo shorts, and brown work boots, and she carried herself with an undeniable air of authority.

Ava stepped between her and Akasha, ready to grab her shockgun, but unwilling to do so. "We're just passing through," she said in a conversational tone that belied her anxiety and her impatience to move on. "Business of our own."

"Business to do with those sirens overhead? We don't want trouble."

"Neither do we." Ava swept her gaze around the settlement grounds. "You're evacuating. Good."

Piles of discarded possessions cluttered the area, but that wasn't surprising given the speed at which people were working to take down tents and haul off the tiny homes. The settlement appeared to have been well organized. The gravel had been raked into level platforms for homesites—more than half already vacated—and a row of what looked to be composting toilets stood off at a distance.

The woman nodded. "When Nolo hit, it flooded out all this place—washed out the peninsula, chewed at the freeway foundation. Not stayin' for Huko. Don't wanna see good people die."

Ava supposed even good people had their reasons for living under a bridge in a shanty town, instead of in the comfort of the sponsored villages. Some had surely been evicted from the villages for behavioral issues, and doubtless others couldn't get housing because they were in the state illegally. Some would have their names on outstanding warrants—*we fit right in on that score*—but others might be here because they wanted to be close to the city, or to the ocean. She noted surfboards and small canoes being loaded onto flatbed trucks along with the collapsed tents, and coops of unhappy chickens.

The woman said, "I don' know your business an' I don' wanna, but no way you can stay here." She pointed to the mangrove growing along Moanalua Stream. "You like my advice? Go down there.

Cross the bridge. Get buses on the other side, in the park. They take you to the stadium, no questions asked."

With that, she moved on to interrogate a couple arguing over what possessions to bring and which to leave behind.

Ava turned to Akasha, who shook her head, whispering, "What the hell have we gotten ourselves into?"

"Shit," Ava answered, side-eyeing Matt. "Deep, deep dirty shit."

"It *is* real isn't it?"

"It could be real."

"And we gotta keep going, 'til we know for sure."

"Yeah. Come on. Let's move before those cops get down here."

Ava felt confident the officers wouldn't spend a lot of time looking—there were more important tasks to deal with tonight—but better for everyone if they stayed out of sight.

She looked again to where the woman had pointed. Beyond the rapidly disappearing encampment, she saw an old man with a stiff gray beard, a small backpack, and a hefty walking stick, disappear into the hedge. Must be a gap there. "Let's cross the bridge," she said. "Re-evaluate on the other side."

She turned to look for Lyric, but didn't see her. She scanned the encampment. Tall, thin, black-skinned, Lyric was an anomaly in this gathering; she should have been easy to spot. But she was nowhere.

"Lyric's gone," Matt announced.

Ava turned on him. "Gone where? If she has transportation, a way out of here—"

"She'll find a way. Easier on her own. She has to get back inside, back under the umbrella of the agency—and you need to decide if you're in or not."

"Like there's a choice? You've burned my career. Akasha's too."

The sound of a police siren, circling around.

Shit.

Ava hooked her fingers at the younger officer. "Let's go." Moving off at an easy run, she made for the gap in the hedge. Akasha and Matt followed.

What to do?

For now, stay out of sight. Get in a secure position. Then reach out, see if she could negotiate *her* way back inside.

A simple plan, but she was doomed to fail the first step as long as she looked like a coastal cop.

Eyeing the abandoned possessions scattered on the ground, she spotted a gym bag, mud-stained and with a hole in the corner. Empty? She grabbed it. It felt empty. Without slowing down, she checked. Found only a couple of candy wrappers.

"What?" Akasha asked.

"I don't want to look like a cop. Find another bag, a backpack, something to stow your gear in."

They kept moving, but they cast around as they did, kicking apart piles of debris. Akasha came up with a kid's green backpack, printed with a dragon's face, one eye gone and the toothy mouth half ripped off.

"Fine. Let's go."

Matt hadn't waited. He'd gone ahead. He didn't look like a cop. With his vest and brown-camo waist pack, he looked like a hard-bodied civilian modeling mercenary chic. They sprinted after him, catching up as he entered the mangrove. Akasha followed him, then Ava. The mangrove's dense canopy cut off the moonlight and the light from the settlement. Just a few steps in, darkness closed around them. One more step, and Akasha slipped in the mud. She fell hard on her ass, cursing.

"Stay put," Ava told her. "We'll change here. Get your shirt off. Turn it inside out to hide the insignia—and stash your belt." She followed her own instructions, wrestling her shirt off, elbows banging against branches, rustling against leaves. Large drops of accumulated rainwater dripped from the canopy, cold against her head and her bare shoulders. And all around her, mosquitos whined.

Working blind in the darkness, Ava reversed her shirt, then pulled it on again, yanking the long knit sleeves down to her wrists. Next she unclipped the flashlight from her duty belt, then stuffed the belt into the gym bag. She zipped the bag up, then shouldered it. Not much of a disguise, but better than nothing.

Finishing ahead of Akasha, she took a few seconds to check her alerts. Ivan had left a message; so had an FBI special agent. Each a request to turn herself in.

Not yet.

"Ready," Akasha announced.

Ava leaned close to whisper. "Let's be careful when we cross. It's supposed to be no-questions-asked on the other side, but if HPD has officers on scene, we need to stay out of sight."

"I'm with you."

"Let's go, then."

Ava triggered the flashlight. She rotated quickly through its white-light and green options, settling for a paltry red beam that would let her eyes adjust to the dark.

The ruby light revealed a muddy path chopped through the mangroves and partly paved with broken concrete blocks. As Akasha's fall had proven, the footing was treacherous, but mangrove stems provided handholds, polished from use.

With the light revealing the way, they moved down the shallow bank to where Matt waited at the water's edge.

"*Damn*, the water's already high," Ava observed.

The stream had risen to drown the path. The start of the floating bridge was now six feet out in the slow-moving current.

Rainfall could not explain this flood. There hadn't been enough rain yet to make an impact. No, either the tide had pushed in, or this was the leading edge of the storm surge.

Matt went first, wading through the muddy water as a misty rain wafted down from moon-limned clouds. Akasha went next.

Ava took off her rain-speckled smart glasses, stashing them in a pocket. Then she entered the water, placing each foot carefully, feeling for the concrete blocks that marked the path. Cold water lapped at the hem of her shorts by the time she reached the bridge.

Despite the clouds, there was light enough from the moon that she could see the old man who'd preceded them, already nearly across. She switched off her flashlight.

The bridge was constructed of aluminum rowboats chained together, each with outriggers for stability. Sheets of plywood had been fitted over the thwarts to level the path for walking, and a single line of taut rope provided a hand-hold.

The first rowboat bobbed as Matt boosted himself onto it. Its stern sank, but the outriggers kept it from going under. He moved quickly, and as soon as he stepped onto the second boat, Ava signaled Akasha to follow. When she was clear, Ava scrambled up, flexing her knees to balance as the plywood rocked beneath her. She advanced with small, carefully measured steps that allowed her to smoothly transition to the second boat, and then the third. Ahead of her, Akasha moved confidently, and Matt had almost reached the other side.

Another wall of mangrove crowded the opposite shore. Glints of light shone through the trees from the park beyond. A gust of wind rocked the branches, sending a loud spattering of water showering off the leaves. And the moonlight brightened—enough that Ava could see someone huddled on the path just above the reach of the water, head bowed and arms wrapped around knees. Her first-responder instincts kicked in at the sound of sharp halting gasps—a woman taken by grief, on the edge of heartbroken weeping.

The old man stood alongside the forlorn figure, gesturing, his grumbly low voice chiding: "Mo' people coming. Mo' gonna come. You like dem see you geeve up? Is hard, sistah, I know, but you not dead yet. Come on now. We go. One mo' night, one mo' day, one mo' miracle. Dis all happening again, no mean it's your turn. You see dat boy again when God wills it. Not before."

Matt slipped past them, a ghost unworthy of even a glance. But Akasha remained solid and real. "Eh, Auntie," she said, bending down to speak. "Come, we help you. No one gets left behind."

Ava switched on her flashlight as she waded ashore. The red beam revealed a bony woman shivering in the rain. Caucasian, though years of sun had left her skin dark and heavily lined, contrasting with white hair tied neatly behind her neck. She looked ancient in the red light, but that might have been more grief and hard living than years. Mud covered her hands, the front of her blouse, and most of her knee-length trousers, as well as her splayed feet and the rubber slippers she wore, the kind that people on the mainland called flip-flops.

Easy to see she'd had a bad fall trying to climb the bank.

Acting on instinct, Ava moved in to help. It's what she'd always done. It's why she'd gone out into the storm in defiance of orders—because when people needed help, you helped them.

Guilt chided: *You still nevah learn, eh, Ava?*

Yeah, maybe not.

The cold equation of mission priority demanded she follow Matt's lead, walk away, don't waste time on this sad, broken woman. But a sense of community, of connection, of humanity, knit this island together. Ava was part of that—and it would take only a few minutes to lend a hand.

"Let's go, Auntie," she said. "You can get warm at the stadium. People there gonna need you to comfort them."

"Dat's right, dees ladies right," the old man said. He wore only shorts and a T-shirt, but didn't appear cold. Reaching out, he pulled the woman to her feet. She was small, maybe five-two. Probably didn't weigh a hundred pounds.

"My things," she said in a whisper.

Ava played the beam of her flashlight around and found two large shoulder bags under the mangrove roots. Designer brands, now covered in mud. She picked them up and handed them to Akasha. More people were coming over the floating bridge. Blue lights flashed through the mangrove on the other side of the stream.

"Let's go, Auntie," Ava said again, extending an arm for the woman to hold. "We're all called to do what we can for each other tonight."

They made their way up the path, to the well-worn lawn of a city-and-county park. More debris on the ground, evidence of another settlement, newly abandoned. A couple of young men stood nearby, enjoying their electronic cigarettes, exhaling clouds of sweet-smelling vapor. They were outliers of a crowd of over a hundred, some in line to board one of two buses waiting in the parking lot under amber lights, others standing uncertainly in small groups. Many of these had dogs leashed beside them. No doubt they'd been told the animals would not be allowed on the buses.

Ava looked for police, but saw none. Instead, a squad of sailors wearing the latest blue-themed revision of the navy's working uniform organized the evacuees, helping them tag and then load their possessions onto a flatbed truck before steering them into the line for the first bus.

The woman had only her two shoulder bags and the old man only his small backpack. "I think you can just get in line," Ava advised them.

Akasha handed the woman her bags, saying, "Take care."

A murmured thank you. The old man nodding, assuring her, "We stay in God's hands."

Ava had felt grounded as she helped the old woman up the bank, comfortable in a world she understood. But as she turned away, familiar reality retreated. A strange sensation swept over her. She felt all the quiet activity in the park contracting, closing in around her. The artificial lights brightened and blurred, the anxious incessant murmur of human voices rose in volume, and the drizzling rain fell slow and warm.

Where was Matt? She looked around, but couldn't see him. Had he vanished like Lyric? Ava remembered how he'd moved like a ghost up the stream bank. The old man had not even looked at him. Maybe he hadn't really been there at all. A hallucination? A fantasy conjured from her lonely imagination? And Kaden . . . uncertainty surrounded him too. Ava swayed, rocked by a sudden sharp suspicion that she'd suffered a break with reality and none of this was real . . .

Deep breath.

No getting out that easily.

Akasha touched her arm, unwittingly anchoring her back in the world. "Look what's coming."

Ava followed the direction of her wide-eyed gaze to see a young sailor approaching with a tentative smile. Slender, no taller than her. The dark-blue ball cap he wore bore a silver submarine warfare badge, and above it a name: *Denali.*

Ava tensed. Her hand twitched as she gauged the time it would take to pull her sidearm.

But there was no aggression in the kid's bearing, no malice in his eyes. She guessed his age to be nineteen, maybe twenty. He spoke to her softly, shyly. "I think I seen you before, ma'am. You the commander's friend?"

Her throat tightened. A simple question with an answer too complicated to convey. She mustered a short nod, then asked, "Isn't your vessel due to deploy?"

"Not s'posed to say, ma'am. But what I can tell you is, me and my shipmates are tasked on an emergency basis to help out with evacuating civilians out of inundation zones." A self-deprecating smile. "We the *non*-essentials."

"I don't think there are any non-essentials aboard an attack sub, son."

He rolled his eyes. "Yeah, we all got our place, but *Denali* can make do for a bit with a skeleton crew."

"You gonna stay ashore for the hurricane, then?"

"That's what I'm told, ma'am. It's gonna be excitin'."

Ava drew a shaky breath, striving not to reveal her inner horror. She glanced around, looking more closely at the other sailors. She counted six, in a range of ages and ranks. Two other youngsters were white or maybe mixed. The others, like this kid, were black.

These would be the crew loyal to the country. None would be members of Sigrún; they'd probably never heard of it. And because of their loyalty—and the risk that they would object to and interfere with a nuclear launch—they'd been put ashore, condemned by Kaden to die in the blast. That was the reality guiding Ava's actions tonight—though she still didn't truly believe it.

The kid's brows knit. "Whatcha doin' out here, ma'am?" he asked, now with a skeptical edge, like it had just hit him how odd and unlikely that was.

She answered in a carefully neutral voice. "Same as you, son. Seeing how I can help with the evacuation. Is Ohta out here with you?"

"Ah, no ma'am. The officers are needed at the dock."

Of course. Every sailor making up the skeleton crew was surely either a Sigrún member or had been flagged by HADAFA as compliant, or sympathetic to their cause. Sigrún had surely planned well. None of those due to sail aboard *Denali* would rise up to stop the launch.

Ava held out her hand. The young man looked surprised, but he shook it. "Thank you, sailor, for helping out. And thank you for your service."

"Yes, ma'am. I better get back to work, ma'am."

She walked away, heart pounding, sensing Akasha trailing behind.

"How you like that for a fucked-up coincidence," Akasha said, just as Matt faded back into existence, materializing alongside them.

"He sent the innocents ashore," Ava told them.

"*Shit*," Akasha said. "I guess that's true. So what do we do now? What *can* we do?"

Ava glanced at Matt, who was eyeing the line of vehicles. More had come in, civilian farm trucks by the look of them, parking behind the flatbed. She said, "Let's get to the stadium and figure it out. There'll be people there, enough that we won't stand out. And the open market should still be operating."

"You want to go shopping?" Akasha asked.

"I want to stay out of custody. Easiest way to improve our odds is to change into civilian clothes. But I don't want to ride the bus there—"

"Yeah, no way. If Sigrún comes after us, or even HPD, it could get ugly fast."

"And any confrontation would slow the evacuation. We are not going to put these people in danger."

"Let's see what those trucks are doing," Matt suggested. "Maybe we can hitch a ride. Once we're there, I'll see about finding us our own means of transportation."

chapter

14

WITH THE GUSTING wind and Huko imminent, people were in a mood to help each other—no questions asked. Two farm trucks—both flatbed electrics, Chinese manufacture—had been brought in by volunteers to evacuate the animals not allowed to accompany their owners to the stadium. Cardboard carry boxes and battered airline crates secured the small dogs, the cats, and a family of rabbits. A few larger dogs were confined too, but there weren't crates for all of them.

So after the driver agreed to squeeze three human passengers onto the flatbed for the short drive to the stadium, Ava found herself comforting a frightened pit bull while she huddled with Akasha and Matt at the hollow center of the flatbed's stacked load. A nerve-grating cacophony of plaintive mewing, whining, and competitive barking surrounded them—and still it felt like a respite.

The truck started to roll, startling the pit bull. It raised its head from Ava's lap. "It's all right," she murmured.

She waited until the truck pulled out onto Kamehameha Highway. Then she leaned in, eyeing Matt. With her voice hushed and the rush of wind to cover her words, she told him, "So talk. We kept you out of Sigrún's hands. We got you out of the hospital. Now what? Tell me you've got a plan that'll keep *Denali* from launching that missile."

"Lyric's working on it." He met her gaze, his bruised face calm, assured. A modern portrait of belief.

"You know that? You've been talking to her?"

"No, but when she gets to a secure position, we'll hear from her again."

Ava considered this. Lyric had deep access into HADAFA, but she didn't have superpowers. If this was all a set-up—if Ivan's intel was right and Lyric really was a double agent working for the Chinese, legitimate officers should have already brought her down.

But if she was loyal? If she was the real thing, despite the fatal game she'd played with Robert Bell? Then the evidence she'd gathered on Sigrún should have triggered an emergency action.

That hadn't happened—and Ava could parse that only by accepting what Matt had said, before they'd left the hospital room: *Somewhere in the chain of command, is Sigrún.*

"What if we don't hear from Lyric again?" Akasha asked.

"It gets harder," Matt said, his gaze still fixed on Ava, so intense it made her feel vulnerable.

She didn't like feeling vulnerable. "You're still thinking you can use me to get to Kaden. *I* think we're past that."

A slight shake of his head. "We don't know that yet—"

He broke off with a distracted look, just as Ava's earbud pulsed a sequence of emergency-alert tones. A male voice followed—not the standard voice she'd selected for her system, but something sterner: "Emergency Management System alert. Warning: The Ānuenue Taxi fleet will end service at 1 AM. All travel must be completed before that time. Hurricane Huko is an extremely dangerous Category 5 storm. Shelter only within hurricane-rated structures. Emergency shelters are available at—"

Ava tapped her earbud, ending the message. Her hand returned to the dog, stroking its head to bleed off tension. They still had time before *Denali* sailed. But what, realistically, could they do with their time? Arm up and storm the main gate at Pearl Harbor? Send Matt over the wire in a commando operation to sabotage *Denali*? Or send in an autonomous drone to do it?

She shook her head. "We're nowhere if we don't find allies."

Akasha shifted beside her. "Yeah. We're in a fucking black hole, aren't we?"

Maybe not. Ava had worked years for HPD. She knew a lot of people there. And Akasha had some link to Hōkū Ala—tenuous, maybe, but real. Maybe they didn't have to do this all on their own.

She glanced at Matt. Found him zoned out on his smart glasses, while Akasha grasped at a wistful alternate history: "Shit, Ava. How did we let this happen? We should be at the coastal park. That's where we belong."

Truth. Right now, Ivan would be organizing a sweep of the beach and the dunes, to clear the park of anyone lingering in the inundation zone. Later, KCA Security would clear the strip and check the lower floors of the hotels to ensure compliance with emergency procedures.

Anger welled up in Ava for the way things had gone. She'd given up her place in the world and she'd taken Akasha down with her . . . but none of that mattered, not in the greater context of what might be real.

The truck pulled off on the side of the highway, just outside the stadium complex. Ava whispered goodbye to the dog, then jumped down, waving her thanks to the driver and her partner. Matt and Akasha set off at a fast walk toward the lights and bustle of the stadium complex, but Ava lingered.

Reach out, she chided herself. Make connections. Tap every potential resource, however unlikely . . . lowest-risk first.

In the momentary quiet afforded to her there on the side of the road, Ava double-tapped her tactile mic and subvoked, *Call Astrid Robicheaux.* She saw no downside in talking to Kaden's college-age daughter—and you never knew what you might learn from relatives.

Gazing southwest toward the glow of Naval Base Pearl Harbor less than a mile away, she waited for a ring tone. None came. The call went straight to voicemail.

Speaking aloud, she left a terse message: "I'm a friend of your father's. There's an emergency situation here in Honolulu. It goes beyond the hurricane. I'm hoping I can get a call back, as soon as you're able."

Kaden was somewhere in that sprawl of light. Probably at the dock, aboard *Denali*. Ava wanted to ask him, to demand to know, *How do you explain any of this to yourself?*

The stadium complex had still felt new when Nolo roared through, ripping apart the roof that shaded the stands, tearing up the seating, and destroying the field lights. But the structure's shell had survived the hurricane, as had the ancillary buildings. A small hotel and a mini-mall, positioned along the rail line, were among the first structures to be repaired and reopened after the storm.

Soon after, the state government decided a community center was desperately needed to boost morale, and the stadium would do nicely, thank you. Volunteer work crews cleared the field of debris and stripped every remnant iron seating bracket from the stands. Audiences made do with what was left, bringing canopies for shade, and their own folding seats or cushions to pad the bare concrete tiers. Ava had been to a few concerts and a couple of amateur games. There had always been room enough, just using the lower courses.

She held the memories of those days and nights, but as she trotted to catch up with Akasha and Matt, the memories felt like they belonged to a different person, a different life.

A bus glided by, moving on past a line of parking structures left dark and unused by the collapse of private automobile owner-ship after Nolo. The bus would deliver its passengers to the bright lights and ubiquitous security cameras surrounding the stadium. Closer, quieter—and less subject to surveillance—was the open-air market.

Established in a re-purposed parking structure close to the train terminal, the market provided a home for an ever-changing assortment of independent vendors. Every day and most nights the first three floors hosted farmers, crafters, resellers, and other entrepreneurs working to supplement their basic income. Most advertised their social ratings alongside their prices, but even those who didn't had reasonably good reputations, because the market's management group didn't allow anyone with a negative rating to set up shop.

"Let's split up," Ava said as they approached the ground-floor entrance. "Not a lot of people tonight, no surprise. We'll be less noticeable if we're not moving in a pack. Get what you need, get changed, and get out. We've got options, but we need to keep moving."

"Look confident," Matt added. "Don't look lost, and don't look like a victim."

"We're fucking cops," Akasha reminded him.

"Right. And don't look like cops."

"Just be back here in twelve," Ava said. "Ping your location if you sense any kind of trouble."

They agreed. Akasha headed in to look at the nearby stalls. Matt split off toward another aisle. Ava watched him walk swiftly past the stalls and the browsing shoppers, heading toward the back of the market like he knew where he was going.

If he found what he was looking for back there, would he drop out of sight? Fail to make the rendezvous?

She doubted it. If he had wanted to, he could have slipped away with Lyric. And if he had, Ava probably would have stayed to meet the cops who'd been looking for them.

She kind of wished it had gone that way. But she suspected part of Matt's assignment was to keep an eye on her, to keep her close, in case it turned out she still had an in with Kaden.

Setting a countdown timer, she headed upstairs.

Lines and numbers had been painted onto the concrete floor to mark out the stalls—each with enough room for the vendor's van or truck, and their display tables. The vendors who sold art, kitchenware, flowers, potted plants, carpets, small furnishings, and packaged or preserved food—all those had closed down, their goods packed up and evacuated.

But at least half the stalls remained open, all offering highly discounted fresh produce and prepared foods—storm sale!—and their supplies were going fast. Ava grabbed three sets of bentos in waxed-lined cardboard boxes—styrofoam and one-use plastic had been banned more than two decades ago. A looming headache warned her she needed to rehydrate, so she picked up a glass bottle of some repulsive-green athletic drink and chugged it. Water would have been better, but you couldn't get it in plastic bottles anymore. She returned the glass to the vendor, then went to the third floor to look for clothes.

The stalls closest to the stairway all sold used clothing. Once Ava figured that out, she bypassed their tables without browsing. If this turned out to be her last shopping expedition, she wanted to spend her money on new stuff, tags still attached.

Money. Her thoughts chased the word. After this adventure— no matter what happened—there wouldn't be any more paychecks going to her ex-husband for the support of her kids.

Shit.

Her own parents were gone. There'd be nothing more from her side . . . but her girls were older now. They had basic income and they were smart. She told herself they'd be all right. Did her best to believe it.

"Hey, sistah," a friendly female voice called out. "Watcha lookin' for? Looks like you caught some rain. Need dry clothes for the night?"

Ava turned to see a smiling, short-haired woman, plump, with Asian features, no more than five-two, standing behind a table stacked with surf-wear. Designer brands. Tags on. Fell off a truck.

Ava crooked a smile, noting that the vendor didn't display her social rating. "Yeah, I got caught in the rain. And more rain coming. You got a rash guard that's gonna fit me?"

"Sure do. What color you like?"

She *liked* black, but that was too close to what she was already wearing, and a light color would be too obvious at night. "Camo?" she asked hopefully.

"Urban gray or desert tan?"

Ava's smile widened at the absurdity of buying luxury goods on the edge of disaster. "Urban gray. A hoodie and lightweight watch cap, too, if you've got 'em."

Ava examined the goods, approved the purchase. Pricey. No doubt marked up for suspected fugitive status.

The vendor hooked a thumb over her shoulder. "You wanna jump in the back of the van to change, go ahead."

"Thanks."

It took Ava just a minute to swap shirts and pull the cap on. Too hot to wear the hoodie, so she stuffed it in the gym bag on top of the food and her duty belt. Damn thing already splitting at the seams. No wonder it'd been left behind.

"Don't stay too late," she advised the vendor as she slung the bag over her shoulder and prepared to leave. "This blow's going to be bad. Nolo all over again."

"Yeah, no worries. Heading home at midnight." She thrust her chin. "How 'bout you? You gonna shelter at the stadium?"

"Can't go home," she said truthfully.

Her little apartment was lost to her. She flashed back on the joy of moving in, achieving running water and electricity on the same glorious day. But all those windows . . . they were made of cheap glass, not hurricane-proof. Even if she'd had a way to board them up, plywood wasn't going to stand up against Huko. There would be no going back anyway, after tonight. Her old life was gone.

"Aloha," she called to the vendor. "Take care of yourself."

"You too, sistah."

Right.

She'd headed downstairs, ready to do what was needed—once she figured out what that was.

Ava's earbud beeped an alert as she reached the landing between the second and third floors. In her exile from HADAFA, the bright, eager female voice of her personal digital assistant had taken over. "Call from Astrid Robicheaux," it announced.

Ava startled at the name. She had not really expected a call back, and certainly not this soon.

"Answer," she ordered, moving to a corner of the landing as an older couple passed by.

A second beep, confirming the link.

"Thank you for calling," Ava said softly.

The voice on the other end was strung high with tension: "Who are you?"

"My name is Ava Arnett. I work for the Coastal Authority. That's like a special police agency for the Waikīkī District here in Honolulu."

"The hurricane hasn't hit yet?"

"No, not yet. But things have happened tonight."

"My dad?"

"He may be involved with something, Astrid."

A cynical grunt. "Yeah, you mean someone finally figured that out? Has he been arrested?"

Ava caught her breath, needing a couple of seconds to process this. "Why do you think he's been arrested?"

Hesitation. Then, "You should know, I haven't talked to him in two years, at least. He writes me, but I don't write back." She sniffed. Tears had started. "He's a bigot, you know. And a crypto-fascist. Devoted to Cornerstone."

"*What?*"

Ava's chest squeezed. A flush of heat. She had not known that. But should she have known? Guessed? Her thoughts flashed back to the sailor she'd talked to, helping with the evacuation. Most of those Kaden had put ashore were black skinned, or brown.

"My mom didn't catch on either," Astrid said. "Not for years. That's what she told me, anyway. I think she didn't want to believe it."

"*Why?*" Ava whispered, not realizing she'd spoken the thought aloud until it was too late.

"I don't know. But it's real. It's deep. Mom divorced him for it. And after she and Farron died—"

"What? Your sister? I thought she was in high school?"

"She should be. She would have been a senior this year, but she and my mom . . ." A shaky breath. "They died in the Endocino Hack. Two years ago now."

"Oh, God, I'm sorry. I had no idea."

The Endocino Hack had been an insider job. An autonomous

taxi company in Charleston, South Carolina, had been compromised. Malware cropped up in the navigation programming. The vehicles had been used in a coordinated terrorist attack, accelerating into crowds of unsuspecting shoppers and kids on school playgrounds, ramming into suburban homes, or driving their hapless passengers into trees or concrete walls. It had been a fucking horror movie, cars possessed by vengeful spirits. But in the end, those spirits had turned out to be a brilliant young programmer of Muslim faith who'd immigrated from Nairobi. In the minds of many, his sins had become the sins of anyone who shared his faith or the dark shade of his skin.

"I was dating this boy at the time. Mixed race, you know? And not the right mix. He got jumped. Beat up really bad. He wouldn't talk to me, after. I know my dad had something to do with it. Him and his asshat friends."

"*Jesus*," Ava whispered. She felt sick, defiled, realizing she didn't know at all the man she'd been sleeping with for two months.

"He hides it well," Astrid said bitterly. "He has to, in the navy."

A long pause. Ava at a loss for words.

Astrid broke the silence. "I know you can't tell me about the case, but you do have him in custody? Right?"

"Not yet," Ava said. "But soon."

chapter

15

DEEP BREATH.

Ava imagined a cigarette between her lips, its papery feel, white smoke curling past her throat and into her lungs—a well-rehearsed mental exercise.

Exhale.

Envisioning the smoke spewing from her lips, no longer white. Turned dark and toxic by the anxiety and ill feelings it had absorbed, and that it now carried away from her. The exercise helped her to compose herself, to settle her mind, to reject a sense of being in the wrong place, of occupying an alternate reality that allowed impossible things.

She stood at the wall of the open-air stairwell, looking out at another bus coming in, and beyond it, Kamehameha Highway, with two lanes of heavy traffic heading out of town. Below the highway, athletic fields, and then the dark water of Pearl Harbor, flecked by glints of reflected artificial light and moon-glow that slipped between the clouds.

If any large ship remained in port at the naval base, she should have been able to pick out its superstructure from where she stood. But the surface fleet had left ahead of Huko, and the submarines would leave in the morning. At least that's what Kaden had said. She knew now that he'd lied to her, more than once.

Deep breath.

The faint roar of a distant jet drew her gaze out over the ocean. She spotted the bright lights of two arriving airliners come to carry away transient visitors and those residents who could afford the ticket and had made the choice to go. She could have gone. Taken Kaden up on his offer, grabbed that seat on a military flight, seen her daughters again . . .

No way.

No way could she have ever lived with herself afterward.

She headed down the stairs again just as her countdown timer went off. A moment later, her earbud beeped, and the chipper female voice announced, "Call from Matt Domanski."

"Answer." She waited for the next beep, then said, "I'm on my way."

"New rendezvous point," Matt said. "I'm pinging you the location."

Retrieving her smart glasses from the pocket where she'd stashed them, she asked, "What's changed?"

"Lyric's back online—and I've got us transportation."

Ava's digital assistant mapped a path to the new rendezvous point—ground floor, far back corner—an area occupied by bike racks and charging stations. Tonight the bike racks were empty and only a handful of scooters were still charging up. With the exceptions of Akasha and Matt, the area was deserted, and the chatter and bustle of the marketplace seemed weirdly far away.

"You're kidding, right?" Ava asked, eyeing Matt in suspicion.

"What were you expecting?" he asked her. "An expeditionary vehicle?"

"An SUV maybe? Or hell, a chartered taxi? Lyric struck me as a woman with resources."

Instead, Matt had taken possession of a trio of electric scooters.

Akasha had already claimed one. She sat on it with one foot on the ground, the other on the scooter's floorboard. She'd changed from her uniform into a form-fitting gray tank top, black leggings, and a charcoal overshirt. She'd released her hair from its service bun, securing it instead in a braid behind her neck. And she'd exchanged her dinosaur backpack for a more dignified black tear-drop style.

Matt tossed a key fob to Ava, telling her, "This is our best option. These bikes are fast, cheap, off-grid, and therefore unhackable."

"Cheap?" Akasha echoed. "You paid three times their cost, new."

"Midnight before a major hurricane? That's still cheap."

"It's not even close to midnight," Ava said. "But it is damn late for us to be standing here, waiting for Lyric to come up with a mission plan."

"I say we go public," Akasha offered.

Ava tucked the fob into a pants pocket. "If Ivan didn't believe our story, why should anyone else . . . except a handful of conspiracy-theory nuts who'll believe anything."

"At least it'd be on the record."

Lyric's voice intruded, speaking through Ava's earbud: "I'm not the only one working the cloud. If you try to put something online, it'll be wiped away before there's time to capture a screenshot."

Ava hissed at this breach. She had not given Lyric access to her system, but the agent was there anyway, controlling her comms. Ava took it as a deliberate demonstration of her reach and it fed her mistrust. Even so, the sound of Lyric's voice brought her a measure of relief. Lyric had designed this game, she'd drawn them into it, and though it hurt like hell to admit it, she'd seen deeper into Kaden's heart than Ava ever had.

That didn't mean Ava had to like her. "So you're back home?" she asked acidly. "Safe in a bunker somewhere? Kunia, maybe? Or bumming a chair from the FBI out in Ewa?"

"She's probably on a flight to California," Akasha said.

Right.

"Lyric's on our side," Matt said. "And we've got a job to do. The goal is to prevent *Denali* from launching a missile, an action that can only take place if all necessary conditions are met." He ticked off those conditions on his fingers. "The sub must be at sea, there must be a launch code from Washington DC, and both the commander and executive officer must be aboard, so they can each enter their own biometrically validated codes to certify the launch. By interrupting any one of those conditions, we can stop the launch."

"So block the launch code," Ava said. "Or assassinate the Sigrún member who controls it."

"I don't know who that is," Lyric admitted. "My best guess is that Sigrún has a means to generate spoofed code outside official channels—though it's possible they have someone on the inside, close to the president."

"Is *Denali* still in port?" Akasha asked. "If not, it's all up, isn't it?"

Ava's thoughts fared briefly back to the afternoon, when Kaden still had her trust and her affection. "Kaden said the submarine fleet leaves tomorrow . . . but tomorrow starts at midnight."

"*Denali* is still in port," Lyric assured them. "It's not due to sail until after sunrise."

"It's the navy who needs to step in," Ava insisted. "Not everyone in the chain of command can be loyal to Sigrún."

"No, but look how hard it's been to convince you of the truth— and you still don't fully believe it, do you? Because you don't want to believe."

"Who would?"

"Exactly."

But Lyric was wrong. Given all that Astrid Robicheaux had told her, Ava knew the scheme *could* be real . . . and Kaden had been so eager for her to leave the island.

Lyric said, "I've tried going outside official channels, approaching several officers who could be in a position to do something, but every one of them has shut me down."

"Like they're supposed to," Ava growled, her own military training weighing on her conscience.

"Robicheaux needs to be aboard the sub," Matt said.

"And he's there," Ava told him. "He left to join his crew before we left the hospital."

"Lyric, can you confirm he's there?"

"I can confirm that," Lyric says. "He is at the dock, along with his executive officer."

"Then we have to lure him off," Matt said. He met Ava's gaze. "That's why you're here."

"I told you before, we're past that. Kaden is not going to talk to me."

"Arnette is right," Lyric said. "That window has closed. Robicheaux's latest HADAFA profile shows he will *not* accept a communication from her, or respond to an entreaty should she get through."

"Hell of a way to break up," Ava said—a bitter façade as she tried to hide, even from herself, the blunt trauma of being summarily cut off.

Akasha spoke up, sounding cynical. "So the last option is to force *Denali* to stay in port, right? Get Matt over the fence. Let him do his thing. Trespass and sabotage."

"Lyric?" Matt asked, appearing unfazed at the challenge of infiltrating a base guarded by both electronic eyes, and armed sailors who were, no doubt, bored out of their minds and eager for action.

Ava shook her head. "No way. Won't work."

"Arnette is right again," Lyric said. "I've run the models through HADAFA. There is no way you can successfully penetrate base security."

Ava sensed where this was going. She'd glimpsed the possibility when they were still on the truck. "But sabotage is still an option, isn't it? If we can enlist the help of allies." She looked at Akasha. "Say, a local insurgent group?"

Lyric backed her up. "Yes. Akasha's compatriots have been working on plans to harass and cripple the fleet."

Akasha's face went slack with shock—then anger slammed in. She left her scooter and backed a step away. Her fierce gaze fixed on Matt as if she imagined Lyric looking through his eyes—and wasn't that true? Matt's smart glasses surely served Lyric as a window onto their activities. "That's what this is really about, isn't it?" she demanded. "You decided I'm part of Hōkū Ala, and you're working a shell game to get on the inside—"

"Akasha, this is real!" Ava snapped.

Akasha's wrath shifted to her. "Did you help set this up?"

"*No.* I didn't know until tonight that you had anything to do with Hōkū Ala. And I'm not sure I believe Hōkū Ala has the means or the talent to take out *Denali*." Although Lyric's interest suggested they did . . .

Had Hōkū Ala been preparing for violent revolution? Like

preppers, stockpiling weapons and accumulating hardware to make their insurgent fantasies feel more real . . .

"Akasha, if there's anything you know, now is the time."

Akasha shook her head. "I'm *not* part of it. I'm not on the inside."

In the army, Ava had spent a year working counterinsurgency. She knew how the game was played. "You're not on the inside, but you know people who are. You've heard rumors about what they're working on. Akasha, if Hōkū Ala has the capability to disable *Denali* and prevent it from sailing—"

"I don't know," Akasha insisted, backing away, frightened now. "I really don't."

Lyric: "My reports indicate Hōkū Ala has the means, but we need a way in. That's why you're here, Akasha. I selected the players who would bring the most value to my operation."

Bullshit, Ava thought. Akasha had come to the hospital because Ava requested it. No other reason.

But then paranoia swept in. How long had Lyric been on the case? Akasha had transferred to night shift less than three months ago. Was that chance? And was it chance that not long after that, Ava found herself seated beside Kaden at the wedding of a mutual friend? Or had Lyric already been collecting and preparing her game pieces?

It doesn't matter.

All that mattered, here, tonight, was that they stop *Denali*. "Can you do it?" Ava asked, meeting Akasha's frightened gaze. "Can you get us in?"

"I don't know. I really don't know what the operation looks like, or who else is involved."

"But you know at least one person."

"He's prickly. Unpredictable." She tapped her head. "He had a bad time, after Nolo. If he's even willing to talk to me, it'll take time to convince him."

"So get on it," Matt said.

"It's not that easy." She edged up to the scooter she'd claimed. "He doesn't talk on the phone. If this is gonna happen, it's gotta be done face to face."

"Give us a direction," Ava said. "Where are we going?"

"First we need to get down to the water. Then head Ewa. The old bike path, you know?"

"There's nothing out there," Lyric said.

"Oh, you're wrong. He's out there."

They needed to get back to Kamehameha Highway, but blue lights marked a pair of patrol cars stopped at the turnoff into the stadium complex.

"They might *not* be looking for us," Ava said, straddling her scooter just outside the open market. "But how about we take another way out?"

"Working on it," Lyric answered. "I've got a potential route through the complex. Take the footpath. Walk your scooters. And stay dark. No headlights."

They skirted the bright lights at the entrance to the stadium, then passed behind a little amphitheater.

"All right, you can ride now," Lyric said. "But stay dark, and go slowly."

"Go where?" Ava asked. "I don't remember an exit on this side."

"There used to be a hole in the fence," Akasha said. "Kids would use it as a short cut out."

From Lyric: "It's still there."

They passed offices and additional parking structures, all dark, with no one around—which meant the three of them would be obvious to anyone watching through a security camera.

"Loading the route now," Lyric said.

A soft green guideline appeared in Ava's field of view. At first it followed the concrete walkway, but then it diverged onto a dirt path that crossed a narrow unlit lawn. Glancing up, she could just make out the top of a chain-link fence against the brighter background of the night sky.

"Drone!" Akasha warned, as Ava registered the faint waspy buzz.

"It's mine," Lyric said. "It's a jammer. Get through the fence. You're going to lose connectivity for the next few minutes, and so is everyone else. Just follow the route. Don't stop for anything. Matt, take the lead."

"Roger that."

Ava's glasses popped up an icon announcing the loss of network connectivity, but the projected path remained. Locally stored on her device, it led away into darkness.

Matt went first, whisking ahead, moving with speed for the first time. Ava followed, and Akasha came behind her.

The path jogged sharply left. Then right. Ava felt the mesh of the fence scrape her shoulder. Then she was through. The path turned again, ninety degrees. She followed it, and to her shock, the ground fell away. She clenched the brake lever. The wheels locked, skidding, sliding, down a steep muddy slope. No way to stop.

The glare of street lights in her peripheral vision blinded her to whatever lay ahead, and she'd lost track of Matt. But she knew Akasha's position by the swearing behind her.

Then she bounced down over a curb. Her teeth rattled as she arrived at what she guessed to be an asphalt road, though no lights illuminated it. Probably a closed driveway into the stadium.

The projected path jogged left. She turned too, and as she did, two blue police cruise lights flicked on not twenty feet ahead. Their cold steady glow revealed a patrol car blocking the narrow, weed-choked drive.

Lyric had known. She'd warned them, *Don't stop for anything.* Matt had taken that advice to heart. Ava saw him again as he yanked his scooter to the side and shot past the car.

The slim figure resting her ass against the hood made no move to stop him. She called out instead, "Ava Arnette, what the hell are you up to? There are quite a few patrol officers who'd like to know."

REACH OUT, AVA reminded herself.

In a split second decision, she resolved to ignore Lyric's instruction. Instead of following Matt, she jammed the brake hard and skidded, bringing her scooter to a stop just five feet short of where Officer Gina Alameda waited. Backlit by the patrol car's cruise lights, Ava could not read Gina's expression.

"You here to arrest me?" she asked, as Akasha skidded to a stop beside her. Matt had disappeared into the dark ahead.

Gina answered using her tough-cop voice. "Maybe."

"And maybe not?"

Ava pushed her glasses to the top of her head, sending them into sleep mode. She gestured at Akasha to do the same. A record of this conversation wouldn't help any of them.

Gina said, "Tell me what's going on."

"I can do that. But you won't believe me."

"Let's hear it anyway."

"Right. And then I'm going to need your help."

"You really believe this, don't you?" Gina asked, after Ava had outlined the basic situation.

"I have to believe it. Maybe there is another explanation, but I can't gamble on that. I've burned my career over this, Gina. Akasha has, too."

"But Ivan doesn't believe it?"

"It's the chain of command, not Ivan. They're telling him it's not real. What's he going to do? He's down there on the beach, trying to keep a thousand tourists alive."

"I know what that's like." Gina let out a slow breath. "Remember when we were in high school and an incoming missile alert popped up on all our phones, telling us we were about to die?"

"I remember," Ava said with a sinking feeling. "False alarm. It wasn't real."

"This feels real," Gina said. "I don't know why. Maybe because the world's gotten more crazy every year. Fucking suicide cults, accelerating us toward apocalypse. *Jesus*, Ava, *if* this is real . . ."

"Yeah. If it is, we'll all be dead, or we'll wish we were, by this time tomorrow. And if it's not, at worst, one submarine will have been disabled. Come on, Gina. I need to know. Are you in?"

"I can't do anything about the warrants."

"But you can put the word out."

"Yeah. The warrants can wait until after Huko. Do what you need to do. And if you need backup, let us know."

An unbroken stream of evenly spaced traffic filled the Ewabound lanes of Kamehameha Highway. With the taxi fleet due to be garaged, people were heading home while they could. Ava straddled her scooter, watching the oncoming headlights from the shadows at the side of the road, waiting for a chance to cross. After a minute, she turned to Akasha. "We don't have time for this. I'm going to trigger the damned safety algorithms."

"Ava—"

"Be ready to follow."

Ava waited a few more seconds, allowing a truck to roll by. Relying on the reaction time of the taxi fleet seemed a reasonable gamble, but she knew better than to hazard a human driver. When all the oncoming headlights shared the same height, the same shape, the same brightness, she rocked her scooter forward. She had a few feet of road shoulder to cross. Time enough for the autonomous taxi fleet to pick up her presence.

The vehicles detected her instantly, reacting in networked alarm. A warning chorus of horns blared as she accelerated toward the outside lane of traffic. Tires squealed against pavement in a concert of deceleration, moments before she jumped the curb. Prickles of fear sweat broke out under her shirt as she bounced down in the traffic lane, in front of an oncoming taxi, its headlights burning into her retina. She breathed in the fumes of smoking tires, felt the soft kiss of a plastic bumper against her left leg—and knew the algorithms had worked perfectly.

Headlights piled up on her left and outraged voices, muffled by closed passenger cabins, called her a fucking idiot as she shot across the inner lane and onto the median.

Akasha joined her there a moment later. "Holy shit, Ava!" she said as the flow of traffic resumed, returning to full speed within seconds. "That was fucking amazing."

Ava laughed. The adrenaline rush demanded it. "Yeah? Well, we just earned a hefty fine and a year of community service. But what the hell."

She looked right, checking the town-bound lanes, but only a handful of taxis were heading into the city. "Let's go."

Once on the other side, Akasha took the lead. She followed an unlit access road down to the shoreline, weaving between potholes picked out by the beam of her scooter's headlight. The road ended in the remains of a small parking lot. Head-high brush grew out of the cracked asphalt. Wind rustled thorny kiawe trees. Insects buzzed and wavelets slapped at the mangrove-lined shore. This was the start of the Pearl Harbor Bike Path.

"Pull up here," Ava said. She looked around by moonlight, but saw no one. "Let's get our belts back on, just in case."

In case they needed a shockgun, or a pistol.

Ava moved quickly, settling her duty belt around her waist, grateful for the weight. It made her feel stronger, more grounded.

"We don't have to go far," Akasha said as she secured her own belt. "Like three miles. No more. *If* he's there. He might have evacuated."

"And you can't contact him."

She shook her head.

Ava thought about it as she hurried to re-secure her gym bag to the scooter's cargo rack. "Lyric thought this Hōkū Ala connection was a good bet. But we're running out of time and we never had many options. If he's not there, to hell with caution. We'll put out word through the coconut wireless. Ask who's seen him—and then chase down the rest of Hōkū Ala if we have to."

"And if Lyric doesn't turn up again? And Matt? You gonna keep going?"

Ava had left her doubt behind, on the stairway landing where she'd spoken with Astrid Robicheaux. "I don't think we've heard the last of them."

She rocked her scooter forward, accelerating toward the gap in the vegetation that marked the bike path. For the first hundred feet they rode through an aisle of brush. Then the shoreline opened up. Makai of the path, tumbled rocks met an expanse of dark water.

Pearl Harbor was a complex, sprawling anchorage protected from the open ocean by a narrow entrance, and divided by peninsulas into distinct bays known as West Loch, Middle Loch and East Loch. Most of the navy's existing facilities lay behind them on the shore of East Loch, and on Ford Island. Concrete remnants dotted the rest of the shoreline—building foundations, bunkers, roads, and eroding piers—all evidence of the military's long presence, but abandoned now and overgrown. Not much had survived Nolo and since then, most of the shoreline had grown wild.

The bike path had been cleared and patched after Nolo, but not much had been done since. Commuters still used it as a quick route to Pearl City, and on to Kapolei, but the path demanded a rider's attention. Time and weather had left much of the paving cracked and broken, and parts of it flooded at every high tide. Ava kept her speed down, and kept up a careful watch for hazards appearing in her headlight beam.

The rocky shore gave way to sprawls of mangrove. Then the path shifted inland. It passed through stands of kiawe trees and under an elevated highway. Then it bisected a vanished neighborhood, recognizable amid the regrowth only by the few scattered concrete foundations and the fading gridlines of streets. Offshore, shards of moonlight and light from the roads glittered against restless water stirred up by the blustering wind.

The wind had been gusting throughout the evening, bringing with it a misty intermittent rain. But as they reached Blaisdell Park, a sudden ferocious gust slammed into them, bringing with it a torrent of rain that felt like it came out of a hose.

"Hey, at least tonight's not cold," Akasha grumbled.

No, it couldn't be, because Huko fed off the overheated ocean, its breath as warm and moist as the breath of a living thing.

After a few minutes, the path retreated again from the shore, this time to parallel the elevated freeway. That's when a flash of light across the rough pavement alerted Ava to someone behind them. She glanced over her shoulder. Saw a single headlight, coming fast.

"Let's stop."

"You think it's him?" Akasha asked.

"Yes." She unsnapped her holster anyway, and rested her hand on the weapon. "Identify yourself," she called out.

The wind carried Matt's voice back to her. "Don't shoot. It's me."

"Glad you decided to come back," Ava said sincerely when he caught up.

Matt just sounded annoyed. "How'd you get away from that cop?"

"*I'm* a cop," she reminded him. "What happened to Lyric?"

"I don't know and I'm worried. She never came back after that jam. She may be relocating, or she may have been arrested. If she's been arrested, we don't have much time."

"So let's *go*," Akasha urged with a bitter edge. "It's not much farther."

They rode through another grove of young kiawe trees, grown up since Nolo. Ava double-tapped her mic, shifting it to tactile mode. *Display current location*, she subvoked.

A map popped into existence on the periphery of her vision. A glowing red point placed her almost halfway across the base of Pearl City Peninsula. The peninsula, only about a square mile in size, extended into the harbor, with Middle Loch on the other side.

Akasha called another halt. They'd come to a shelter, built of four steel posts embedded in the corners of a rectangular concrete pad. A slanted roof made of corrugated plastic held off the rain.

"Wait here," Akasha instructed. "He lives out on the peninsula, but I have to go in alone. I'll call you, if he says okay."

"Let's all go at once," Ava said. "Leave him no choice."

"*No.* You think he doesn't have defenses? Just wait here, out of the rain. Let me convince him. I know he's been waiting for a chance like this."

Matt sounded guarded when he asked. "How much time do you need?"

"I don't know. I'll call."

Akasha continued on her own for fifty feet or so. Then she turned off the path. Her headlight bucked as she crossed rough terrain. She switched the light off and disappeared into the darkness among the trees.

Ava sighed and walked her bike under the shelter. Matt followed her, grumbling, "I don't like this at all."

After a few minutes the wind calmed, but rain continued to fall, loud against the slanted plastic roof. Ava had left her scooter's headlight on and with the rain passing through it, its white beam looked like a shimmering other-dimension.

A distant roar drew her attention farther afield. A jet engine? No, just a fresh gust blustering in across the mangrove and the kiawe, filling the low forest with motion and spraying rain beneath the shelter. Tiny kiawe leaflets fluttered in the aftermath.

Ava took off her smart glasses, using a wet sleeve to wipe the water from her eyes. "And this is just the beginning."

A shiver ran through her. She'd been warm enough while she kept moving, but now, with her wet clothing and the wind picking up, a chill had set in. So she shoved her glasses in a hip pocket, and retrieved her newly purchased hoodie from the gym bag. It felt damp, but she slipped it on and zipped it.

Matt said, "We'll get this done in plenty of time to get to shelter."

"You think so?" A cynical note. "How long have you worked with Lyric, anyway?"

"More than three years and I'm still alive. She knows what she's doing."

"Puppet master," Ava said in soft contempt, remembering Robert Bell and his frantic search for a way out that didn't exist, and herself, here, tonight, by Lyric's design.

"What was that?" Matt asked.

But her earbud beeped, her digital assistant announcing, "Call from Kaden Robicheaux."

Ava caught her breath. Her hand trembled as she reached for her smart glasses. She slipped them on, though she didn't need to. The call was voice-only.

"Answer," she whispered.

She heard the confirmation beep but said nothing, half-expecting the caller to be someone else—FBI maybe?—using Kaden's device.

But it was him.

"Ava, damn it. You haven't checked in at the airfield."

She realized she'd never heard him angry before. She moved away from Matt, her mind racing as she struggled to grasp the meaning behind this call. He couldn't really have expected her to take that flight out tonight. He had to know what had gone down at the hospital after he'd left; he had to know she wasn't going to play along.

Or—another blast of rain across her face—*was there room for second thoughts?* As theory hardened into reality and he faced head-on the monstrousness of the deed, had he reconsidered? Had he rejected his role?

Or had *he* only been playing at the villain's role all along . . . like Matt, an undercover operator?

She wanted so much to resurrect the man she thought she'd known.

But how could she, after hearing the testimony of Astrid Robicheaux?

Hoarse with suppressed emotion, Ava finally spoke, not to answer him, but to accuse. "Earlier tonight I met some of your sailors, the nonessentials, the ones you ordered to stay ashore through the hurricane. They were helping out, aiding civilians in the evacuation. Good people. Every one of them."

"Of course they are."

Was that suspicion in his voice?

"You left them behind," she said.

"They have their duty."

"And you? What's your duty?"

Matt had come around to look at her, the faint glow of his smart glasses illuminating worried eyes and lips silently shaping words: *Is it him?*

She nodded.

Find out where he is!

She knew already where he was—with *Denali*, and his skeleton crew.

"Kaden?" she asked when his silence had stretched through many seconds, long enough for hope to stir from its grave. Please let him reconsider . . .

But he let her question pass unanswered. Instead, he returned to his hours-old argument: "You have children, Ava. They still need you."

She drew a trembling breath. "And what about the thousands of children here? Do their lives mean nothing to you?"

An even longer pause this time, before he asked, softly, "Will those children grow up to wear a Chinese uniform?"

"Don't do it, Kaden. Don't do it. For all our sakes."

A hollow silence, and then the call dropped. She slipped her glasses off, wiped her eyes on a wet sleeve.

"It's happening, then," Matt said.

"Yes."

They stood in silence as the wind eased. The rain backed off to a mist, and in the lull something ratcheted past the shelter on clattering wings.

Startled, Ava dropped into a crouch, catching a glimpse of the device as it swooped low to pass through the beam of her scooter's headlight. A mechanical dragonfly, three times the size of the real thing

The dragonfly doubled back, appearing again, this time at a hover as it studied her and Matt with electronic eyes.

Ava stood slowly upright again, her heart slowing as she shook off yet another adrenaline cocktail. "Looks like Akasha made contact."

Matt eyed the device, his hands half raised, body poised for action. "I hope that thing doesn't have kamikaze capabilities."

"Too bad, yeah, it does," a tinny male voice answered. "Shut off all your comms now, if you don't wanna see it in action."

Shit. But they were the uninvited guests.

Ava took off her glasses, her hands shaking a little. She powered them down and shoved them into a pocket. Next, her tactile mic and linked earbud. Then she dug out her tablet, unfolded it long enough to take it offline, then turned it off too. Matt stowed his gear in his waist pack.

"Done," Ava said. "Is Akasha all right?"

A woman's voice, distorted by the tiny size of the dragonfly's speaker, but recognizable: "Gideon's an asshole, but I'm all right. He says you can come in."

"But this better be real," Gideon added—a low threat that made the speaker buzz.

Akasha again: "Make sure you turn your headlights off as soon as you cross the fence. And don't turn them on again."

The dragonfly ratcheted away down the road in the direction Akasha had taken. Ava scrambled onto her scooter and followed, with Matt close behind her. She heard the dragonfly before she saw it again, hovering at what she guessed to be the point where Akasha had left the road.

"I presume we turn here," she told Matt.

"I'm with you."

Their headlights picked out the ruin of a fence lying flat on the ground: bent steel posts and woven wire, a small rectangular sign, bleached white, attached to the top strand. Ava remembered: The

Ewa side of this peninsula was supposed to be a protected wildlife refuge.

They bumped across the rusty fence. In the beam of her headlight, Ava glimpsed what might be the start of a path through the kiawe, but she couldn't see more than a couple feet along its length before it angled into the trees.

Remembering Akasha's instructions, she switched her headlight off. Matt did the same, and darkness enveloped them. She heard the dragonfly ratcheting away on its noisy wings, and then another gust of wind roaring in over the trees. No way could they see well enough to find a path through this tangle.

"What now?" Ava wondered aloud.

As if in answer, specks of blue light winked on among the kiawe, a few feet apart and just inches above the ground. Ava leaned down to look at the nearest. She caught her breath, eyes wide with surprise. Matt left his scooter, crouching to see.

"Cyber firefly," he murmured in admiration.

Not really a firefly, but it was a living beetle with a tiny LED light on its head and a single long black antenna curving over its back. Ava gulped at the humid air, her heart beating a fast pulse as she sat back up again. She wondered: Had the beetles been positioned to illuminate a path? Or—given the wildly uneven spacing between them—did they exist in such numbers that only the handful along the path had been selectively illuminated?

Matt said, "I'll go first."

chapter

17

THE BLUSTERY AIR smelled of salt, with whiffs of organic rot and traces of some sulphuric chemical. They rode slowly, their tires making grotesque sucking sounds against the muddy path. The tires slipped in the mud, or got stuck in it. Then Ava would have to feel with her feet for solid ground, or a root, something to push off against to pull the scooter free. And she quickly learned to put a foot down every time the path zig-zagged, to keep the scooter from sliding out from under her.

She could never see more than a few meters ahead. At first she thought it was because Matt, having taken the lead, blocked her view of the blue illuminated beetles that marked the way. But when she paused to look back, she saw only darkness. The lights behind them had gone out. And when she leaned to look around Matt, she counted only three points of light. But as he advanced, a new blue glow winked to life, and then another.

The constant turns overwhelmed her sense of direction and with the heavy cloud cover she could not orient to moon and stars—or even to the occasional sound of wavelets against the shore, because they were on a small peninsula with water on three sides. She knew they could not have gone far, yet it seemed far, and a profound sense of isolation closed in around her, enforced by the rustling of leaves and the pattering of rain that together made a constant background noise, muffling almost all sound from beyond the forest.

How long had they been riding, anyway? With all her devices off, Ava had no way to precisely measure time, but surely several minutes had already passed.

"Hold up, Matt," she called softly.

He stopped and looked back. "You thinking what I am? This place is a maze."

It had to be. The peninsula was no more than a mile long, its perimeter reduced from its historic norm by sea level rise. Before Nolo, there had been military housing at its southern tip, but the storm surge had scrubbed that, depositing a layer of harbor mud over the streets and concrete foundations. No one had suggested rebuilding.

Since then, the mangrove habitat had merged with a tangle of low jungle nurtured by years of steadily increasing rainfall. On a still night, the air would have been buzzing with swarms of biologically confused mosquitoes, but with the wind pulsing in hard gusts, no insects flew, and the mechanical dragonfly did not show itself again. Even so, Ava felt sure they were observed.

Light drew her gaze downward, in time to see a slender foot-long snake slide past her booted foot. Its body, translucent as clear jelly, gleamed from within, the circuitry of its artificial nervous system illuminated by tiny embedded LEDs. The LEDs flashed in a shifting gradient of fiery colors—red, orange, amber, yellow— divided by a dark dorsal line.

Out of instinct, Ava drew her boot back. The snake reacted to the motion. Six hair-thin spines bobbed erect from its dorsal line. An obvious warning of toxic menace.

"*Nice*," she breathed in a sarcastic overtone.

After a few seconds, the spines lay flat again and the menacing little robot went on its way, slipping into a patch of head-high rustling elephant grass. Its light winked out, and all the beetle lights went out too, leaving them swathed in a velvety humid darkness.

"Stop fucking around," Ava warned in a strong, clear voice. "We don't have time for it. We need to get this done now, or we fail."

Something jumped from branch to branch in the kiawe above her. She ducked instinctively, almost toppling the bike over. Even so, she caught a glimpse of the thing—small, long-limbed, agile, gleaming with a ghostly pale luminescence—and soon gone from sight.

"Probably a rat," Matt said.

"You didn't see it." A slight tremor had worked its way into her voice. "It was a monkey bot."

She pressed a fist against her chest in a vain attempt to calm the rapid beating of her heart. Did Gideon think this was a game?

Okay, maybe he did.

He had to be strange. Weird. A wild eccentric more than half cracked to be out in this proto-swamp, pumping fake biology into the world.

She flinched again as the beetle lights winked back on.

"This is bullshit," Matt said with a soft bravado that failed to fully mask the tension in his voice.

"Or a setup?" Ava suggested.

It would be so easy for this Gideon to take them out with a pair of explosive kamikaze bots.

"Fuck it." Matt rolled his bike forward, resuming his pursuit of the blue lights. "Let's get this done."

The rain fell in a slow misty drizzle. The path turned, and turned again—and then they were there, at a break in the trees that opened onto a small muddy clearing.

A tent crowded the available ground, tall enough to stand in and printed in jungle camouflage. The front panels were rolled open and inside, a red light hung on a hook, dimly illuminating the interior. A moped and a little box trailer with two wheels made from bicycle tires occupied more than half the floorspace. Akasha stood silhouetted at the entrance, looking out. Another figure sat cross-legged on a towel at the back of the canvas floor.

No doubt this was Gideon.

Long, loose black hair veiled his face as he hunched over what Ava guessed to be a tablet. He wore baggy olive-drab shorts and a matching T-shirt that hung loose on his bony shoulders. His arms and legs were so thin they looked fragile. Dirty toenails poked through the fabric uppers of a battered pair of reef shoes.

"Sorry about the bullshit," Akasha said.

Gideon looked up, shaking the hair back from a startlingly

young face. He looked like a teenager. "It's not bullshit, you jack-boot. It's cool." His was the voice of the dragonfly, but a high-fidelity version.

Ava left her scooter in the rain, alongside Akasha's. She grabbed the gym bag, which held the food she'd bought at the stadium. But she hesitated before stepping inside.

Reading her mind, Akasha said, "Leave your shoes on. It's a mud pit in here."

Ava stepped inside, where she dripped onto the already damp and dirty floor. She crooked an eyebrow at Akasha, who responded with a grimace and an eye roll. The tent was only nine by nine, the windows all zipped closed against the rain. When Matt came inside, it felt crowded.

Gideon glanced up from his tablet to ask Ava, "What's in the bag?"

"Food," she told him, crouching to open it.

"Good, I'm hungry."

Even in the dim light, she was struck by the familiar lines of his face. He appeared to be a Eurasian mix, with light eyes and a scattering of freckles across his nose and cheeks. But there was something in the shape of his eyes and his eyebrows, and in the angle of his chin, that made her wonder if she'd seen this kid before . . .

Matt worked it out before she did. "Hey, Akasha. Is he your brother? He looks just like you."

Akasha rolled her eyes, lip curling in disgust. "This little weirdo doesn't look anything like me."

"He *does* look like you," Ava said. "But I've seen your profile. Your brother is supposed to be dead."

According to the official record, Gideon Li had been with his parents during Nolo, sheltering in their Manoa Valley home when massive landslides broke from the valley's steep walls, roaring through the neighborhood, burying homes under ten to twenty feet of eroded lava rock, mud, and crushed vegetation.

Before that day, Gideon had been a prickly genius on scholarship at Punahou School. Afterward . . .

"Legally, he *is* dead," Akasha said. "He likes it that way."

Gideon eyed his sister warily . . . until he noticed Ava's gaze.

"You weren't at home," she said.

"I told them the house wasn't safe," Gideon growled, with that same lip-curling expression of contempt Ava had seen so often on Akasha's face. "They didn't want to evacuate."

Akasha said, "He went to sulk in the bedroom. Nothing unusual about that. We had to share that room, and he was always sulking."

"Shut up."

"By that time, it was raining torrents. Too late to get to a shelter, that's what I thought. But you couldn't tell him no. He took his skateboard and climbed out the bedroom window." Her face scrunched up. It was clear the next words cost her dearly. "The brat was right to leave. I went after him. It's the only reason I'm still alive. I meant to bring him back. I mean, he was only twelve years old. I was fifteen. But I didn't have a skateboard and I couldn't keep up. He disappeared in the storm, and I ended up in the gym at Punahou. Afterward, I couldn't find him on any of the survivor lists. You know how it was. If people didn't check in, they got logged as dead. Two years later, I saw him on a moped. He didn't stop though, even when I yelled at him."

"I wasn't in my right mind," Gideon muttered.

"You've never been in your right mind."

"But you need me now, don't you?"

Akasha scoffed. "You're sitting here at ground zero, idiot. If you want to keep your little kingdom, then you better help out."

"Huko's going to wipe me out anyway. You're lucky you came when you did or you would have missed me. I've got a few more things to get off the houseboat, then I'm out of here."

"So you don't live in this tent?" Matt asked. Surely a facetious question.

"Shit, no. This is the garage."

"Not that his houseboat looks much better," Akasha told them.

"You could stay and clean it up for me."

"Love you too, brother."

Ava sighed, grateful for once that she'd been an only child. She pulled out the bento trays. "I need to eat. I only bought three bentos, but me and Akasha can share. Then, Gideon, you need to show us what you've got."

Fifteen minutes later they were walking single file through lashing rain, following Gideon as he led them on a muddy trail towards East Loch, the wind rising and falling in long monstrous breaths. Kiawe and elephant grass eight feet tall overhung the path, rustling, sighing, creaking in a velvety darkness that smothered the red beam of Ava's flashlight. She walked behind Gideon, who carried his red LED lantern. Akasha followed with her own light, helping Matt to keep to the trail.

Matt had argued for the use of his smart glasses: "Come on. The infrared illumination is just a slight signal—less than the flashlights—and it'll let me generate a guideline so I can stay on the trail."

But Gideon denied the request: "Every device is a window for some faceless creep to look through—and I like my privacy."

Ava had thought of Lyric and silently agreed. But now she wondered, "Don't you get civilian drones flying in here, poking around? I mean, people have to know you're here, and people get curious."

Gideon slowed, looked back. Raised his finger and moved it in a small circle. "Navy no-fly zone."

"Convenient," she conceded. "I guess they haven't noticed your dragonfly?"

"I keep it below the treetops."

"What about human trespassers?"

A cold chuckle. "Nolo stirred up toxic sludge from the bottom of the harbor. Shit that goes back to World War II. Maybe even before. Storm surge dumped it on the shore. Nowadays, step off the bike path and you could get hit with fumes that'll leave you sick and dizzy."

The toxic sludge was well documented and quite real. Still, Gideon's tone stirred her suspicion. "You started the rumor about the fumes, didn't you?"

Another glance back. "It's not a rumor. I've got gas bladders all along the periphery."

"You must have a record low social rating."

Behind her, Akasha snorted. "*Shoots!* If he *had* a social rating."

As they moved on, the rain passed and the wind eased. After a few minutes, Gideon stopped, turned around, and said, "Now we go dark." He switched off his lantern.

"We're not going to be able to see anything," Ava objected.

"Trust me."

"That'd be crazy," Akasha murmured, but she switched off her light anyway. Ava did too, plunging them into darkness—except it wasn't all that dark anymore.

Ahead, in the direction they'd been going, distant electric lights shone through the vegetation. From the freeway, probably, and the stadium on the other side of East Loch. Some of the lights might even be from the navy's docks . . . or maybe not. Ava wrestled with the geography, suspecting Ford Island lay in the way.

Then Gideon moved aside, revealing a paler illumination.

"Whoa," Ava said, wonderstruck. "What am I seeing?"

At her feet, a black glassy surface, curving away for at least fifteen feet before it disappeared within the shoreline mangroves. Beneath that surface, scattered patches of white light—she counted seven—alive with slow sinuous motion. Only one lay close to where they stood.

18

It took several seconds for Ava to make sense of what she was seeing. The glassy surface was a pond—no, an inlet—and the white objects glowing beneath the water's surface—

"Are those robotic gels?" Matt asked.

"No," Ava said. "They're bioluminescent jellyfish."

She had watched a bloom of party-light jellies dying in the surf only last night. The round mantle of the closest one was at least two feet across, with a dark spot the size of a quarter just off center.

Gideon said, "This big one's the prototype."

Ava crouched in the slick mud at the water's edge to get a closer look and noted smaller spots—she counted three, but there might be more—scattered at irregular intervals around the edge of the mantle.

"This is your weapon?" she asked, looking up at Gideon—and trying to stave off disappointment.

"Yeah. And it's really cool." He stood beside her, his feet half sunk in mud. "My asshole friends swore they were serious, that there was gonna be a revolution before the handover treaty was signed. A fucking declaration of independence. Targeted military action to back it up. They wanted me to come up with something. So I did." A contemptuous *tsk*. "You can guess what happened next."

"No revolution," Ava said. "They wised up and called it off."

Another *tsk*. "They called it off, anyway. That's all I really know." He shrugged. "They were probably watching too much Netflix to begin with. A lot harder to pull off a revolution in the real world."

"But they didn't give you a reason?" she pressed, wanting to better understand the scope of the aborted insurgency, and any options that might remain.

Gideon shook his head. "They're tight with details. And I haven't talked to them in a while. *I* gave 'em a working weapon, but I don't think they got much out of their other developers. It's not like they have a big talent pool to draw on. So the cops and the guard probably decided they didn't want to go along with it." He cracked a cold smile. "Or the kupuna heard about it and told them to sit their asses down before the grandkids got killed."

Akasha disregarded all this, demanding, "What's it do?"

"It blows shit up." Gideon crouched beside Ava. He gestured at the jelly. "You wouldn't know it by looking at them here, but jellyfish are strong and fast—and these party-light cultivars are common enough they don't draw much attention."

"Except from sea serpents?" Ava asked him.

"Well, yeah. The snakes keep the population in check. Serpents are fast, but I couldn't use them because every serpent is tracked and monitored by HADAFA."

"Really?"

"Yeah. They're artificial lifeforms."

"Sure. Just like the jellyfish. So tell us what you've got."

"You've weaponized them," Matt said, eyeing the crouching kid with a predator's intensity.

"No. Not the jellies. They're just a vector." In the upwelling light, Gideon looked both smug and diabolical as he peered at Ava. "Remember what it used to be like at New Year's, when the whole fucking city would light up with illegal fireworks? You have *no idea* how many sealed shipping containers filled with fireworks survived Nolo, all of it smuggled in past Homeland So-Called-Security. No way was I going to waste all that potential—"

"Wait—you unpacked fireworks? You're lucky you didn't blow yourself up."

Gideon scoffed. "Remote operation. That monkey bot's not just a toy, you know." He stood up, and Ava stood up too. "So anyway, I did a lot of experimenting. Best thing I've come up with so far is robot fish. Easy to print, assemble, and program. They use standard batteries and carry a decent payload of salvaged gunpowder."

"Navy is on to that," Matt said, sounding disappointed. "The harbor's patrolled by robot tuna. You're not going to get a drone fish past them."

"I can get a *swarm* of aquatic drones past them," Gideon said. "It's not hard, because the robot tuna are looking for free-swimming devices."

He'd brought a telescoping rod with him. He extended it now, and, crouching again, he used it to reach into the inlet's water, poking at the curtain of three-foot-long tentacles beneath the prototype jelly. The tentacles writhed as he touched them, and some wrapped around the pole, allowing him to lift them to the water's surface.

Embedded among the glowing tentacles, Ava counted eight opaque white shapes, each six or seven inches long, bullet-shaped, with dorsal and lateral fins, and a vertical fish tail. "The payload," she murmured, starting to see how this might work.

"The swarm is passive when it's with the jelly," Gideon explained. "But when the jellyfish gets past security and is close on the target, the swarm activates and the components strike like one." He lowered the tentacles back into the water. "It'd be better if I had access to C-4, but when the swarm packs together, they'll still manage a solid bang. Pretty cool, huh?"

"Damn cool," Ava agreed. "*If* it works."

"How do you steer the jellies?" Matt asked, sounding skeptical.

Gideon stood up again. "That part's not great, but it's good enough. Party-lights are CRISPRed, too. Their sting doesn't do much to humans, but they're good at feeding on other jellyfish. You know, to keep the water safe for people 'cause we get so many wild jellies these days, like they're the last thing surviving in the ocean.

"Anyway, party-lights were designed so they stay near-shore and close to the surface. A side benefit is that it makes their population easy to monitor. You just have to have an aerial drone count the glowing mantles. Another side benefit, for me, is that I can get a radio signal to that hub at the top of the mantle."

With the rod, he indicated the dark central spot Ava had seen before. As she looked at it again, she noticed a wisp of wire protruding from it.

Gideon pulled out his tablet. Ava leaned in to look at the screen. A green line traced a complex path against a black background. It took her a few seconds to recognize the display as a map of East Loch. A labeled point marked the inlet where they stood.

Gideon expanded the map. The point grew into a circle with six hash marks around its perimeter. He said, "Jellies are predators, but they get eaten, too. Sea serpents are the main problem for big party-lights. I can fake a serpent attack by using an electric shock. The jelly responds by swimming away from the jolt."

He tapped the screen. The jellyfish at their feet pumped its mantle and bobbled away from the shore. Ava watched it with a little shiver of horror.

"Sweet Jesus," Matt murmured in her ear. He'd moved in close to get a look at the screen over her shoulder. "This is monster-movie shit—and this is the best we've got?"

With the wind and the rustling leaves, Gideon, fortunately, hadn't heard him. That was clear when he turned to Ava with an impish grin. "So where's the target?"

Just like that . . .

She straightened up. "You've got just the one?"

"Yeah, like I told you, the revolution got called off. I'm working on my own here."

"And you've done impressive work," Ava assured him, ready to elbow Matt if he started to say anything else too critical. "We saw that on the way in, but . . ."

She should have worried about Akasha, not Matt. "What she's trying to say, dear brother, is this whole setup is comic book, not real world."

"It's not that," Ava said quickly. "But . . . you haven't tested it, have you?"

If he had, HADAFA would surely have observed the explosion and issued a report.

Gideon backed off a step, looking annoyed. "I've never actually blown anything up," he admitted. "But I've tested all the components, if that's what you're worried about. I've run this jelly across the loch and brought it back again. It *will* work."

Ava looked to Matt, her chest tight with anticipation. "We might as well try it."

He nodded, but sounded glum: "Yeah, if there's any chance at all." He turned to Gideon. "Let me give you the target. All we want to do is disable the submarine, force it to stay in port."

"And let Huko batter it?" Gideon asked.

"Yeah. Cost of treason."

A minute later, Ava watched as the luminous jellyfish shivered and thrashed and then retreated, its wide mantle coiling and snapping, propelling it erratically down the inlet. She trailed after it, edging along the shore, feeling her way, and discovering a path there.

The other jellies in the inlet roused as the augmented one passed by. One by one, they began to follow it, a parade of party-lights.

Ava went with them around the curve of the inlet. The augmented one moved more gracefully now, its mantle working in slow, steady, fluid motion. Its serenity a sharp contrast to her own tangled nervous system.

She glanced ahead. Mangrove leaned in over the mouth of the inlet, framing the bright lights of the eastern shore. She went no farther, but stayed to watch.

The companion jellies did not share their leader's motivation and they soon fell behind. But the augmented jelly moved with steady determination as if on a mission. Or did she see it that way only because she knew it was true? Without that knowledge, would its behavior still seem aberrant? Would the robot tuna tag it as suspicious because it moved with more purpose than any jellyfish should?

She crossed her fingers. *Let this work. Please.*

The jelly entered open water. She watched it until it was just a faint glow some two hundred feet offshore. Then she drew a sharp breath and turned, making her way back to the others.

"How long will it take to get there?" she asked Gideon.

The faint, upwelling light of his tablet revealed a thoughtful frown. "All the way to navy docks? At least a couple of hours."

A couple of hours before they knew if the tactic would work . . . a couple of hours to come up with a backup plan when this one failed.

"Have you got *anything* else?" she asked.

"Nothing that'll get past navy security."

Matt said, "You mentioned other developers working for the insurgency."

"I can't tell you who."

"Can't or won't?"

"Can't. Because I don't know. Security protocol, right? In case some jackboot comes asking."

"But you could get word out," Ava said. "Contact your contact."

"Why? I don't think they've got anything."

"But you could ask," she pressed.

"I told you," he said, his voice low and defensive, "it's been a while since I talked to them."

"Ah, geez," Akasha said. "You had a meltdown, didn't you, when you heard the revolution was off? And they dropped you. They cut you off. They're not taking your calls."

He shrugged, but didn't deny it—and Ava felt an avenue of opportunity close.

"I gotta go by the houseboat," Gideon said. "Take care of something before I head out. You guys might as well come. It's not far. And anyway, if you take off on your own, you're gonna get lost."

With his red lantern lighting the way, Gideon led them up the eastern side of the peninsula, to a little cove bordered with the ubiquitous mangrove. The houseboat was moored close to the trees, a dark and angular silhouette against the bright lights across the water—headlights, streetlights, and a cluster of pinpoint blue lights flashing silently as HPD attended to some unknowable emergency.

Gideon followed a path down to the water and waded in, thigh-deep. Ava followed, so wet already it didn't matter. She felt clouds of fine silt rising from the bottom with every step.

The houseboat had a flat deck with a little plywood-walled cabin occupying the middle half. The cabin's flat roof extended out to cover the open deck on both sides. The nearest side was furnished with a tiny round patio table and a matching chair. And at the edge of the deck, a pile of . . . something.

Gideon tugged at the something. It spilled over the side: a ladder made of plastic-coated cable and three plastic steps. Still clutching his tablet in one hand, he climbed up with practiced grace. Ava followed more awkwardly, grateful to get under a roof. Across the water to the south, she saw the dark wall of another heavy rain band moving in.

"Welcome to my former base of operations," Gideon said quietly as Akasha and Matt came aboard. "I don't know where I'm going to rebuild, after, but it won't be here. The boat won't survive and the peninsula is gonna get scrubbed into an empty mudflat again, if anything's left at all." He sounded dejected—a display of emotional vulnerability that surprised Ava after all his bluster.

A moment later, he shifted back to chipper cynicism. "Okay, so who wants to drive the jelly while I finish up here?"

"I'll do it," Matt said, taking the proffered tablet. He scowled at it. "But your jellyfish is moving damn slow."

"High tide and storm surge. What do you expect? Just keep hitting it. Big jellies can move against the current."

Ava eyed him, trying to imagine how he'd survived on his own . . . how he'd protected himself. "Have you always been by yourself out here?" she asked.

"I like it that way."

"You're not worried about . . ." Her voice trailed off. She didn't know quite how to phrase it.

"Creeps and weirdos, like me?"

"That's not what I meant."

A flash of teeth. "I know. You're a lot nicer than Akasha. It's actually been good here. Quiet. No one comes in by land and the handful of people like me, living on the water, are here because they don't want anybody's nose in their business. And anyway, there's a rumor along the shoreline that the one time a zombie thought it would be fun to mess up my boat, he left with a nasty dose of Angel Dust eating at his lungs."

Ava considered this, considered what she'd already seen, and then asked, "That's just a rumor . . . right?"

"You asked what else I had." He cocked his head toward the cabin. "Come inside."

"*Hey*," Akasha said. "You've never let *me* inside."

"And I'm not letting you in now. Wait here."

Ava wasn't entirely sure she wanted to see what Gideon kept hidden, but neither did she want to piss him off. And if he had another device that might be useful against *Denali*, she needed to see it.

So when he opened the door—just a few inches, clearly determined to frustrate Akasha's attempt to peer inside—Ava slipped past him, into the lightless interior.

She heard him follow; heard the door close. A dull red overhead light came on.

"You like red."

"Saves the night vision."

The day's heat lingered in the interior. No windows looked out. No source of ventilation. A second door, on the opposite side, would open to the houseboat's back deck. With both doors open, there would be the hope of a breeze, but the doors were closed. Despite her wet clothing, Ava started to sweat.

A glance around showed her everything there was to see, which was mostly nothing. A wide wooden shelf on one side had probably served as a workbench, but it was empty now. So were the two bracket-mounted shelves above it. Underneath the bench, small circles and lines of dust on the rough plank floor showed where other objects had been recently removed. A couple of raggedy hand towels hung on a laundry line. She wondered why Gideon had brought her inside.

"God, it's hot in here," he said, over a sudden clatter of rain on the roof. "The AC unit went with the rest of the equipment. It's all stashed in a village dome house—and I'm planning to ride out the storm with it. Only one thing's left here."

Ava cocked a skeptical brow.

From him, a slight, anxious smile. "It's hidden."

"What is it?"

"Nothing clever. Call it a mistake. I was going to leave it. Let Huko chew it up. But hell, we're talking nukes now. My mistakes don't seem so bad."

Ava did not like the sound of that.

"Is there any way you or somebody else can physically get to that submarine?" Gideon asked.

"I don't know. I mean, not me. Matt, maybe. Why?"

He knelt, put his finger in a little notch at the end of a floorboard, and lifted it up. Water glistened a few inches below. He reached in, felt around under the floor, and came up with a chain. Small steel links, clean and shiny. Couldn't have been in the water for much more than a day. He pulled it up.

The chain was only a couple of feet long. Attached to its end with a locking carabiner was a small, squat, stainless-steel, wide-mouth vacuum bottle, the kind hikers use to carry whiskey or a cup of hot coffee. He unscrewed the lock on the carabiner, and unshackled the bottle, which looked as clean as the chain.

"What's in there?" Ava asked uneasily.

"Nasty shit." He grabbed one of the towels from the laundry line and used it to dry the bottle. "That zombie who died of Angel Dust? I didn't kill him on purpose. He went after me. Beat the shit out of me for no reason. Then broke in here. Went through my stuff. Infected himself."

"You were working with Angel Dust." Her skin crawled as she stared at the bottle; adrenaline shivered her heart.

"I didn't kill the zombie, but I was not in a good place at the time." He tapped his forehead. "You know. Up here."

Ava weighed her options as he unscrewed the top. The door behind her was probably locked, while he stood between her and the door they'd used to come in. Could she get past him before he released whatever was in that bottle?

He said, "I'm in a better place now. Like I said, I was going to leave it to Huko to take care of, but if you want to take it, if you can find a way to use it, it's yours."

The cap came off. Ava held her breath. She couldn't help it.

Gideon dumped out the contents of the bottle on the built-in bench. Six clear-plastic ampules, an inch long, with snap caps. A dark substance half-filling each. Not a gel, because it flowed. And not a liquid. Only a powder could settle like that, at an angle within each ampule.

"Angel Dust," Gideon said, the contrition in his voice letting her know he regretted the whole enterprise.

She gestured at the ampules. "How did you manage to collect all that without killing yourself?"

"How does anyone? I used a remotely controlled bot, of course, just like with the gunpowder." He held up his hands, thumbs and forefingers tapping together. "Pinching appendages, controlled by gloves. The only hard part was harvesting ripe spore sacs without popping them open."

"And the dust is viable?" she asked.

"Yes. I mean, I haven't tested it on anybody lately, but the zombie popped an ampule and sniffed it—must have thought it was a designer drug—and went down hard."

"I saw that report. The body turned up on the grounds of the old Waiau Power Plant. There was speculation about an infestation in the underground piping—but I guess nothing was ever found?"

"Probably not."

"That had to be, what . . . eight or nine months ago?"

"Eight months. But I kept the dust in the freezer until I took the unit out a few hours ago."

"And what do you think I can do with it?"

"Nothing, if you can't get to that submarine. But if you can, if you drop it into an enclosed atmosphere like that, with all those jackboots rebreathing each other's air, no one would last very long."

Ava's skin prickled with the memory of Robert Bell on his knees, his shoulders rising and falling in short spasmodic jerks as the fungal toxin shut down his ability to breathe. "Put it back in the water. I don't see how it could work."

He gathered the ampules. Dropped them back into the vacuum bottle.

"No, wait," Ava said. "What if that bottle survives the storm, or some of those ampules?"

"I don't have a safe way to get rid of it."

"Then give me the bottle. I'll turn it over to hazmat as soon as I can."

"Assuming there still is a hazmat, after the nuke hits."

She hissed softly. "*Right.*" She took the bottle, secured it to her belt. It hung awkwardly against her hip.

Gideon kicked the chain into the water, replaced the floorboard, and then they went back outside.

Akasha looked around reproachfully. She was holding the tablet now. With a slight thrust of her chin, she indicated Matt. "He's back online," she said, raising her voice to be heard over the rain. "And I don't think it's going well."

Matt didn't even register their reappearance. He stood by the houseboat's corner post, staring out over East Loch through the lens of his smart glasses, fist clenched as he demanded answers from someone not present. "I don't care if you're on the move! Get my comms cleaned *now.*"

"He's compromised," Gideon concluded, all his cocky bravado gone. "Idiot! Come on." He crossed the deck, his glance taking in Ava and Akasha. "If you don't want to go down with him, you need to get out of here now." He slipped with hardly a splash into the water.

"Go," Ava told Akasha. "Keep the tablet safe. I'll be right behind you."

Akasha nodded, and followed her brother.

Ava flicked on the red beam of her flashlight. "Matt!"

He didn't answer.

She stepped closer. Touched his back. For just a moment she felt the heat, the hardness of the muscles beneath his shirt. Then he jerked away, half-turning to eye her with a dangerous gaze.

"Just me," she snarled. "And we need you. So leave your gear and move out. *Now.*"

"I can't leave the gear, but it's being scrubbed. Let's go."

Rain fell hard as Ava slid first into the water. She waded to the shore, the red beam of her flashlight picking out Gideon's well-worn path. Matt followed a step behind.

"What happened?" she asked as the blue beetle lights came on to show the way.

"The EmLoc—the Emergency Locator—responded to a rogue signal as soon as I went online. That access has been closed, but my position is known outside the circle of trust."

Her feet slipped in the mud with every hurried step. "So what's coming? *Who's* coming?"

"My guess is, navy security. Not that they're part of this. They're just doing their job."

"And Lyric? She's still on the outside?"

"Status unknown." Bitterness in those words.

"You're kidding?" Ava blinked against the rain, moving as quickly as she could without falling down. "Who were you talking to then?"

"Tech support," he growled.

An answer so mundane that doubt clutched at her again. She rejected it. *This is real.* Kaden had denied nothing.

Past the sound of her breathing, beyond the squish of her footsteps, and the fast patter of rain, a new noise reached her. A low hum, felt as much as heard, familiar from her years on the battlefield. A stealthed quad-copter. *No, probably more than one.* Large enough to contend with the weather, and no doubt well-armed.

Ava switched off her flashlight and unholstered her gun.

chapter

19

A VOICE BOOMED down through the rain: "Officer Arnett. Lieutenant Matthew Domanski. You are both ordered to stop. Stop *now*. You have been duped into cooperating with a highly skilled enemy agent. Do not continue. Turn yourselves in voluntarily, and all possible consideration—"

A gun went off behind Ava. She dropped into a crouch, looking over her shoulder. Another shot. Another. The muzzle flashes revealing Matt, firing slowly and deliberately in the direction of the voice as it continued to boom.

"—will be given to your motive for involving yourselves in this affair."

The low hum surrounded them now, a vibration in the rain, in the impenetrable darkness. At least three quad-copters, Ava judged. Their lights off, utterly invisible.

"Don't stop," she urged Matt. "Keep moving. Keep under the vegetation."

The tall cane and the rain would obscure their profiles, making it harder for thermal imaging cameras to track them, but even so, they were far from invisible. And it didn't help that the blue sparks of the beetle lights advertised their escape route through the entangling vegetation. The only real question: How soon before the quad-copters started shooting?

The answer arrived without delay. A low buzz, a wet *thwop!* as if a water-logged towel had been dropped in a sink, and she heard Matt go down with a grunt.

"Knives out!" he barked. "They're shooting webs."

Instead, as a glint in the sky drew her gaze, she raised her pistol. Holding it in a two-handed grip, she fired three swift shots, each a few degrees apart. The second and third threw sparks and changed the frequency of the surrounding hum—but the quad-copter she'd targeted did not go down.

Thwop!

A painful slap against the back of her right hand, across her exposed wrist, and halfway up her forearm. The sleeve of her shirt did nothing to soften the blow. Sticky webbing: It writhed like a living thing, random motion meant to bind and seal. She yanked her left hand away, an instant before the webbing locked it down.

Ava had trained with webbing, both in the army and with the police. Keep a hand free and you could cut away the tendrils as they hardened. Right now, the tendrils were binding the pistol, keeping it secure in her right hand. Probably not the outcome the drone's overseer had wanted.

She heard Matt moving, grunting. "You free?" she asked, shifting her position, moving a few more steps along the path to get deeper into the cane.

"I'm up. *Run.*"

A challenge, given the darkness, the rain, the mud, the down-draft from hovering quad-copters—or was that just the swirling wind? She fixed her gaze on the next blue light and bounded toward it, arms raised to protect her face in case there were low-hanging branches. She prayed she would not twist an ankle, break a leg, or impale herself on a broken branch.

Thwop! Thwop!

"You hit?" she yelled without turning back.

"No, the veg is shielding us!"

For now. But how long before the quad-copters shifted to hard ammo? The vegetation would be no defense against that, and with Huko coming in, no one need ever know that four bodies had been left behind in this swamp.

She made it to the next pinpoint of blue light, and the one after that. Then the lights went out. "Damn it, Gideon!" she shouted.

"I'm re-mapping!" he yelled back, startlingly close.

Then she saw him, his down-turned face and dancing fingers faintly lit by the screen of his tablet. She pulled up sharply so she wouldn't run into him, at the same time yelling at Matt, "Hold up!"

An incoherent oath as Matt bumped up against her. His hand gripped her shoulder.

Panting, her heart racing, she tried to pinpoint the quad-copters by sound, but the wind-combed rattling and rustling of the cane drowned out their engine noise. "Where's Akasha?" she asked.

"I'm here." Her voice placed her on the other side of Gideon. "They went after the bikes, shot them full of webbing. So we're on foot."

Maybe it was better that way. Headlights would give them away, and riding fast in the dark was a damn good way to kill yourself.

"Where are they now?" Ava wondered as she worked to pry away the strands of webbing on her gun hand.

"Probably surveying the peninsula," Matt answered. "They know they've got us trapped, but they don't know who else might be out here, and they don't want anyone slipping away."

"We're not trapped," Gideon said as the tablet's light went out.

The blue beetle lights came back on at the same time, marking a path beneath the trees that angled away from the direction they'd been going.

"Go!" Matt barked.

Ava wrenched her gun free, though her arm still trailed strands of hardening gunk. With the tablet dark, she couldn't see Gideon anymore—but she heard him up ahead: "You owe me big, Akasha!"

Akasha already sounded distant when she answered, "We'll settle it after the storm!"

"Rain's backing off," Ava observed as she lingered in place, gazing up into the sky.

"Yeah." Matt stood rooted beside her. "And here they come."

The rain had eased enough that Ava could see low cloud bellies brushed with the gleam of city lights. Outlined against the clouds, two circular shapes moved slowly, black and humming, no more than ten feet above the trees. *Fricking flying saucers.*

"Westside's mine," she said quickly.

"I got east."

They both fired multiple times. The low elevation made the quad-copters easy targets. Sparks fountained as bullets connected with the vulnerable rotor blades. The even hum became high pitched and discordant. One quad see-sawed erratically; the other wisely chose to retreat. No sign of a third drone.

"Let's go," Matt ordered.

Ava moved out, holstering her pistol as she did. Without breaking stride, she grabbed her flashlight and switched on the red beam. No time for groping in the dark. They needed to get out from under the foundering quad-copter and get off the peninsula before the navy shifted to more lethal options. Navy jurisdiction was limited. If they could make it to suburbia, they ought to be okay—for the next few minutes anyway.

Something popped in the air behind them, followed closely by a high-pitched shrieking whine and a double flash of golden light. Then shrapnel came flying, ripping through the brush. Ava shifted to a run, hearing the bulk of the damaged quad-copter hit ground with a crunching, grating noise. A final splash placed it at the water's edge.

Thwop!

Ava's legs tangled. She went down hard, landing on her elbows, dirty rainwater splashing into her mouth and her flashlight rolling away, its red beam dulled by mud.

That hum. Singular now, and not so close.

"I've got you covered," Matt said.

She groped for her folding knife. Snapped it open. Felt for the shape of the webbing that bound her feet together. Slid the blade under a strand. Jerked hard to slice through it. Once. Twice. And again. Ripped the rest of the webbing off. "I'm good."

The hum sounding closer now.

"Incoming," Matt said softly.

Ava snapped the knife shut. Holstered it. Drew her pistol. Then looked up. A pale white light crept across a kiawe branch overhead.

The monkey bot.

As the quad-copter closed in, the little bot leaped at it, found a grip somewhere, and in the space of three seconds, swung itself up, over, and into one of the propellers. A horrible crunch. Debris showered the forest as the quad-copter wobbled and rotated, lifting away.

With a whispered thank-you to Gideon, Ava grabbed her flashlight from where it had fallen in the mud. Then she picked herself up, and ran.

Matt kept pace behind her.

The blue beetle lights led them on until they came to a wide break in the vegetation that turned out to be an unpaved road. Lights from the elevated freeway, two-tenths of a mile ahead, glinted against the wind-rippled pools of rainwater that filled the road's deep ruts.

On the other side of the road, Ava could just make out what had to be a tree nursery. Some brave soul, believing in the future, had planted rows of coconut and Alexander palms. None had yet grown even six-feet high. Their fronds thrashed and rattled in the gusting wind.

"We're over here!" Akasha shouted from the edge of the palm plantation.

Ava sprinted through the open to join her. "Injuries?"

"We're good," Akasha assured her.

Ava played her light over them anyway. Akasha looked surprisingly clean. Gideon looked stone-cold angry.

"Thank you for sending the monkey bot," Ava told him.

He nodded shortly. Then he jerked his chin in Matt's direction. "I lost my moped, my trailer, and the fucking monkey bot because seal-team-six here didn't stick to our deal and keep his comms off."

"There's more at stake tonight than just your gear," Matt said, no apology in his voice. "Have you got a status on your jellyfish?"

Gideon gave him a dark look. "Okay, so it's having a hard time," he admitted. "The tide, the storm surge—"

"But it's still in play?"

"Sure. It can go all night if it needs to."

"It needs to get inside the security perimeter before *Denali* leaves."

"I know that! I understand. I'm doing what I can. More than you're doing."

"Yeah, sorry. You didn't sign up for this, but if it doesn't work—"

"We find another way," Ava said. "That's all. Now let's move. Navy's not going to be in a good mood tonight, and I don't want to be here when some stealth unit shows up."

"You mean real navy seals?" Gideon asked with a sneer.

"Roger that."

The rain persisted as they followed the dirt road. It washed away the mud from Ava's face, her hands, even her clothing. But the constant wet left her skin shriveled and fragile, rubbed raw under the weight of her duty belt, with blisters forming on her heels.

She didn't slow down. Not until they'd gained a little elevation, enough that she could look back, out over the wind-lashed waters of East Loch. No boats out tonight. No traffic on the freeway. Everyone else had gone to shelter.

But we're still here! Still trying to save the world! The wretched world. *My* world.

She wished to God she could get back to yesterday. But there was no way back. There never would be, no matter what happened.

From up ahead, Gideon shouted. "Ah, *fuck*." He turned around, his thin figure backlit by streetlights. "They got it! They *got* it!"

Ava's heart skipped as she turned to look again out over the Loch. Two small boats had appeared, their navigation lights on. They raced past Ford Island, heading for the peninsula.

"How do you know they got it?" Matt demanded.

"No signal! Signal's gone. It's not there."

"Could have been a sea serpent," Ava said. Like it was better to lose the jellyfish to an accident of nature, than a deliberate attack? "Shit, it doesn't matter. Can you still trigger the swarm?"

"Don't have to. If they lose the mothership, they go. But they're still outside the security perimeter! And they don't have the battery power for evasive—"

Far away, a cluster of eight tiny white geysers silently erupted from the black water. The robot tuna had found their prey and induced the entire swarm to detonate.

"*Fuck!*" Gideon screamed. "*Fuck* these assholes. I'm going to get the word out. Get people away from here."

"Sigrún is ready for that," Matt told him. "They'll scrub anything you post online."

"You think I don't know that? I know how this works. It's word-of-mouth. The coconut wireless."

"You can try, but it'll get online in a heartbeat, and then Sigrún will issue counter rumors claiming it's a hoax meant to start a panic so people will go running out into the storm. And which interpretation sounds more plausible to you?"

"So what?" Gideon demanded. "What do you want me to do? Just sit here and wait for it to happen?"

Ava groped for an answer. It was surely too late for anyone not already booked on a flight to get a seat out. If they didn't find some way to keep *Denali* in port, they would all be left waiting for the light. No, not *just* waiting.

She turned to Akasha. "What I want you both to do is to survive. Go with Gideon. Take him to headquarters. Convince Ivan this is all real. Convince him to convince the navy. And ride out the storm there."

Akasha was shaking her head even before Ava finished. "No way. I'm in until this is done."

"No, Ava's right," Matt said. "There's nothing more you can do here. Lyric fucked up when she brought you into this. And Gideon needs you."

To Ava's surprise, Gideon was agreeable. "Come on, Akasha. Let's go. If they use a low-yield device, and Pearl is the real target, then we might be able to survive the blast over there."

"No, that's not good enough," Akasha insisted. "We can't let it happen *at all*."

Ava answered, her voice breaking. "Then convince Ivan to persuade his navy contacts that they're being conned into a war they don't want and that they're not ready to fight. The chain of command could still stop this with a word . . ." She trailed off as she wondered if that was true—or had it gone beyond that?

Kaden was at the dock with a hand-picked skeleton crew loyal to him, loyal to his cause. If ordered to stay in port, would he obey?

"Hell, it's worth a try," Ava concluded. "What time is it, anyway?" She'd left her gear powered down, worried it had been hacked along with Matt's.

"Two twenty-eight AM," Gideon said.

"Way too late for a taxi then, but you can get the train." Ava gripped Akasha's shoulders. "You'll be okay. HADAFA will tag you, but it won't matter, because there's nothing to link you to what just went down. Navy security is not going to be looking for you, and HPD has promised to look the other way."

The tears glistening in the younger officer's eyes reflected Ava's own, and maybe they shared the same thought, too: *Will we ever see each other again?*

They traded a quick hug. Then Akasha and Gideon headed off through a ghost neighborhood, where the broken asphalt streets and cracked concrete sidewalks still enforced a rough geometrical order on the brush and the small trees.

Matt said, "I would have asked you to go with them—"

"Not possible. Navy security knows my name."

"Yeah. That, and I'm going to need you as a distraction."

Her pulse quickened, wary of some desperate last measure. "What are you thinking?"

"Back to the basics. Get on the base. Sabotage the sub."

"You're dreaming."

A bitter edge to his voice. "It's what I should have done when we left the stadium, but Lyric wanted to be clever."

"No, she didn't want to waste you on a brute force solution. A *non*-solution. She gave the scenario to HADAFA to analyze—"

"And the AI said it couldn't work! I know that. So she gambled on Gideon." His lip curled, revealing a flash of white teeth in the dark. "But HADAFA isn't always right—and neither is Lyric. She overestimated Hōkū Ala. It's not often she gets played." He wiped at the accumulated rainwater on his face, then stared down at Ava. "You willing to cause a distraction?"

Fatigue and frustration shortened her temper. "Like what? Steal a car? Drive it through Makalapa Gate? Do something stupid, just to do something? How is that going to help you?"

"It won't. I need you to go over the wire. Full stealth. Like you're trying to make the hit yourself. My window of opportunity happens when the hammer comes down on you."

"This is our last shot, but we've still got a couple of hours," Matt said. "So let's find some place out of the rain. Take time to map things out. Get the details right."

Ava felt the tug of momentum, pushing her to sign on to Matt's berserker plan, even if she didn't believe in it. She eyed his waist pack. "You're carrying explosives, aren't you? That's what you've got in there."

"C-4," he confirmed. "Enough to disable the sub, prevent it from sailing. I'll get in while security's tied up with you."

She tried to imagine it, but the scene wouldn't play. "Matt. This isn't—"

She broke off as a cluster of distant lights winked out behind him. Stepping around him to get a better look, she spotted a large shadow gliding fifty feet or so above the dark shoreline.

"Quad-copter," she whispered.

He looked around, then motioned her down.

The rain and the gusting wind cloaked the copter's rotor noise, but it gave them cover too. Staying low, creeping through the jumble of elephant grass and invasive weeds, they retreated inland. The faint ambient light helped them find their way.

After a few minutes, Matt signaled that he'd heard the quad-copter off to their right. They angled away from it.

"Military patrols are not supposed to extend into civilian areas," he whispered.

"But who's going to know tonight?"

"Yeah."

When they came across an abandoned shipping container, partially collapsed, they slipped inside, thinking to outwait the quad-copter. They hunkered down amid puddles of rainwater and fragile flakes of rusting metal. But nothing could be heard past the hammering rain. They had no way to know if the quad-copter was close. So after a few minutes, they set off again, still angling west, almost paralleling the elevated freeway.

Then, past the sound of rain and wind, Ava heard a distant *phoomp!* followed immediately by a hollow *pop*, much closer.

"Stingers!" she warned as she dropped to her knees.

"Not in the rain," Matt objected.

"Trust me."

She'd heard that sequence of sound too many times in urban combat to mistake it now. The first beat marked the release of a hollow shell from a grenade launcher. The second was the sound of that shell popping open, to deliver a swarm of three stingers in the vicinity of the target. And Matt was wrong. Stingers could be used in heavy rain. Ava had used them that way more than once, despite what the manual said. It wasn't ideal. Rain weighed down the little winged drones. It degraded their ability to navigate and maneuver, but it didn't make them useless.

She moved to protect herself. Experience told her she had three or maybe four seconds at best. She pulled up her hood, then hunched over, legs folded beneath her torso, hands tucked under her chest, her face pressed against the sodden grass as she strained to hear past the rain.

There!

A flutter like the sound of panicked bird wings, but played back soft and at three times the natural speed. Then a faint tug on the fabric of her jacket, near her right shoulder. Her hand darted out. She twisted and grabbed. Fifty-fifty chance the stinger's antenna trailed down, not up.

Got it!

She yanked at the thin wire, pulling the stinger off her shoulder, whipping it down into the grass but not letting go. The antenna wire jerked in her hand as the stinger writhed. She got out her shockgun with her other hand and used it to pound the little winged marauder into submission. Then she pitched it away into the brush.

"Matt?"

"Yeah, I got mine." He sounded chagrined. "You okay?"

She sat up—too quickly. A wave of dizziness passed through her, accompanied by a faint stinging sensation on her shoulder, where the stinger had landed. "Touched," she said. "Low dose, I think." Her tongue felt thick. "But I'm feeling it."

She got to her feet. Matt grabbed her elbow, steadying her. "You were right," he conceded. "Let's go, before they decide to try a second round."

Three steps and she stumbled. Her legs felt shaky. Stingers packed a paralytic. Not fatal unless the target received multiple stings, though the swarm intelligence wasn't supposed to let that happen. A full dose dropped the target within two or three seconds, but even the low dose Ava had taken messed up her coordination.

"Keep going," Matt murmured. "If it hasn't put you down yet, it's not going to."

Ava wasn't so sure, but couldn't work her tongue enough to argue. A few more steps. Then, from out of the dark, a burst of accelerated fluttering. *The third stinger!*

Ava envisioned it: loitering in the area, poised on a kiawe branch to preserve its battery, its tiny electronic mind assessing the situation, tracking their position and their direction of movement, calculating the perfect time to launch an ambush.

She twisted free of Matt's grip and dove again for the ground— but she wasn't the target.

Matt grunted. Cursed. A crackle of twigs and a thump as he went down.

Ava groped for him. Found the hard warmth of his shoulder. A stinger's preferred target was the neck. Her searching fingers discovered the device there. With its payload delivered, it was harmless. She grabbed it, crushed its papery wings, and pitched it away, wanting some separation from its location beacon.

Then she hunched over, giving in to another wave of dizziness.

Time passed—a minute? two? Maybe longer, before her head began to clear. Time enough, that she'd gotten chilled. Her hands shook with cold—or maybe that was an effect of the drug. Her stomach felt queasy, and her head ached.

She didn't try to raise her head. Stayed down instead, and spent another minute just listening. Heard the hiss and wash of the wind and the ceaseless patter of rain. But no hum or buzz of drones, no flutter of mechanical wings, no rustle of enemy soldiers moving through wet grass. She sat up slowly, sniffing the air, but detected nothing but rain.

Damn it, move! she chided herself.

The smart thing to do was to put distance between herself and the site of the stinger's ambush—but that meant leaving Matt. No way could she drag him or carry him in her present condition.

Leave him.

That's what he would do—but then what?

She needed Matt, because she did not have his knowledge of the base, its security systems, and its vulnerabilities. No way could she get to *Denali* on her own. She'd be better off crashing a car through the front gate and screaming, *We're all going to die!*

Yeah, and maybe it would come to that. But not yet.

She had to get Matt on his feet.

"Hey." She shook his shoulder. "Matt, come on. Come out of it." Magical thinking. She'd never seen a captive who'd taken a full dose come around without stimulants in less than half an hour.

But maybe Matt had a med-kit in his waist pack? A med-kit with stimulants?

She rolled him half over, so that cloud-filtered moonlight glinted in his unblinking eyes. To save his vision, she followed procedure and closed them. His skin felt hot. His breathing was fast, shallow, and labored. She pressed her fingers to his neck.

What the hell?

His pulse hammered at an unsustainable pace. That made no sense. Stinger toxin put you under, it didn't send you over the top.

Matt definitely didn't need a stimulant.

She unzipped his pack anyway. Inside the main compartment, her flashlight's red beam revealed the packets of C-4, a tiny phone, a cash card. No med-kit, but two foil packets, one already torn open. As she struggled to read the label in the dim red light, Matt stirred, lifting his hand as if to reach for the flashlight.

"*Hey,*" she breathed. Matt had taken a full hit. No way should he be coming around already. She looked again at the empty packet. "What the hell are you on?" she murmured, her tongue still thick with stinger toxin.

To her shock, he answered in a long exhale: "*O– ver–drive.*"

"Ah, Matt, that stuff will kill you."

A pained half smile. "Feels . . . that . . . way." His throat bobbed as he swallowed. "Help me . . . up."

She zipped his pack closed, then supported him as he sat up. The exertion combined with the stinger toxin still in her system to send her own heart racing.

"Navy . . . be here . . . soon," Matt whispered.

"Yeah, and we need to be gone before then. Let's see how you do on your feet."

With his arm over her shoulder, he managed to stand—a moment only. She flexed her knees, taking more of his weight as she felt him sag. "Do I need to carry you?"

"Shu' up."

He took a tentative step. Then another. They both struggled not to trip in the weeds. More steps. "Where . . . ?" he asked.

"A little farther."

Every step she took demanded more effort than the last. She felt wrung out, exhausted. Her legs trembled and her spine ached from bearing Matt's weight. Her stomach churned and her pulse hammered against her skull. But she kept going.

They left the weeds. Stumbled along a dirt road. *Navy be here soon*. Yet she saw no sign of pursuit. No quad-copter, no searchlights, no barking dogs.

Another few minutes, and a square structure loomed out of the moon-flecked darkness. A shed, on the edge of a banana grove. They needed shelter. A short time-out. So she steered Matt toward it, feeling him drift into unconsciousness, more and more of his weight bearing down on her until she snapped at him, "Focus, soldier!"

A hasp held the shed door closed. Ava had been ready to shoot off a padlock, but there was none, so she pulled the door open and shone her light inside.

Empty, except for a cardboard box stuffed with trash. Everything valuable—down to the padlock—must have been taken out ahead of the storm.

She steered Matt inside. He wilted to the floor and she went down beside him, her flashlight tumbling from her hand.

That dream again:

Two little girls clinging to the smooth bark of a wind-stripped rainbow shower tree. Half submerged in rushing water, the unrelenting rain pouring down on them, they cried for help in haunting, high-pitched voices as Ava struggled to reach them.

These little girls were not her daughters. Not this time. Nine years had passed since she'd confronted the reality of their faces—the wind whipping their black hair into tangled streamers, their beautiful dark terror-filled eyes looking on her to save their lives, their pleading voices begging her to *hurry, hurry.*

Ava tried—but movement came hard. Each step a battle, frustration mounting as she waded through a tangle of rain-soaked weeds toward a distant dock, the huge black hull of a submarine lying beside it like a sleeping whale.

Hurry!

One step ahead of panic. Reality now fluid, slippery, allowing impossible things: The submarine had gone.

No, she whispered. *No, no, no.*

But it was already too late. She had failed again to save the little girls and they knew it. They looked at her with accusation in their eyes, an instant before light exploded around them, ten thousand times brighter than the sun.

Ava's eyes snapped open on the dull red glow of her flashlight, her heart racing, breath trembling. *My God, my God.*

Pressing her hands against a muddy plywood floor, she pushed herself to sit up. *Was* it already too late? Had *Denali* sailed?

Matt lay prone beside her, head turned in her direction, his smart glasses fogged and a thread of drool running from his half-open mouth as he breathed in uneasy rhythm. Ava shuddered and hugged herself. How much time had she just lost? Rain hammered on the shed's roof and splattered through the open door. Still dark out there, but dawn came late this time of year.

Fatigue gripped her. Her head still ached and her mouth felt sour and dry—but her heart fluttered in caged panic. *We need to move!*

"Matt," she croaked, her voice hoarse. She reached out and shook him. "Matt, come out of it."

He stirred and groaned. Behind his fogged glasses, his eyes fluttered open. "Where?" he whispered without raising his head.

"A farm shed. I don't know what time it is."

His focus shifted. Checking his display?

"'s late," he whispered, his voice still a little slurred. He rolled over onto his back. Drew in a deliberate deep breath, and then another.

She pressed her fingers to his neck, measuring the thready beat of his heart. "Still fast, but way better than before. I was afraid you were going to have a heart attack."

Another deep breath, and then a cynical half smile. "Yeah, me too."

Given what he'd been through over the past twenty-four hours, it was a miracle he could function.

He lifted his forearm to his mouth and sucked on the wet fabric of his sleeve. "God, ah'm thirsty."

"Same."

She crawled to the box of trash, dumped it out, and found a crushed soda cup, still sticky with syrup. She reshaped it and then put it outside, under the curtain of water running off the shed roof. After it collected a few swallows, she shared it with Matt.

"Has Lyric checked back in?" she asked, the terror of the dream still haunting her.

"Nah yet. Bu' I messaged her."

"She must have been taken out."

"No. Nah true. She's s'ill workin' things."

"You really believe that, don't you? Well, damn it, Matt. She's not magic."

That half-smile again. "Yeah, she is." He rolled to his side, then sat up, scooting to rest his back against the shed wall. He slipped his fogged-up glasses off. "Navy never showed, huh?"

"Guess not." And how crazy was that? "They had us with those stingers. They could have walked right up and shot us. Why are we still here?"

He polished his glasses with a damp cleaning cloth from his waist pack. "Lyric's magic."

"Bull. Shit."

He slipped his smart glasses back on. "Try dis, then: Navy security's nah authorized to use stingers off base. Nah their jur-iss . . . dic-shun."

"Come on. You're saying someone got gung-ho, violated regs, and now they're trying to avoid a reprimand?"

"I've heard crazier stories."

Ava grimaced. "Right. I've heard crazier stories just tonight."

He got his feet under him, and with one hand against the shed wall for balance, he stood up. "Less get going."

Ava grabbed her flashlight, then stood too, so she could try to catch him when he fell. "What can you do, Matt? Look at you. You're sick and exhausted."

"No, I jus' need to move. Work this shit out of my system. You with me?"

She shuddered, seeing again the accusing eyes of those little girls, nine years gone. "There's not much time. You still think we can get over the wire?"

He froze, light glinting in his smart glasses. "*Holy shit.* I tol' you she's magic. Link up. Lyric's back online."

chapter

21

AVA GRABBED HER tactile mic from the pocket where she'd stashed it when they'd entered Gideon's realm. She powered up her smart glasses and slipped them on. "Here's hoping my gear's not hacked."

Of course, it *had* been hacked. Lyric had hacked it. Proof of that came when she was automatically linked into an ongoing explanation, Lyric's voice saying, ". . . the blast door locked and I've got a Marine general with a contingent of volunteers standing guard. I've never seen anything like it, Matt. It's blown up into a civil war in cyberspace, and here, in the halls and stairwells—all without the knowledge of the American people."

"You're not alone anymore?" Ava asked.

"I wouldn't say I have a lot of allies."

Matt made a fist. "You need to get me on that base. I don't want to hear any reasons why not. I've still got the C-4. Just get me past perimeter security and I'll disable the sub."

"That is not going to work," Lyric told him. "You're a wanted man. HADAFA will tag you and throw an alarm as soon as a networked camera detects anyone who *might* be you—"

"So fix it. Clean my record."

"I don't have the reach anymore. There's a lock on your profile and that means you aren't going to get near the base. Even if you could, it's on lockdown. High alert. Nothing goes in or out. They had an attempted terrorist incident. Averted, but too close for comfort."

Matt turned to Ava, teeth gritted. She felt a blush stinging her rain-chilled cheeks. "That was us," she volunteered. "Bad luck it didn't work."

"Bad luck it's made our job even harder."

"How much time do we have left?" Ava asked. She hadn't meant it as an existential question, so she clarified: "I mean, before *Denali* sails?"

"*Denali* is scheduled to depart at oh-seven-hundred."

Ava checked the time. Already 6:00 AM, despite the darkness. Less than an hour, and their fate would be decided.

Okay, maybe she *had* meant it as an existential question.

"Come on, Lyric," she pleaded. "There has to be someone already on the inside you can use. Or some*thing*. A security drone—"

"I don't have the reach! But I am working with the chain of command to get *Denali*'s departure delayed."

Matt asked, "What good is a delay if we can't get someone in there? Damn it, Lyric. Get me a car. Get me over there. Let me try."

"Nothing goes in or out," Ava murmured, thinking aloud. "But what if something happened? An incident that demanded Kaden's presence off the base . . . would he have the authority to leave?"

"He's not going to leave," Matt snapped. "Not now. Conrad owns him."

"Conrad?" Ava echoed, thinking about the leader of Sigrún. Daniel Conrad had still been in Honolulu as of late yesterday.

Matt said, "Yeah, this is Conrad's scheme. He recruited Robicheaux—and Robicheaux is devoted to him. You must have heard him talk about Daniel Conrad."

"No. Or, *yes*. But only yesterday afternoon."

Even then, it had been Ava who brought up the topic of Conrad, because he'd been in the news, come to speak against the handover treaty. And when she'd made her contempt clear, Kaden had responded with a gentle accusation: *You don't like it that you agree with him.*

Ava had never hidden her political opinions from Kaden, but he'd never wanted to talk politics—a silence she'd attributed to his station, assuming that as an officer, he felt obligated to remain neutral. Little did she know.

"Is it possible Daniel Conrad is still in Honolulu?" she asked.

"No way," Matt said. "He's got to be long gone."

But Lyric grasped at the chance. "Checking." Seconds passed. "Got him. He's at the airport in a private lounge. I don't see him scheduled on any commercial flight . . . okay, I've got an association with a chartered jet, business class. *Yes*. It's being ferried over from Maui. It'll need to top off its fuel tanks before departing from Honolulu. That gives you time. Forty-five minutes, maybe."

"Get me a vehicle," Matt insisted.

"You can't be the one to go, Matt. HADAFA will initiate a lockdown the moment you try to enter an airport terminal."

"I didn't mean Matt should go after Conrad," Ava objected, her words running together in her haste to get them out. "Even if you got past HADAFA, got past Conrad's bodyguards, and forced him to order Kaden to stand down—do you think Kaden would listen? *No*. It's gone too far. But you talked before about luring Kaden out. If he's not aboard the sub, there's no way the operation can go forward. Right?"

"His presence is required to launch," Lyric confirmed. "But where are you going with this? You burned your relationship with him."

"Right. I know. He won't come for me, but what about Conrad? Lyric, could you fake a message from Conrad? And push it through to Kaden? Have Conrad demand to be taken aboard the sub, a ride-along because he wants to witness the historic action. I'm surprised that arrogant dick hasn't already arranged it. Kaden would have to leave the base himself, pick up Conrad, escort him back through security—because no one else in his crew would have the authority to defy the lockdown and bring a civilian on base."

Matt nodded. "This could work, Lyric. But we'll need a deep fake. A really convincing video message. If you lure him out, I'll ambush him on the road."

Lyric instructed Matt and Ava to make their way to Kamehameha Highway. "It's not far. Once you're there, wait out of sight. I'll contact you again when the operation is good to go."

Ava tallied her ammunition, thinking about Kaden, how he'd been her lover only yesterday. "I've got four rounds left," she told Matt.

"Lyric will resupply you."

He tore open the second foil packet of Overdrive.

"Matt," she said disapprovingly. "You're in no condition to handle another dose of that shit."

A half-smile, an amused grunt, as he pushed up his sleeve, revealing an old medical patch. "You're thinking long term. All I need is a couple more hours of clarity." His smile faded as he swapped out the old patch, replacing it with the fresh one from the packet. "This is a no-fail mission. You know that."

"Right."

Deep breath.

He added, "And you're here for backup, if I go down."

She nodded, imbued with a sense of calm tension familiar from her time in the army.

They headed out through the banana plantation, the huge leaves of the banana trees rustling, rattling, and snapping as the wind shredded them to ribbons. After that, the road they followed crossed a section of abandoned land, overgrown with kiawe and weeds. The setting moon gleamed yellow past the fringes of rushing clouds—and Ava thought of her daughters.

They'd be awake now in their Spokane home, chided by their stepmother to hurry and get ready for school. She was a good woman, a good mom. They'd be all right. Ava's heart ached all the same, for all that had been broken—in her, in the world.

Why did we choose this future?

It *had* been a choice. People had voted against their own long-term interests, returning to office corrupt politicians whose only goal was to sell them out, to sell their futures. Or people had failed to vote at all, too anesthetized by the grind of daily life to lift their heads and really see what was going on around them.

And so the seas rose, the winds raged, fire swept the forests, once-verdant fields turned to dust, and innocent children who'd never had the chance to choose, drowned in floods or were buried in mudslides.

Never ask, *Who knew?* We all knew.

She staggered as a gust of wind, stronger than any before it that night, roared through the brush, slamming against her back. Branches whipped around her and a confetti-swirl of plucked leaves took flight, shimmering with the sideways rain in the refracted glow of lights from the freeway—all of it blurred into unreality by the water sheeting across the lens of her smart glasses.

They passed under the freeway, continuing on toward Kamehameha Highway as Lyric had instructed, stopping at the edge of the brush, outside the reach of the traffic cameras.

Ava looked out at the highway, the nearest lane some thirty feet away. The imposing edifice of the elevated rail track divided the highway, but no train was in sight, and not a single vehicle moved on the usually busy road. The streetlights still shone and rain danced on the pavement, but there were no cars, no bikes, and no one else on foot—an absence that felt surreal, like an apocalyptic movie set. Everyone but a few stragglers already gone from the world.

Not yet. Not if I can help it.

She glanced at Matt, standing motionless in the shadows. "You doing okay?" she whispered.

"I'm good."

She imagined Lyric, merged in dark communion with HADAFA, setting up the operation. *How long would it take?*

To ease her nerves, she turned to the ritual, imagining a dancing flame, a lit cigarette, a burn in her throat as she inhaled soothing white smoke. When that exercise grew stale, she focused on the sound of the wind, the pattering rain, seeking to maintain a state of calm ahead of the coming mission.

Twenty-seven minutes after her last communication, Lyric checked back in. "It worked," she said. "Robicheaux's on the move. And I've hijacked Conrad's phone number. If Robicheaux tries to confirm, he'll only get voicemail."

"I'm not in position," Matt objected. "I'm still stuck here on the side of the road."

"Vehicle is on the way," she assured him. "Ninety seconds out. Once you're onboard, you and Arnette will have another ninety seconds to gear up and get in position."

"No hurry, then."

"I need you to take him alive," Lyric said, ignoring his sarcasm. "I want to cauterize this infection. That means I need him as a witness, to testify to what he intended to do, and to name everyone who helped."

"I'll do what I can. No promises."

"Matt—"

"I said I'll try! What weapons have you got for me?"

"Since this is not a kill, you're going in light—"

"Damn it!"

"You've got a Carousel shotgun, with slugs, light-weight shot, and webbing in the cartridge wheel. Ammo for your handgun, and for Arnette's. A spike strip, and aerial kamikazes. Robicheaux is not alone. He's got two armed sailors with him—"

"So he's suspecting something," Ava said.

Lyric answered, "The whole base is on edge after the attempted terrorist attack—"

"Right," she conceded.

"—and Robicheaux has more reason to be on edge than most. He's been instructed to meet Conrad on the upper level of the airport terminal, east end. Don't let him get that far. Try to detain him on the road before he reaches the airport, but do not detain him in the vicinity of the base or you will not be able to control the situation."

"That's a narrow window," Ava said. "The base entrance is only a couple of miles from the airport. You need to call for police backup. Get them to close all vehicular exits—"

"We're outside the law on this one," Lyric reminded her. "The only thing a heads-up to the police will achieve is advance warning for Robicheaux."

"Vehicle incoming," Matt said. "Is that us?"

"Affirmed. Matt, you will enter via the back door. Arnett, take the front."

Matt turned to Ava, his fist raised. "No-fail mission. Do what's necessary. *Whatever* is necessary."

Her heart rate soared as she lightly touched her knuckles against his. "Confirm," she said, hoarse with tension.

The vehicle raced toward them: a big, dark-gray SUV with federal plates, its windows coated to reject the probing gazes of standard surveillance cameras and curious onlookers. A hundred feet out it braked hard, swooping onto the shoulder, coming to a rocking stop exactly in front of them as they darted from the brush to meet it.

Ava yanked open the front passenger door. Both front seats were empty. A passage between them allowed easy access to the back where the seat had been removed.

She scrambled in, slamming the door shut. The back door slammed a half second later, and the car accelerated hard, swerving onto the road.

She twisted around in her seat to see Matt clinging with one hand to a grip, using the other to unclip a shotgun from a ceiling rack. Two small quad-copters waited in racks on the floor.

Lyric's voice: "Arnette, there's a vest on the driver's seat. Ammo in the dash compartment."

Right.

Ava grabbed the armored vest. Got it on. Popped the dash compartment open and found three magazines. She ejected the almost-empty one from her pistol and slammed in a fully loaded one, pocketing the other two.

"You coming up front?" she asked Matt.

"Yeah." He leaned over her shoulder, bulked up in his own armored vest. "Move behind the wheel. Be ready to take over if you need to."

The stadium complex loomed ahead. Ava made the shift, then braced as the highway curved south, following the coast of East Loch.

Matt took over the passenger seat, sliding it back as far as it would go to give himself room to maneuver the shotgun. Behind his smart glasses, his expression was grim.

"You've missed the first window," Lyric announced. "Robicheaux has just exited the base ahead of you. So you've got a pursuit, not an ambush."

Ava heard an odd, amused note in Lyric's voice. It snapped her focus, kicking her loose from the present, sending her back to that scene of Robert Bell, trapped in the basement laundry. Doubt pounded against her rib cage. Had Lyric deliberately mistimed this? *No.* This was real. It had to be . . . unless Kaden too had been misled from the beginning?

No.

"Why don't you just hijack their ride?" Matt asked. "Make it easy for us."

"I would if I could."

Ava braced as she felt a shift in momentum. She glanced at the dash. "Hey, why are we slowing down?"

"Yeah, what the hell?" Matt demanded. "What are you doing? We need to be closing on Robicheaux."

"I want you at legal speed so you don't draw attention from the guards when you pass Makalapa Gate. If Kaden gets additional support you won't be able to take him alive."

Their progress felt horribly slow, though it was not. They approached the turn-off to the gate. As they passed, Ava looked down the side street, but she couldn't make out much through the rain-blurred window, just a patch of light illuminating the area outside the guard booth.

Their SUV picked up speed again, rapidly accelerating.

The windshield wipers worked frantically, but the rain had begun to hammer, and each pass of the wipers yielded only a half-second clarity of vision. Even blurred, the sudden sight of red taillights ahead made her catch her breath.

It was him. Kaden. Her focus tightened despite a flare of anger. She had never loved him. She'd only loved the illusion of him. *And I don't regret anything.* Yesterday's words, but still true. If Kaden had not brought her into this, she would not be in a position to stop it.

With each swift beat of the windshield wipers, the taillights brightened, and the interval between Kaden and her shrank. Would he look back? Did he know there had been no traffic on the highway just moments before? Would he be suspicious when he caught sight of a single vehicle rapidly closing with his?

"Something's off," Lyric announced. "I'm hooked into surveillance cameras in the terminal, watching Conrad. He's left the lounge. He's moving quickly with a carry-on bag, phone to his ear. But it's not his phone. Not his registered phone."

"Secondary line of communication," Matt said. "Is he talking to Robicheaux?"

"Unknown, but he's in a hurry."

"Even if he *is* talking to Kaden," Ava said. "Even if Kaden has figured out this is a setup, why is Conrad moving? Is he heading to his plane? Is it ready to board?"

"Checking," Lyric said.

Then: "Conrad is *not* going to his plane. He's exiting the terminal."

"*What?*" Matt demanded. "Why?"

Lyric hissed, and then she laughed. "Well, fuck me. Conrad's flight has been canceled. The outbound traffic queue is so long, the charter company calculated they'd never get off the ground again before the airport closed—so they turned their plane around and sent it back to Maui. Conrad must be about to piss his pants right now."

"He's already got a new exit plan," Ava said, with bitter triumph. "We gave it to him. He's going with Kaden."

"New battle strategy," Lyric decided. "Hang back. Trail him into the airport, but make no move until Conrad gets picked up. Then take them both at once."

chapter

22

RED TAILLIGHTS CLIMBED the ramp that led to the Liliuoka-lani Freeway. Ava watched, anxious to close the gap, but Lyric kept the SUV following at a respectful distance.

Less than a mile later, Kaden shifted onto the long curving bridge that was the exit ramp to the airport. As his car rounded the curve, she saw it in profile for the first time. Another dark-gray SUV, identical to the one she rode in.

They took the exit too, but at a much slower speed. "We're letting him go for now," Lyric said. "We won't lose him. I've got him through surveillance cameras."

The ramp divided. Ava leaned forward, glimpsing Kaden up ahead as he disappeared down a lane that led to arrivals. They took that lane too. She looked for him, and as they reached the ground level, she caught sight of his SUV one more time. His vehicle had shifted into a lane turning left. A moment later, she lost sight of him again.

This time, they didn't follow, but instead kept to the right, taking a different route.

Ava exhaled, bleeding off tension. She told herself Kaden had not gotten away, that Lyric knew what she was doing, that they were on the same side.

They rounded a curve, entering the lower level of the terminal building. The rain cut off. The wipers swiped a few more times and then settled out of sight. Lights shone in the baggage claim areas, but no one was there. No one was outside on the sidewalk either, and there were no cars.

They rounded the next curve, then accelerated, speeding past another eerily empty terminal. Ava gripped the armrest. At this speed, it would be only moments before they reached the return ramp to the freeway.

"Fill me in, Lyric," Matt said. "What's going on?"

The SUV braked hard, coming to a full stop beside the center island—and the world went strangely quiet. There was no sound of traffic, no tire noise. And because they were still under the shelter of the terminal building, there was no drumming rain. It was quiet enough, that Ava could hear the faint, distant roar of a jet taking off. A lonely sound, dividing those who would escape from those left behind.

"Kaden's being cautious," Lyric said. "He passed the lei stands and circled back up to departures. He's moving fast now."

"He noticed us on the road," Ava said softly as she rechecked her pistol. "He'll be looking for us when he exits."

"Assume it," Matt agreed.

"Get ready," Lyric warned them. "He's almost right above you."

Deep breath!

"Let's get this done," Ava whispered over the rapid pounding of her heart.

Lyric said, "Here we go . . . They've made a hard stop at the curb. And here comes Conrad, grinning like a drunk . . . Okay, Conrad is inside the vehicle, backseat. Door is closed. I couldn't see how Robicheaux placed his bodyguards, but best guess from his profile is that he's in the driver's seat, with one of his bullyboys riding shotgun, and the other in back, on the left."

"Got it," Matt said.

"And here they come. They're taking the freeway ramp."

The side windows, front and back, slid open. Matt reached out, grabbed the side mirror, and folded it out of the way. Then he raised the shotgun, so the muzzle extended outside. Ava slipped off her smart glasses and pocketed them, not wanting to contend with more rain on the lens. She still wore her mic.

Lyric started a countdown: "Four, three, two, one—"

Ava braced herself against the seatback.

The SUV shot forward, hurtling out into the rain. A short sprint across level ground. Rainwater, thrown up by the tires, struck the undercarriage with a crunching roar. More rain lanced in through the open window, needling Ava's face, and soaking her all over again.

They reached the ramp, and raced up the incline into the first gray gleam of dawn.

A buzzing from behind the front seats announced the launch of the kamikazes. Ava twisted around to see the two little quadcopters—just fifteen inches across—lift from their racks on the floor. They darted one after the other out the open window on the left, to fly alongside the SUV.

Just ahead, the ramp leveled out and merged with another traffic lane coming from the left. No taillights, but Ava's eye was drawn by a blur of dark motion as a blocky SUV merged less than a hundred feet ahead of them.

"That's him," Lyric said.

The kamikazes shot away, pursuing their target. At the same time, muzzle flashes erupted from both sides of the fleeing vehicle—and the kamikazes blew up. Halfway between the two SUVs, they burst into balls of orange and white flame, generating a double concussion that Ava felt in her chest. The SUV bucked and her head snapped back against the headrest. She felt the heat of lingering flame, and caught the scent of spent explosives as they shot past the point of detonation.

Matt leaned forward, the shotgun braced against his shoulder, and started squeezing off carefully spaced rounds, each blast painfully loud.

Ava couldn't get a clear shot from her side, not without leaning halfway out. She started to do it, when a hail of bullets frosted the armored windshield. She jerked back inside.

Kaden's vehicle skewed right. It slid toward a ramp that would take him east, away from Pearl Harbor and toward the city.

Did he really mean to go that way?

"It's a feint," Lyric said. Calm, confident. "He'll try to cross back at the last second. Block him—"

"No, he means it," Matt said. "Follow him."

Ava wanted to do more than follow.

Just as Matt had predicted, Kaden took the ramp. Their own SUV shifted lanes to go after it, but it dumped speed as it did.

"No way!" Ava shouted. She reached for the dash and toggled the switch that shifted the vehicle from remote to manual control. Lyric yelled a protest. Ava growled back, "I've got this."

She stomped the accelerator, skimmed past a concrete divider, and shot onto the ramp. The SUV hydroplaned, sliding sideways on the wet, oily surface, tires screaming, but at the same time, rapidly closing with Kaden's vehicle.

More white blossoms on the windshield, obscuring her vision, and then a spatter of blood, immediately washed away by the rain.

"Right-side shooter is hit," Matt said, leaving his seat and moving into the back.

"Hold tight," Ava warned him. "It's gonna get rough."

"Just drive."

She couldn't see him, but she sensed him right behind her. Proof came with a shot that sounded like it was to the back of her head. Matt said something. Missed? Maybe. Didn't matter. She was out of time. The ramp was about to merge onto a wide-open freeway.

She aimed the nose of the SUV at the gap between the ramp's concrete wall and the left side of Kaden's vehicle, intending to force him against the right wall. But the car's proximity alarm went off, the accelerator disengaged under her foot, and the SUV rapidly slowed to the posted speed limit as its automated accident-avoidance function took over.

"What are you doing?" Matt screamed, while Ava swore and hammered on the dash, watching helplessly as Kaden's vehicle raced away.

"Reset, reset, tell me how to reset," she murmured, scanning the dash while the SUV continued at a sedate fifty-five miles an hour. *There.*

The steering-control toggle had shifted back to remote-autonomous mode. "Goddamn nanny state."

She returned it to manual as Matt dropped back into the passenger seat. Far ahead, the dark bulk of Kaden's SUV took the ramp down to Nimitz Highway, passing over the site of the encampment Ava had visited so briefly last night.

"You secure?" she asked Matt as she closed the windows and set the air-conditioning to blow hard and cold so water vapor wouldn't cloud the glass.

"Gun it."

She pushed the accelerator all the way down, feeling the tires float on the film of rainwater flooding the freeway. Beside her, Matt reloaded the shotgun.

"Lyric!" she shouted. "Why is Kaden going this way?"

"I don't know. I don't know what he's doing. This doesn't make sense."

For the first time, Ava heard uncertainty in Lyric's voice—and it made her skin crawl. Lyric was the puppet master, the oracle of HADAFA. She knew what people would do before they did.

"There's something else, isn't there?" Ava asked as she took the ramp down to Nimitz. The traffic lights ahead were green. "What is it? What's happened?"

"*Denali* has left the dock. It's sailed—ahead of schedule. Robicheaux has left himself no way out."

"That can't be right," Matt said.

"It's verified. It's true."

"But that means it's over," Ava said. Hope stirred, a strange, warm sensation around her heart. "You said Kaden had to be aboard the sub to authorize the launch. If he's not there, there won't be a launch."

"That's how it should work," Lyric confirmed. "But if they managed to transfer his authority—"

"*No.*" Ava rejected the argument. "He's not suicidal and I don't think Conrad is either. Run their profiles. Confirm it if you need to. Is either one of them willing to lay down his life here, now, to further the cause?"

"No," Lyric said, her voice now low and hard. Vengeful. "That's an unlikely behavior for Robicheaux, and incompatible with Conrad's profile. They must have cancelled."

"No way," Matt said. "It's now or never for them. Too many questions are going to be asked after this fiasco. At the least, Kaden will lose his command. He cannot abort. He has to have another way out."

"He *does*," Ava said as revelation washed over her, a rising tide of unwelcome memory. "He's planning to join *Denali* at sea."

Kaden had shown her the scheme, hadn't he? That day after they'd met. She'd been there for the demonstration of a special-ops midget sub, newly assigned to *Denali*. It had been a dog-and-pony show prepared for a congressional representative . . . one from the Cornerstone party.

Thinking out loud, Ava said, "Kaden must have set up a rendezvous. The midget sub will come in, pick him up . . . at a harbor, maybe?"

It had to be in a harbor. It couldn't happen anywhere else. The midget sub was designed to carry special forces personnel close to shore, allowing them to exit and enter underwater. But with the storm surge and the massive surf generated by Huko, Kaden couldn't expect to swim to it from a beach, or from a seawall facing the open ocean—especially not with Conrad slowing him down. He would have to meet the sub in sheltered water.

But he was already passing the sprawl of docks at Honolulu Harbor without slowing down. In moments, he'd be blowing by Harbor Station. What was left after that? The old moorings at Ala Moana had not survived Nolo, and there was no other harbor on this side of the island.

"It doesn't make sense!" Ava protested, feeling suddenly cold—shivering—in the blast of the air-conditioning.

It made no sense for Kaden to run east—not if Ava's understanding of the situation was true. But if all of this was a crazy fantasy woven from the mind of a puppet master, playing a bizarre game of her own . . .

That sense of dissociation, of having lost all anchors to logical reality. Ava only knew *Denali* had sailed because Lyric had told her. She had no outside means of confirming that claim.

She had spoken to Astrid Robicheaux and believed her to be

the real thing even though her description of Kaden contradicted everything Ava had believed about him. Was it possible Astrid had been a deep fake?

Kaden himself had all but confirmed his own treasonous role: *Will these children grow up to wear a Chinese uniform?*

But had they been talking past each other? What had he really meant by that?

Don't do it, Kaden, she'd pleaded with him. *Don't do it. For all our sakes.* And he'd let her go. He'd ended the conversation because he didn't want to acknowledge the truth, to face his own guilt. That's what she'd assumed. But what if he'd ended the call because he thought *she* was compromised? Or crazy?

It doesn't matter!

Ava could not allow it to matter. It had all gone too far. The stakes were too high. Even if it was all a crazy fantasy spawned from Lyric's machinations, she had to play it through, keep Kaden ashore. No grave harm would be done by that; her own jeopardy could not be made worse than it already was—while quitting now would put the lives of a hundred thousand innocents at risk. And if the missile launched and all those people died? Millions more would be lost in the engineered war that would surely follow.

And still, she mistrusted Lyric—enough that she kept manual control of the SUV.

Ava peered past the bullet-scarred windshield, looking for patches of pooling water that could send the SUV hydroplaning out of control; she watched for the dark shape of Kaden's vehicle, now past Harbor Station; and she tapped her tactile mic, whispering, "Call Gina Alameda."

"End current call?" her digital assistant queried in its upbeat voice.

"Yes."

The link to Lyric closed.

"What are you doing?" Matt wanted to know.

"Asking for help."

Gina picked up after one ring. "You saved the world yet?"

"I need a spike strip, *now*," Ava told her without preamble. "Ala Moana corridor—"

"I'm nowhere near. Stand by."

Ava again lost sight of Kaden as his SUV rounded a curve in the business district. They were on Ala Moana Boulevard now. Two empty lanes ran in each direction, with the streetcar median between them, fenced by low hedges of naupaka.

"I've got the nearest unit linked in," Gina said. "What are we looking for?"

"Federal SUV, dark gray, proceeding at high speed toward the Coastal district. Four occupants, one known to be injured. They are in possession of assault weapons—and they know how to use them."

"*Shit*," a male voice said. "Really didn't need this today, Ava."

"Sorry. We're coming behind, same vehicle type, half-mile separation."

The male voice again: "Got you both on camera."

Ava heard a grunt and a car door slamming as he rushed to get the spike strip from out of the patrol car's trunk. Breathing audibly now, he said, "We might have just enough time to do this."

Matt could hear only her side of the conversation, but that was enough to understand. "This going to work?" he demanded.

"Gotta try." A curtain of white water spewed from beneath the tires as she took a curve too quickly. Backing off the accelerator, she let the SUV slide across empty lanes until she felt the tires grip the road again—then she eased the pedal down, reclaiming her speed.

Over her earbud, she heard the rattle of the spike strip unrolling.

Instantly, past the blur of rain on the windshield, she saw the red warning-flash of brake lights a half-mile out, near the west end of the Ala Moana seawall. She maintained speed for a few more seconds, the distance between her and those lights rapidly closing. Then Kaden's SUV pulled a one-eighty, the chassis rocking. Ava found herself facing its dark windshield. She pressed the brake, holding her breath, waiting for Kaden to accelerate straight at her.

Instead, his SUV wheeled around and lunged over the curb of the median, plowing through the naupaka hedge and bouncing over the streetcar tracks, ending up in the westbound lanes.

The patrol car was on that side, parked across the lanes and partially blocking them, but Kaden found room enough to slip around it. Once past, he took off again.

The cop—Ava still didn't know who he was—stood on the median, at a gap in the hedge where pedestrians could cross. He yanked the spike strip out of her way. "Sorry, Ava," he said as she rocketed past.

"Thanks for trying."

"I'll be right behind you."

"Get your vest on," she advised him, and muted the call.

She still didn't know where Kaden was going, or why.

She said to Matt, "There's a traffic barrier at the Ala Moana Bridge. He won't be able to get past it into Waikīkī. He'll have to make a hard left on Atkinson. That's your chance."

"Understood."

"If he fucks up and fails to do that, we trap him in front of the barrier."

"Confirmed."

Blue lights flashed in the rearview as the patrol car joined the chase.

The failed blockade had given Ava a chance to close the distance to Kaden's car. No more than a hundred fifty yards separated them now, though Kaden remained on the other side of the median. She opened all the windows again, then leaned over the wheel, straining to see past the scarred windshield and the currents of rain, watching for him to make the turn onto Atkinson—but she saw no reassuring glow of red brake lights.

She glanced at Matt, already leaning out the open window, weapon braced on his shoulder, squinting against the rain. She said, "If he doesn't slow down he's not going to be able to make the turn."

Ava decided to bring her own speed down. Better to hang back and avoid the debris of a crash when Kaden took the turn too fast. No way would he try to run the barrier. The double line of steel bollards would shred his SUV.

"Don't slow down!" Matt yelled at her. "The fucking barrier is going down. He's gonna cross."

"*What?*"

The barrier was controlled from KCA headquarters. The bollards could be lowered at any time for emergency vehicles, or at fixed times for maintenance and delivery vans—but not for random speeding maniacs.

"It can't be!"

"It *is*. Maybe Coastal gave him a pass, maybe Sigrún hacked it. I don't know. It doesn't matter. But if you don't make it across with him, we're going to be left behind."

Ava couldn't see the barrier to confirm. She couldn't make it out past the ruined windshield. But she leaned on the accelerator anyway, making the choice to trust Matt—though her stomach lurched as she flashed on the horror of what would happen if he was wrong and she hit that barrier at speed.

"Which side?" she asked frantically. Kaden was still on the left side of the road. "Which side is open? Right or left?"

"Both, I think. Definitely right."

"Okay."

Finally, a flash of brake lights ahead. She tapped her brakes too.

"No!" Matt yelled. "Close the gap. Do it now!"

She clamped her teeth together and blindly pushed the accelerator down. They shot past Atkinson, closing on Kaden as he went the wrong way into the roundabout, his lead now less than fifty feet.

The shotgun went off.

Kaden's SUV slalomed, but it didn't slow as it sped over the retracted barrier and up the low arch of the bridge. Ava followed, on the righthand side of the road. Steel plates rattled under her tires as she passed the barrier. A glance in the rearview showed the bollards beginning to rise again, swinging up out of recessed sockets in the tiled paving. Farther back, the patrol car made a skidding turn onto Atkinson.

"Lost our backup," Ava said as she followed Kaden's vehicle in parallel, down the bridge and onto the pedestrian mall. No humans in sight, but at the sudden appearance of the two vehicles, green parrots, scarlet macaws, and white pigeons burst from their roosts and took flight, their feathers catching the gray morning light.

Ava strove to see past the scarred windshield as she jerked the steering wheel right, left, right, slaloming down a serpentine path between coconut palms and concrete benches, driving as if she was in a video game—and she caught up with Kaden. Only the streetcar tracks divided them now.

The shotgun went off behind her, startling her badly. She'd been so focused on driving, she hadn't even noticed Matt moving to the back.

"Got him!" Matt yelled.

Instinctively, she tapped the brake. Then she looked left—and stomped the brake hard.

Kaden's SUV came plowing across the streetcar tracks. Its shattered side windows had gone white with ruin and condensation, the front tire was shredded, the back tire nearly flat, and a jet of flame shot from the undercarriage.

Ava turned the wheel hard, skidding sideways as she fought to avoid a collision—and failed. Her vehicle slammed side-to-side into Kaden's. Air bags blasted her from the front and from the door. The horrible low crunch of crumpling metal, and the carriage rocking.

Three stunned seconds as the airbags deflated. A battery fire hissed. Rain hammered down. And wind raged, roaring through a forest of trees, lifting flights of leaves, and twirling them in the air.

The collision had brought them to a stop where the pedestrian mall passed through Fort DeRussy Park.

From the floor behind her seat, there came a grunt of pain and a string of whispered curses.

"Matt!" she yelled, finding her voice again. "Status?"

"Banged up. Not broken." Then he added, "*Fuck*."

"Then get moving!" she ordered. "Get the fuck out! There's a fire!"

With her door jammed up against the other vehicle, she needed to exit on the right. She started to rise, then froze at the sight of two figures, bent low and moving swiftly away from the other SUV. One was obviously Dan Conrad, a big bulky man wearing slacks and a red-themed aloha shirt that purled in the wind where it wasn't held down by the straps of a shoulder holster. As he fled, he shrugged on a slender plastic backpack.

The other figure caused her a moment of surprise and a dagger of heartache. She'd expected to see Kaden in uniform. Instead, he wore black—a wetsuit that embraced the familiar, erotic terrain of his body from neck to feet, and on his back, a pack like the one Conrad had just put on. An air supply.

Ava took a second, two seconds, sorting the implications. Lyric had lured him from the base with a faked message, but he had gone out ready to enter the water. That must have been his plan from the start, or an alternative to use in an emergency. Either way, he was ready to do this. This was not some desperate last measure. Kaden had a way to reach the midget sub, despite the massive storm-churned surf.

As if he sensed her watching, he turned—and aimed a pistol at the bullet-scarred windshield through which she gazed.

Ava didn't think he could see her. It wasn't personal. Not yet.

She threw herself down between the seats as three more bullets struck the windshield. It gave way at last, spilling a handful of glass cubes across her legs.

"It's Kaden and Conrad!" she snapped at Matt as he lay on his back, reloading the shotgun amid a scatter of empty cartridges. "They're rabbiting."

"Two rounds left," he told her.

"And two sailors unaccounted for," she reminded him. One of Kaden's bodyguards had been hit in the first exchange of fire, but with the extent of the injury unknown, they had to assume that individual could still pull a trigger. A glance up showed her flames rising inside the other vehicle. "If they're alive, they're outside," she said with grim certainty.

Her skin crawled as she imagined the two creeping around the wrecked vehicles, positioning themselves to gun her down, along with Matt, the moment they exited.

She squeezed past the seat to the right-side front door. Got up on her knees and risked a glance out the open window, warm rain sluicing over her face and the fire's radiant heat pressing against her back.

No sign of the two sailors. But Conrad was running makai, deeper into the park, moving with the toddling awkwardness of a man who has doubled his weight since the last time he'd pushed his pace beyond a walk. In contrast, Kaden, in his black wetsuit, followed with a leopard's grace, shielding Conrad while looking back, watching for pursuit.

From these two clues—the wetsuit and their retreat into the park—Ava guessed where they were going. "It's the pirate tunnel," she told Matt, raising her voice to be heard over the pounding rain and the dull roar of the fire.

"The *what?*"

Now that she knew where to find Kaden, she could be patient. No point making herself a target. Better to wait, give him a few more seconds lead-time—and figure out where the two missing sailors were.

She told Matt, "There's a tunnel running through Komohana Point."

"That peninsula, at the end of the beach?" he asked as he crawled to the side window. He peered out, but kept checking the SUV's rear window, too.

"Right. The tunnel's twice as long as the peninsula. It goes out to deeper water. The lower section is flooded, but Kaden's got an air supply. He can use it to get out under the waves."

"No fucking way. This is a resort. A tunnel like that has to be sealed."

"Sure. Gates at both ends. But are they still locked?"

Recent experience said no.

She checked her weapon, reassuring herself that the magazine was full. Then she glanced at Matt. A ribbon of blood, bright in the gray light, seeped from his temple to his ear before it was diluted by the rain coming in the window. How hard had he hit his head? Was he dizzy? Did he have a concussion?

She didn't ask, because there was no way he could take a time-out now.

She hooked her fingers around the door latch. What did it mean that Kaden's sailors had not followed him? Were they dead, or injured? Or had they stayed behind to ensure there was no pursuit?

"Ready to exit?" she asked.

"Confirm. I go first. I'll cover. You get clear."

He pulled the latch, kicked the rear door open, and jumped out, firing off a round toward the back of the SUV—but he took a round at the same time. It knocked him against the open door, while an anguished scream erupted from behind the car.

Ava shoved her own door open and jumped out, dropping to her knees in the spongy lawn. The scream devolved to panicked gasps. She aimed her pistol in that direction and saw a figure on the ground, hunched over, face down . . . wearing a wetsuit. Kaden's sailors had also come prepared. She squeezed off a round. The sailor went limp.

A glance toward the front of the SUV revealed no movement. So she scrambled to Matt. He sat on the muddy ground, his back against the open door, head lolling, but he still held onto the shotgun.

"Talk to me, Matt."

"I'm alive," he croaked. "Vest stopped it." He grabbed the door-frame and started leveraging himself to his feet. "Why are you still here, anyway? Get going! I'll finish this and come behind you."

"Right."

One more glance around. Probably, the other shooter was badly injured and immobile—*fingers crossed*—but she'd have to take the chance of a bullet in the back.

Still gripping her pistol, she took off across the park's sodden, slippery lawn, her duty belt bouncing against her hips with every step. She didn't follow Kaden, but took a more direct route to the tunnel door.

Behind her, a pistol cracked. A fraction of a second later, the shotgun answered.

Ava had left her smart glasses in her pocket, but she still wore her tactile mic and its linked earbud. "Call Matt Domanski," she said as she ran beneath the wildly tossing canopy of a monkeypod tree.

The call went through. The ring tone pulsed. But she got no answer.

He's busy. That's what she told herself, unwilling to believe anything else.

Seconds later, her earbud beeped an alert.

It's him! Or maybe Lyric?

But it wasn't.

"Link to Dispatch established," her system's voice announced.

"Really?" she whispered.

Akasha must have persuaded Ivan to restore her credentials—temporarily anyway—putting her back inside the Coastal Authority network.

"Yes, really," a familiar voice assured her as she splashed down a concrete path slippery with thousands of pea-sized fallen banyan fruits. The dispatcher added, "You're having an exciting shift."

"You got that right," she answered, floating the words out on a quick low-voiced exhale—all the breath she could spare.

"Officers are on the way to secure the scene of the accident. And backup is inbound to assist you in the pursuit."

"Meet me at . . . pirate tunnel," she snapped between breaths, running uphill now, to the coastal promenade.

"The pirate tunnel? Confirmed. But why there?"

Ava stopped before she emerged onto the promenade. Squinting against the rain, she looked right and left, but saw no sign of Kaden, so she crept across the tiled walkway, to look down on the other side. As she moved, she sketched, in as few words as possible, her theory of the midget sub, concluding, "If he can get out under the waves, he can make it."

"Umm . . . *got it*," the dispatcher said doubtfully.

Wind rippled the water of the lagoon below her, the westernmost in the park. It tore at the fronds of the surrounding coconut trees, and lifted a mist of wet sand off the dunes.

Komohana Point lay just Ewa of her position. It had been made to look like a natural peninsula, constructed of concrete tinted and sculpted to imitate smooth dark lava rock. Pockets of sand softened the rock, and plantings of naupaka shrubs and small coconut palms gave it a tropical feel. Nothing in its outward appearance suggested the presence of a tunnel within.

On most days, kids swarmed the point, climbing the rocks and jumping from them into cool, deep water. On that day, the feeble morning light showed only a single visitor.

Daniel Conrad.

His red aloha shirt shone like a beacon in the gray rain. He stood with his back to her, at the far end of the bridge spanning the lagoon. Twenty feet farther on, a high grass-stabilized dune spilled over a few of the outlying false lava rocks at the start of Komohana Point. A footpath wound up past the dune's toe and into the rocks. She did not see Kaden. But past the roar of the wind, she clearly heard a distant harsh rattling of steel, like a madly wild prisoner shaking a cell door.

Staying low, using a hibiscus hedge for cover, she moved quickly toward the path that zig-zagged down to the lagoon and to the bridge that spanned it.

Dispatch spoke: "You were right, Ava. Subject in the wetsuit is at the tunnel door. But it's locked. I confirmed that. He's got no way to get it open."

Ava murmured, "He has a way."

Kaden wouldn't be there if he didn't have a way in. He would have planned for things to go wrong. He probably had multiple contingencies, but it had come down to this: a crazy scheme pursued out of the existential necessity of getting Daniel Conrad out ahead of the storm Sigrún meant to launch.

Now Ivan spoke in her earbud, just as she reached the end of the hedge. "Hold your position," he warned. "Do not go in alone. I'll be there with backup in a minute and a half."

She hunkered down, breathing hard, debating the wisdom of the order. "I don't think we have a minute and a half."

Conrad had already moved farther away, past the dune's toe and into the rocks. He could be at the tunnel door in twenty seconds.

The steel door was in a sheltered alcove that budded off the footpath. The alcove used to be shaded with a vine-covered pergola. Grand doors had guarded the pirate tunnel and only the most elite among the resort's guests had been able to buy their way in—to a dark, coldly air-conditioned passage decorated as a secret smugglers' cave, a haven of pirates. Not inappropriate, given that many of the guests had accumulated their wealth through government and regulatory corruption, and by hostile corporate takeovers.

Near the end of the peninsula, the tunnel descended to below sea level, emerging onto the seafloor. During the day, round windows in the tunnel walls had looked out onto sunlit waters. At night, underwater lights had illuminated the dark sea, drawing in planktonic creatures that in turn lured in feeding manta rays.

At the tunnel's end, a wide acrylic arch, like an aquarium tunnel, had housed an underwater restaurant, where diners enjoyed luxury meals surrounded by the sight of the living ocean.

The restaurant had been spectacular, but it had lasted less than a year. The seafloor proved unstable. Subsidence kept cracking the seals. Leaking salt water spoiled the kitchen. The restaurant closed, and its acrylic shell was removed, presumably sold off to some other resort. But the tunnel remained, flooded now where it passed below sea level. A heavy steel grate at the underwater end kept out large fish and curious tourists. At the tunnel's dry end, the grand doors had been replaced by a plain steel maintenance door, tan-colored, marked with a sign that read:

NO ENTRANCE
Authorized Personnel Only

The crazy-mad steel banging noise stopped. Conrad's back was still turned to Ava as he gazed up the footpath. Kaden must have told him to stay back.

"Ah, shit," she whispered to Ivan. "He's going to blow the door."

She darted from behind the hedge and down the path.

"No, Ava!" Ivan shouted in her ear. "Hold your position."

"Can't. He'll be inside the tunnel before you're here."

She followed the path across the strip of beach that bordered the lagoon, and then onto the bridge. The roaring wind and the pounding rain covered any sound she might have made—and Conrad's back remained turned. *Idiot.* Kaden had surely told him to guard their rear, but he was failing to do it.

Ava followed Conrad's gaze, up the footpath. From the midpoint of the bridge, she found she could just see into the alcove. When the banging started up again, this time accompanied by an eerie moan, she saw that it was caused by the steel door, jumping and rattling in its frame—as if trying to throw off the dual charges fixed beside the bolts that held it closed.

She saw Kaden too, a black silhouette in his wetsuit, retreating from the alcove.

She ducked below the bridge railing while bringing her pistol to bear. Slim odds of making the shot, given his distance and the raging wind, but she gripped the pistol in two hands and took aim anyway, forcing herself to see Kaden as just a target. Anonymous. Impersonal. Not the man she'd made love with less than twenty-four hours ago.

Praying for divine intervention, for the goddess of the storm to guide the bullet, she squeezed off a round. Intervention came, but not in the way she'd hoped.

Boom-boom!

Twin explosions, just as she took the shot, the dual concussion covering the sound of her pistol. The steel door slammed open, rebounding against rock, as if an imprisoned demon had shoved it out of the way.

Ava had missed her shot, but Kaden hadn't heard the pistol; he didn't know yet she was there.

He yelled at Conrad, "Come on! Follow me." And disappeared into the dark of the tunnel mouth.

Conrad didn't follow right away. Shoulders hunched, he turned to look back, revealing a face flushed and angry. Ava guessed he was not enthusiastic about Kaden's escape route. But she had no time to take satisfaction from that.

Conrad's gaze met hers. His flush deepened. His brows drew together as he reached for his shoulder holster.

Ava shot before he touched the weapon—and missed by inches. The bullet hit the concrete rock behind him, showering him with fragments. He stumbled, crab-walking toward the alcove, eyes wide, mouth open, fumbling to get his weapon out. She fired again. This time she didn't miss. The bullet hit him in the gut. He doubled over and disappeared inside the tunnel.

She sprinted in pursuit, off the bridge, up the footpath, then across the alcove to the tunnel mouth, gambling Conrad was not waiting just inside to ambush her.

No shots came out of the dark.

She pressed her back against the wet stone beside the open doorway. Her breath came hard and fast. Even so, she sensed a faint vibration in the stone, generated by the pounding of storm waves. And to her astonishment, a moaning wind was blasting out of the tunnel, tasting of salt. That wind had knocked the door open when Kaden blew the locks. But why was there wind in a tunnel closed by water?

She hesitated a second, pondering this, and in that interval, motion drew her gaze across the lagoon. Two motorcycles sped down the path from the promenade: Ivan and company.

Ava leaned over, looking cautiously into the tunnel, eyes narrowed against the outflowing wind. Little emergency lighting panels, set two feet apart on the tunnel floor, threw a red glow against walls made to look like rough lava rock. She did not see Conrad, but then the tunnel turned just twenty feet in. It was possible he was right around the bend—and surely he had gotten his pistol out of its holster by now.

The wind's hoarse voice worked together with a low rumbling roar of moving water reverberating from deeper in the tunnel, to cover any sound of footsteps, or strained breathing. But then the wind out of the tunnel hesitated, slowed, a held breath. Seconds ticked past—and the wind reversed, drawing atmosphere back into the tunnel with the sound of massive lungs.

Wave action. It had to be. With each massive swell, a surge of water shot up through the tunnel, displacing the air ahead of it, generating the wind—and when the sea pulled back, the wind reversed.

Ivan rode into the alcove, bringing his motorcycle to a skidding halt. "Dispatch reported you wounded the big one."

"Gut shot," she agreed. "I don't know if it's serious."

The second officer came in behind him. *Akasha.* When Ava realized it, she wanted to curse. What was Ivan thinking? Akasha had been out and on the move all night. She had to be exhausted—and Ava had so wanted to believe the young officer had gotten safely into shelter.

But all she said was, "Where's Gideon?"

Akasha answered, "Keeping himself busy at HQ."

"All right. We've got two perps, both armed, possibly with additional explosives. And we cannot let them reach the water. Let's go."

chapter

24

Ava led, stepping into the tunnel and moving quickly to the first turn, peering around it as the wind rushed at her back.

Nothing.

She moved farther in.

The walls cut off the sound of rain and of the storm outside, but the moaning, indrawn breath of wind remained, blended with a distant rumble of moving water, and overhung by Dan Conrad's booming voice: "I'm hit! I'm bleeding out. I can't go into the water." Hard to tell how far away.

Kaden answered, anger, even disgust, evident in his voice. "You want to live, you don't have a choice."

Ava advanced to the next turn as the argument continued.

"I'm telling you, Robicheaux. Call it off. Call it off *now*."

"*What?*"

Ava peered around the next bend, but did not see them.

"I'm not going to be able to make it out—"

"Then I leave you here."

"Damn you! I *am* Sigrún. This is my operation and you will do what I tell you."

"I am doing it—at the cost of my career, my love, my future, a hundred thousand lives. There is no going back, Daniel. We both swore to it. Our lives, our fortunes, our sacred honor—"

"I am ordering you—"

Bang!

Ava jumped as a gunshot echoed up the passage. She bumped against Akasha who had moved up, to stand just a breath behind her.

There was nothing more to hear of that argument.

Ava traded disbelieving looks with Akasha and Ivan. Then she mouthed, *Let's go.*

As she sprinted to the next bend, the wind reversed again.

Ava slowed only a little when she saw Conrad. He lay face up, his back arched over the pack that held his air supply. His aloha shirt, sagging with the weight of blood seeping from his belly wound, puckered open between the buttons, exposing the mound of his gut. But it was a head shot that had killed him. Kaden's bullet had shattered his broad forehead, leaving his wide, astonished eyes staring at the ceiling and his mouth frozen open in shock.

Coward!

In his own mind, Conrad must have cast himself as a hero, a great leader, imagining that this dangerous last-minute escape would become a story he'd tell over and over again, a testament to his manhood, to the testosterone-fueled determination that would reshape the world and place him at the helm of a new American hegemony—and to get there, he'd been okay with the murder of a city and a hundred thousand innocents.

But he hadn't truly believed in the cause because he'd abandoned it, the moment he'd begun to fear for his own survival.

Kaden's resolve would not be so easily broken.

There is no going back, Daniel.

She ran on, Akasha and Ivan just behind, with the sea's breath blowing in a gale against their faces.

The ragged passage began to slope down. The floor took on a wet sheen. And suddenly water a few inches deep surged past, carrying with it lines of foam tinged red from the upwelling illumination of the emergency lights.

A lull in the wind.

A moment of relative quiet admitting only the hiss of disintegrating foam and the splash of booted feet in shallow water.

Then the sea's breath reversed. An inhale. The gale at Ava's back as she chased the receding water.

In a low voice between ragged breaths, Ivan warned, "We're at the end of the peninsula."

Only seconds left to catch up with Kaden.

A wet sheen could now be seen on the walls, a high-water mark. At first, it reached only inches above the floor. But as the passage continued downward, the sheen rose—knee-high, and then thigh-high. Ava had to run more carefully, bounding over a clutter of debris: broken sticks, plastic floats, clumps of seaweed, even a tangle of fishing net—objects too large to have gotten past the gate at the tunnel's mouth, if the gate was closed as it should have been.

A tidal reek filled her lungs.

At the next turning, a change in the light. A faint gleam of gray daylight. Ava held up a hand, signaling to Akasha and Ivan that she meant to stop. She crouched at the turning. Peered around. The passage straightened, angling steeply down to a watery glimmer, the light welling up from below the surface, coming in through the tunnel's underwater windows.

Kaden waited down there, sheltered in a dark nook off the main passage, where the restaurant's reception podium used to be. He stood immersed to his waist in swirling water, with a respirator hanging over his shoulder—and he held a pistol aimed in her direction.

Ava ducked back behind the rock as Kaden fired. The bullet buzzed past where she had just been. It hit the wall, ricocheted. Akasha cried out, spasmed, then collapsed into silence. Ivan caught her, cushioned her, as Ava reached to find a pulse. "*Akasha.*" A whispered plea.

There! Her chest rose, fell, rose again. Just visible past her black, bloodied hair, a fragment of the spent bullet lay embedded in her scalp, looking like a bit of red bone in the glow of the emergency lights.

"Ava?" Kaden shouted, his confusion echoing up the tunnel. He had not expected her to be there. Who then had he been expecting?

Kaden answered her unspoken question: "It's on you, then, Domanski!"

"No, Kaden!" she shouted, peering out again. "Matt's not here. It's just me."

A blast of wind roared up the passage.

"Run, then!" Kaden shouted, backing deeper into the nook, bracing himself against its smooth walls. "The water's coming in. Get out *now*!

A flood surged from the submerged passage. It swept past him, toward her. She turned. Ivan already had Akasha's limp body over his shoulders in a fireman's carry. He started up the passage— too late. The incoming jet of water hit the wall where the passage turned, and then the flood rebounded, shooting up the tunnel, knocking them both off their feet.

Water churned past Ava's chin as the flood dragged her, scraping her thigh against the concrete, and slamming her shoulder into a wall. A slopping backwash slapped her in the face and she choked. Salt water burned in her nasal passages and in the back of her throat. But she kept her head up, kept her gaze on Akasha as Ivan lost his grip on her and the unconscious young officer went under, the current carrying both her and Ivan away up the tunnel.

Oh God, no. Not Akasha too.

Her recurring nightmare, brought to life. Another friend stolen away by a violent flood. Nolo, all over again.

No. Let me find her. Please. Please.

Instead, the current again slammed Ava against the tunnel wall. Her fingers clawed at the rough stone, defying her desire to follow Akasha, to find her, and bring her back above the surface before it was too late—because didn't she have to get to Kaden? He was the priority. A hundred thousand lives.

Right?

Ava clung to the bumps and knobs sculpted into the imitation lava rock, bracing with her legs, cursing silently at the weight of the armored vest she still wore. A quick last breath as the water rose to fill the passage and she was submerged.

The current slowed. Stilled. Eyes closed against the salt, Ava released her grip on the rock just long enough to pull off the vest so it couldn't drag her under. Then she grabbed the rock again.

Waiting . . . waiting . . . waiting . . . lungs burning.

Then—*at last!*—the current reversed. The water drained away as swiftly as it had come in. Ava got her head above the flood. She gasped and let go of the tunnel wall, riding the current back down the passage and around the bend.

Where was Kaden?

There. Still braced in the nook, his face wet, mouth twisted in anger and disbelief. He reached out a hand as the current swept her past him. She grabbed his wrist. His hand locked around her arm and he pulled her in against him as the water drained away.

Ava realized she'd lost her pistol in the flood, but she still had her duty belt and one free hand. She pulled her shockgun from its holster.

Kaden saw it and slapped it away into the receding current, his grip on her wrist so tight her hand had already gone numb. "He recruited you, didn't he? Matt Domanski. Do you know who he is?"

"Someone who's trying to stop you," she said in a low salt-roughened voice.

Kaden leaned in, eye to eye. "Domanski was Sigrún, too, Ava. He proposed this operation. I argued against it, but I was voted down—and then I was handed the duty to do it."

"And you accepted that duty!"

"I did. And in the end, Domanski lost his nerve. You should have let him drown."

"Don't do it, Kaden," she pleaded as her free hand groped for her folding knife, finding its handle still sticky with threads of webbing. "*Don't.* You know it's wrong." And in an echo of Daniel Conrad, "Call it off. Please."

"You want to think that's still possible."

Concealing the knife under the water, she struggled to get it open, but she couldn't do it with just one hand.

Kaden noticed her effort. He grabbed that wrist too and twisted her arm, forcing her to drop the knife, still folded.

"You can't stop it, Ava. It'll happen whether I'm there or not."

No. She did not want to believe that. It couldn't be true. The launch protocol required him to be there.

But as she gazed into his eyes, she saw it *was* true.

HADAFA should have foreseen Kaden's potential for subversion. It should have detected Sigrún's operation even before it was underway—but HADAFA had been subverted first, made into a false prophet. It had been corrupted by secret-keeping and the ability of those with deep access to modify, sequester, limit, or delete the information on which the system based its assessments.

HADAFA, designed to expose reality, had been used instead to cloak it.

The air grew still. The water swirled, pulling back farther than it had gone before. In that moment of suspended time before the next flood rushed in, Ava saw only truth in Kaden's eyes. Lyric and Matt had both been wrong. Sigrún, operating under a veil constructed by HADAFA, had cracked and compromised national security, rewriting the launch protocol so that it did not need to rely on the presence of any one man.

The revelation hit hard. Even if she stopped Kaden here and now, it wouldn't stop the nuke.

Hope stole away. She sagged in his arms, drained by fatigue and dragged down by the bitter inevitability of defeat.

Another gale of moist, salt-laden wind blasted past, pushed by the next incoming flood—and Gideon spoke to her, his flinty, cynical voice half-heard in the wind's white noise: *Angel Dust . . . drop it into the enclosed atmosphere of that submarine and no one will last long.*

Ava had not seen a way to do that—not then—but she'd taken the vacuum bottle with its ampules of Angel Dust and secured it to her duty belt.

The ocean surged in, curling around them. She wrenched her left hand free of Kaden's, but clung with her right as the current tried to carry her away.

The water rose to her shoulders, her neck. He held on to her, gripping the wall with one hand and bracing with his legs as he strove to keep them both within the shelter of the nook.

She groped for the vacuum bottle with her free hand, found it.

"You can survive this," he told her as she unscrewed the lid. "After I'm gone, just hold on to the wall. Wait for the water to go out and then run. Get to shelter. *Everyone* will be sheltering because of the storm. The death toll will be minimal. And afterward, it will be a new world. I promise . . ."

The lid came off. Her fingers fished in the canister. She clutched a floating ampule, a single ampule.

"Hold onto the wall," Kaden repeated.

Instead, she brought her free hand up, out of the water, holding the ampule hidden in curled fingers, her gaze fixed on his. "I loved you," she told him. And as if she meant to caress him, she brought her trembling hand closer to his face.

The current rested. The passage was flooded now almost to the ceiling.

Now or never.

She sucked in a sharp breath, filled her lungs. Then she used her thumb to pop the top off the ampule, snapping the powdery contents out into his face as she ducked under the water. Using her legs for leverage, she wrenched her wrist free of his grip and pushed away.

The current reversed, sucking her with unholy force down through the lower half of the passage.

An instantaneous mental calculation warned Ava not to resist. If she fought the current in the hope of riding the next inflow back to the upper passage, she would exhaust the oxygen in her system within seconds; she would be dead before the current reversed. So she arrowed her body instead.

Arms extended beyond her head, one hand atop the other, feet together. She kicked hard in mermaid fashion, shooting down the straight passage with her eyes open, salt-stung, her vision a watery blur but good enough to perceive the round windows on either side. Dull gray daylight gleamed behind them, guiding her. A gray glow of open water at the passage's end became her sacred goal. Reach it, and live.

With every kick, a mental chant:

Don't panic.

Don't panic.

Don't panic.

And don't think about the burning explosion building in your chest. You're going to make it out. You can do this. And the gate will be open. It has to be open. All the debris in the upper passage guarantees that. So *kick*, and—

Don't panic.

She saw the gate ahead of her. It was arched like the passage and it was open. *Open!* Standing open at an angle so that its dense steel mesh looked ominously solid in the blur of her vision. Sand swirled around it as the outflowing current eased.

Oh God, no.

Within seconds, the current would reverse. She had to be clear of the passage before then, or she would drown.

She kicked harder, pulled at the water with her hands. Darkness loomed on the periphery of her vision. She ignored it, all her intent, her effort fixed on the necessity of reaching open water.

Don't panic.

She shot past the gate, into a cloud of sand grains stirred up from the shallow sea floor by an incoming wave. Within that veil, just feet away, two dark aquatic shapes—six feet? seven feet? eight feet long? One darted toward her. She recoiled, tumbling back as the force of the wave took her, shoulder crunching against the sandy bottom.

Deep instinct controlled her now. Survival mattered most. She kicked off the sea floor, rocketing toward a foam-laced gray daylight even as her brain noted the presence of a third dark shape appearing out of nowhere to join the other two.

Ava burst past the surface into a driving rain. She had emerged in the long trough between two massive breaking waves.

She filled her lungs with a wrenching gasp, forcing air past a salt-swollen throat, and then she blew it all out again. Breathed in, breathed out. In and out, forcing oxygen into her blood stream.

Then she ducked under the water again, diving for the bottom ahead of the oncoming wave, so that the brutal chaos of its foaming break passed above her.

Even so, the rolling force of the wave dragged the bottom, tumbling her. She didn't fight it. She relaxed in its grip, shaping herself to its flow, riding it, kicking at the water and pulling when she could, surfacing only when the boiling white water had safely passed.

Cold rain sluiced over her upturned face as she breathed, deliberately hyperventilating. The weight of her duty belt forced her to kick hard and paddle at the water just to stay at the surface. She could have popped the buckle, but she didn't, because the belt's weight would make it so much easier to return to the relative safety of the bottom.

She dove again as the next breaking wave bore down. She rode its vortex, swimming when she could. And when it left her behind, she surfaced. Breathed. Looked for the next oncoming wave—still several seconds away—and then turned to gauge the distance to the shore.

The smooth back of the last wave loomed like a blue mountain. Beyond it, she saw the peaks of crumbling dunes, and then hotel towers. Off to her left, at least a hundred feet away, maybe more, waves crashed and fountained against the artificial stone of Komohana Point.

Astonishment coursed through her. The usual longshore current ran east to west, from Diamond Head toward Ewa. If she'd been caught in that, she would have been swept west past the point, toward the Ala Moana seawall—and away from any chance of ever making it alive to shore. But in that raging sea, the usual current had reversed, running west to east, carrying her with it as it paralleled Waikīkī Beach.

She drew another breath, and dove, stroking hard under water, then tumbling in the surge of the passing wave.

Usually, the largest waves came in sets with a relative lull between them. Ava would have waited for that lull before trying for the shore, but in that wild sea she could not judge the wave height. Her only strategy was to keep going. Dive, then swim hard underwater as the seafloor grew shallower—and then it became so shallow there was nowhere left to dive.

Pummeling white water swept her up, rolled her, slammed her against the bottom, lifted her again. Sand got into her mouth, her ears, her eyes. Then the worst of it passed. All along her body she sensed the force, the direction, the velocity of the foaming water. Flattening her hands, she used them like fins to stabilize her body in a wild ride as the wave carried her up the beach. When she felt her momentum slow, she struggled to get her feet beneath her, finally standing up into wind-driven rain.

The wave reversed. Its powerful backwash streamed past, threatening to drag her back into the sea. She leaned in to counterbalance, her shoes sinking into water-logged sand, helping to anchor her. As the water subsided, she pulled her feet free and staggered up a beach strewn with bits of vegetation and plastic, small fish, crushed jellies, and even the long, pale blue corpse of a sea serpent. Seaweed trailed from her duty belt.

She looked for a path inland.

Wave action had undermined the dunes, collapsing their seaward slopes, leaving towering cliffs of sand that she didn't dare try to climb. With that much sand, if it gave way, she would die beneath it. Instead, she ran down the beach searching for a low point, where a paved path had been.

Another wave washed up, fountained past her ankles—a small wave, compared to those marching in behind. The roar of the sea filled her mind and she felt the power of those waves as a vibration in her chest.

There!

A low point in the sand cliff, only a little higher than her head. Ava bolted for it as a massive wave roared onto the beach, flooding it with white water. She clawed at the vertical face, using hands and feet. The sand gave way as she scrambled over what proved to be a narrow ridge, formed by the collapse of the dunes on either side. She splashed down onto a sand-covered path where rainwater pooled. Momentum carried her on for a few more steps before she dropped to her knees, bent over in exhaustion.

After a minute, after her breathing calmed, she remembered the canister on her belt and reached for it, fingers groping inside. *Empty.* All the ampules gone.

She hoped the sea would open them and kill the spores of Angel Dust.

Her tactile mic was gone too, of course.

And Kaden was gone.

She'd seen him, hadn't she? That dark shape that had seemed to come out of nowhere. He'd emerged from the tunnel just seconds behind her. Two divers had been there waiting to meet him.

So he would live, for a time.

And what of Akasha and Ivan? Had they made it out of the tunnel?

And where was Matt?

Kaden's bitter voice echoed in her memory: *Domanski was Sigrún, too, Ava. He proposed this operation.*

But Matt worked for Lyric. The call for Sigrún to carry out a false-flag operation must have begun with her.

Ava straightened up as best she could in the fierce wind. She looked up at the hotel towers, with their windows of hurricane glass. There, only a little farther east, the Pacific Heritage Sea Tower.

She got to her feet and stumbled through the dunes to the line of lagoons, wet sand pelting her legs. Palm fronds, ripped from the whiplashing coconut trees, cluttered the path. She started across the bridge, her head down against the wind until someone yelled her name.

"Ava!"

Looking up, she saw Ivan running toward her—and dread slammed in. "Where's Akasha?"

"Upstairs, with a massive headache. She'll be okay."

They met in the middle of the bridge. Ivan gripped her shoulders, gazing into her eyes as if he could read some truth there, his own eyes narrowed against the rain. "When you didn't come out of that tunnel I thought we'd lost you." His grip tightened. "You went after him?"

She nodded.

"Damn it, Ava. Do you know how crazy that was?"

"No choice in it. Had to try."

A hollow note in his voice: "You couldn't stop him . . . could you?"

"In the end I didn't want to. I hope he made it out. I hope he's taking out his regulator and coughing out Angel Dust into the cold air of *Denali*'s lock."

If Kaden had breathed in the spores and if the spores were viable—then how long would it be before the deadly fungus spread throughout his skeleton crew?

chapter

25

Ava stood in the locker-room shower, hot water sluicing over her body long past the time when all the salt, sand, and bits of seaweed had been washed away.

Still not warm.

She shivered as she dressed in the spare uniform she kept in her locker: long-sleeve black athletic shirt with her name and the glinting badge part of the weave, and black knee-length cargo shorts. Ivan could fire her tomorrow. If they had a tomorrow.

She combed her wet hair, then picked up her shoes, rinsed clean in the shower but still wet. Shoes in hand, she rode the dedicated elevator up to the operations center.

Ivan had warned her, when they were safe in the ready room, "From now until the storm has passed, no one goes out no matter what."

"No matter what we see on camera?"

"Yes."

"But you went out after me—and you saw me on a camera, didn't you?"

"Gideon spotted you. But the wind hasn't reached hurricane force yet."

"When it does, maybe we should turn the cameras off, so we're not tempted."

"No. I won't close my eyes. I know you don't want to, either."

The elevator doors opened. Ava stepped out past the little Christmas tree with its colorful LED lights, and into the operations center, where she was met with a barrage of hugs, good wishes, and the repeated phrase, *We thought we'd lost you.* Besides Ivan, there was a shift supervisor, a dispatcher, a researcher, and two officers on duty—all from day shift. The rest of the staff had been sent home.

Akasha lay in a cot beside the observation window, her head propped on a stack of blankets, wound glue gleaming on her scalp where her dark hair had been clipped away.

She gazed at Ava with the wide-eyed look of someone who'd been cursed with a vision of apocalypse and couldn't get it out of her head. "It was all real, then?" she asked as Ava crouched beside the cot.

Ava nodded. "It was real. *Is* real."

Gideon sat cross-legged on the floor at the foot of the cot, a tablet on his lap. He studied Ava with narrowed eyes. "You figured out a way to get the Angel Dust on that submarine." A twitch of his lips that might have been a smile. "Hope it works."

She turned, to gaze out past the rain-hammered windows to the raging sea . . . until she remembered to ask, "Where's Matt?" A pistol had gone off as she ran through the park—but his shotgun had instantly answered. "He's okay, isn't he? I need to talk to him. Confirm some things."

"Too late for that," Gideon said. "They got him. He's dead."

"*Oh* . . . please, no."

Ivan came over and confirmed it. "The two armed males in the vehicle you were pursuing—both were found with gunshot wounds, severely injured. But one could still pull a trigger." Ivan touched his throat. "Domanski took a bullet right here. It's too bad. I had questions for him, too."

This news grieved Ava—she'd liked Matt—but it stoked her anger, too, and left her feeling cheated. She wanted the truth, *all* the truth, and with Matt gone, she didn't think she'd ever get it.

"What about the two sailors?" she asked. "What's their status?"

Ivan shrugged. "Both were critical when they reached the hospital, but we're not going to know any more than that. The navy's claimed them, and they're untouchable."

"I found your secret agent," Gideon volunteered.

"You did?" That was something. "Show me."

Ava moved to his side, kneeling to look at his tablet. It displayed a still image, taken at a distance, of a tall woman who resembled Lyric only in her height. This woman was heavyset, with large breasts, her hair thick, long, and wound into a neat twist down her back. "That's not her."

"It is," Gideon said. "Here."

He shifted to a night shot taken along Nimitz Highway. "Image is from a public traffic camera. This is right after she disappeared from that settlement. See, she gets into a cab. And then . . ." He scrolled through a succession of still shots: a cab on the airport viaduct; a cab on the airport exit ramp; a cab at the curb of the airport terminal, with a heavyset woman exiting it.

"She had her get-away set up," Gideon concluded. "She must have hacked the cab, pre-loaded it with her gear, and then pulled off a quick change on the way to the airport. Voila! When she gets out, she looks and walks like someone different. But it's her."

Ava looked doubtfully at Ivan.

"HADAFA denies any connection between the two women," he told her. "But I've gone over the sequence and I'm convinced. Whoever that woman is, she's got high-level connections and a security rating that lets her use HADAFA to fake her identity, or hide it altogether."

Stolen credentials? Or legitimate? Either way, it only proved again that HADAFA could not be relied on to interpret truth.

Ava asked, "Where did she go after that?"

"Into the terminal," Ivan said. "That's what the outside camera showed. But by the time we got authorization to access the internal surveillance, the subject wasn't there. HADAFA had scrubbed her presence from the record."

Ava grimaced. "And changing her appearance protected her from private cameras and eyewitness recollections. So we don't know if she caught another cab, or got picked up . . ."

"Or if she had a seat booked on a flight out of here," Ivan finished for her. "She could be anywhere, this time tomorrow."

Ava squeezed her eyes shut as a blush rose in her cheeks, pushed by a heated combination of embarrassment and anger.

Deep breath.

She stood up again and stepped to the window, to look out at the storm. Lightning flickered on the horizon. "We talked to her, Matt and I. She claimed she'd recruited a Marine general who was standing guard at the door of the facility where she was working." Her stomach knotted. "She was probably drinking champagne in first class at the time."

Ava pressed her fingers to the heavy, hurricane-proof glass, steadying herself as a mental haze descended over her. What was real? What was a lie? And who was Lyric, really? What side had she been on? What was her game?

Kaden had said Matt was first to propose the idea of using a nuke to kick off a "cleansing war."

Had Matt done it at Lyric's direction?

Had the puppet master been playing both sides of the game from the very start? Had Lyric ignited the scheme and then, when it got out of hand, scrambled to quash it?

And when would it be game-over?

Despite Ivan's philosophy of eyes-open, Ava resolved not to watch any camera feeds, fearing she'd see the ghosts of two little girls drowning all over again. Instead, she got a couple of blankets out of the supply room and made herself a nest on the west side of the observation deck, alongside the floor-to-ceiling window. From that vantage, she could look out over the shoreline, where the wind tore at the summits of the dunes while the storm surge and the crashing waves eroded them from their base. And—between the passing rain bands—she could see the west half of Waikīkī, along with Ala Moana, Kaka'ako, the airport, and Pearl Harbor beyond.

Stupid, to sit by a window waiting for a nuclear detonation. Ivan pointed this out. "I want everyone not on duty to move downstairs. It's safer there, with no windows."

Ava helped Akasha down, but then she returned to the observation deck, and bundled up again in her blankets. One of the officers brought her a hot meal from the kitchen. Sometime after that she dozed, only to waken, startled, her fingers clawing at the floor as she felt the building swaying. Wind roared past the window. Rain hammered. Lightning flashed. She could not see more than a quarter mile and it was so dark outside it looked as if dusk had fallen.

"What time is it?" she shouted, voice cracking in panic.

Someone answered from the pit: "11:30 AM."

"My God."

Was the city still out there? Or had it already happened?

Surely I would know if it had happened . . .

She walked around the observation deck, trying to calm her racing heart. Her only company, the researcher and the dispatcher still at their stations in the pit, monitoring the video feeds.

"How are the cameras holding out?" Ava asked them.

The answer came back, "Surprisingly well. We're prepared this time. It's not going to be like Nolo. We're going to get through this, and be okay."

Ava wanted to believe that.

Satellite images mapped the progress of the hurricane. Ava dropped into the pit every twenty minutes or so to check the latest. Huko stuck to its projected path, its center on course to plow across O'ahu. But it moved faster than expected, as if it wanted to escape any part in Sigrún's conspiracy.

In late afternoon, everyone came up from downstairs to witness as the eye of the hurricane skirted the coast. The curtain of rain drew back first, and then the wind abruptly eased. Sunlight broke through. Blue sky appeared directly overhead, decorated in streamers of thin high-altitude clouds. But the ocean still raged, and all around there stood an ominous dark cloud wall.

Ava watched the sky, though she knew if the missile came it would be too small, too fast for her eyes to follow.

After half an hour, the wind returned, shifting direction, roaring again like a jet engine, and within a few minutes every tree along the promenade and every coconut palm around the now sand-filled lagoons snapped and broke. Branches hurtled through the air and broken stumps wobbled on the lawns . . . but somehow they were still alive. The city still lived. The missile had not come.

Not yet.

The light faded long before the sun went down. Ava continued to watch and wait, well into the night.

Akasha came up to stand beside her. "It's almost over."

Ava nodded agreement. She didn't want to say it out loud, but surely it was too late for Sigrún to strike. They'd waited too long. They'd lost the cover of the storm. Or maybe, in the end, Kaden had changed his mind?

She hoped that was the reason.

Successive satellite images showed Huko steaming away to the north at a furious pace. The wind's roar eased and the clouds broke apart. The moon and a handful of stars shone through, mirrored by a few surviving lights out beyond Harbor Station. Lightning still flickered, but far away.

Her gaze shifted to the shoreline below, visible now in the moonlight, and barely recognizable.

All up and down the length of Kahanamoku Coastal Park, the massive dunes had been worn down, reduced to low berms. Their sand, redistributed inland, had filled in the lagoons and frosted the promenade.

Beyond the eroded dunes the ocean still churned, white foam lacing the dark water. Tumbling waves washed up a wide beach strewn with debris, some of it identifiable, even at this distance. A tree trunk, a couple of tires, the broken-off prow of a small boat, a long section of two-by-four. Most of it, though, lay anonymous in moonlight.

Directly off the tower in which she stood, the white hull of a crushed fishing boat lay grounded in the shallows, each incoming wave crashing over it, throwing spray into the air. Off to the east, a fountain of white water marked another casualty.

Ava crossed the observation deck to get a better look. Diaphanous moonlit clouds scudded across the night sky above Diamond Head's familiar profile. Halfway to that landmark, a massive dark shape lay in the wave-churned shallows, far bigger than the fishing boat.

Another fountain of spray caught the moonlight as a wave broke against it.

Ava's tired mind strove to understand what she was seeing. Was it an exposed reef? The beached carcass of a great sperm whale? A freighter's overturned hull?

Recognition swept over her.

"Oh God," she whispered, flush with horror.

She rushed for the rapid-access ladder. Slid down it into the pit. "Get a tracker drone into the air," she snapped at the dispatcher. "We've got a large vessel aground. Vicinity of the Imperial Garden. I want eyes on it now."

"Hey, that's *Denali!*" Akasha shouted from the observation deck. "It's gotta be. *Denali* has run aground!" She appeared at the top of the ladder. "You did it, Ava. It worked."

Ava rejected this with a wave of her hand. "We don't know what happened. We don't know for sure that's *Denali*. And if it is, we still don't know what went on inside that hull."

Ava meant to find out, though. She would do her best to find out, before the navy locked the truth away behind impenetrable walls of classification.

She headed for the elevator. "I'm going out there. Look for survivors."

"Yeah, I'm going too."

Ava turned back in time to see Akasha slide down the ladder—and wince as she hit the floor.

"You're injured, you idiot."

"And you don't have working comms," the dispatcher reminded her. "You can't go out, either."

True enough, about the comms. Ava had come ashore with her smart glasses still in her pocket, but they'd failed to turn on. Her tablet and tactile mic had been lost in the water.

Akasha caught up with her, passed her. She slipped her smart glasses on, then slapped the button to open the elevator doors.

"You're in no condition to go," Ava insisted.

"I'm going."

The glint in her eyes promised an argument Ava didn't have time for. "Fine. You're my comms."

She turned back to the dispatcher. "If you need to talk to me, relay through Akasha or through the tracker drone. Record everything. And keep a local copy. Keep it somewhere HADAFA can't reach."

Open-mouthed shock from the dispatcher. "How am I supposed to—"

"I don't know," Ava interrupted. "But I know you can figure it out—and let Ivan know where we're going."

She joined Akasha aboard the elevator. They descended with ear-popping speed. In the ready room, she picked up her dive mask and her regulator. Akasha started to do the same.

"*No.*" This time, Ava insisted. "You are not going in the water."

As she spoke, the elevator opened again, delivering Ivan to the ready room. "Neither of you are going in the water," he said as he stepped out.

Ava grabbed a scuba pack from the wall rack anyway. "Got no choice, Ivan. We've got to check for survivors."

"That's your excuse?"

"Sworn duty." With practiced hands, she secured the regulator's first stage to the pack, adding, "No real hazard from Angel Dust, since I'm bringing my own air."

He tried one more time. "You're too tired for this."

"We're all tired." She looked up. Met his gaze. "You coming with me or not?"

He gritted his teeth. His lip curled. "Hell, why not?" He got his own dive equipment out, grabbed another scuba pack. "I want to see how badly we were played. Let's get there, before the navy shows up."

They took the motorcycles, weaving past fallen trees and broken lamp posts, headlights supplementing moon glow as they made their way down to the beach.

The ocean still churned and rumbled. Waves still broke hard against the sand, carrying debris up and down the shallow slope of the beach—but the waves no longer reached all the way to the eroded feet of the dunes.

Left behind by the ocean's retreat was a strip of compact wet sand where Ava could ride, dodging mounds of fishing nets tangled with plastic trash and seaweed. Driftwood too, and green branches, palm fronds, even a plastic bumper cover from a car and a section of asphalt-tiled roof. Chunks of foam insulation cluttered the sand, along with dozens of coconuts, and dead fish everywhere. Each object appeared briefly in the beam of her headlight as she zig-zagged past.

Akasha called out from behind her: "Hope none of this shit is radioactive!"

Ava kept on, to where the submarine lay just offshore. Then she brought her bike to a skidding stop.

They weren't the only ones to have noticed the grounded vessel. A small crowd of fifteen or so, a mix of hotel staff and guests, had ventured outside. They'd gathered just above the reach of the waves, talking excitedly among themselves, talking on phones, taking videos as another breaker churned past the sub's black hull. No one had entered the water yet, not that Ava could see, anyway.

"Akasha, secure this area. Keep everyone back."

"Got it."

Ivan said, "Amber and Van are a couple minutes behind us. They'll help you set up a perimeter."

Another breaker rolled in. Ava watched it sweep the length of the hull. It took some time. The vessel was *huge*. Maybe four hundred feet in length? The sail towered into the night sky, a cluster of sensor masts rising above it.

No visible name, of course. This was a stealth weapon, its curved hull a black box designed to hide its very existence within the lightless depths of the ocean. A deadly weapon, capable of taking the lives of millions. Now awkwardly exposed.

What had gone on inside? Who had caused the vessel to run aground? And why?

Ava's mind raced with hypothetical scenarios. She envisioned a faction, struck by the enormity of what they were about to do, rising up, initiating an internal struggle for control of the boat. Or maybe it had been a single crew member, stirred to action by a troubled conscience as the moment drew near, committing an irrevocable act of sabotage.

Or had her own desperate move succeeded? If success was the right word for what she'd done. Had there been panic among Kaden's crew as spores of Angel Dust spread among them?

Red light washed over, accompanied by the hum of a tracker drone, the sound abruptly audible over the grumbling waves. She looked up at the device hovering six feet overhead. The dispatcher spoke through it: "HADAFA has confirmed the identity of the submarine as USN *Denali*. A navy helicopter is incoming. No one is to approach the stranded vessel ahead of the navy's arrival."

Ava scanned the horizon for navigation lights but didn't see any. She didn't hear the rhythmic beat of an approaching engine. "They're not close," she concluded. "And we need to check for survivors."

"Agreed," Ivan said. "Get a light on that hull."

Out over the water, a light flicked on: the white search beam of a second tracker drone. As the froth of a passing wave drained away, the beam explored the black hull, beginning at the prow, sweeping toward the stern.

No one visible. Hatches still closed.

"No panicked egress," Ava observed. "And the sensor masts are deployed. Someone would have to do that, don't you think?"

"I don't know. Maybe it's an automated system. Or maybe they *are* okay in there. If so, they'll wait for the surf to drop before they open up. They won't want to flood the interior."

Ava pulled on her mask, her voice going nasally as it sealed against her face. "We have to check it out. They've got a three-sixty view through one of those masts. They'll see us coming. If they need help, if they're desperate enough, they'll open up."

"Yeah, I want to know too."

Fins in hand, Ava followed a retreating wave down the beach, the weight of the scuba pack dragging at her shoulders. Popping the regulator into her mouth, she strode for deep water, slipping on the fins between one wave and the next. The tide helped to pull her out.

A few minutes later, she surfaced alongside the submarine—and heard the beat of helicopter rotors over the sound of the surf. At least two incoming. Probably three. She looked around for Ivan, but didn't see him. No time to wait.

Another swell was rolling in, not quite breaking. She let it lift her up along *Denali*'s smooth side. Just like riding a swell up and out of the ocean along a rocky shore. She'd done it a hundred times. This time, she hauled out at the midpoint of *Denali*'s long hull.

Never turn your back on the ocean.

She checked for the next swell. Saw it rising at the stern of the submarine, but not high enough to submerge the hull. She slipped off her fins and stood, feeling *Denali* subtly shift as the wave rolled past. One tracker hovered with its spotlight fixed on the hatch just behind the sail. The other dropped close to Ava. The dispatcher spoke through it. "Motion detected. Someone's coming out."

Ava bit down hard on her respirator and moved toward the hatch as it began to lift, pushed slowly by a trembling hand. A man emerged to his shoulders within the white glare of the spotlight, his face familiar despite the reddened eyes and a complexion mottled with capillaries freshly burst just beneath the skin. Fuzzy white flecks infested the dark line of a cut in his lower lip. *Tyrone Ohta.*

Did he know who she was? Could he recognize her, standing outside the spotlight's narrow beam, with her mask still on and her lips sealed around the respirator that she held clenched between her teeth?

No.

A grunt of sound came from him as if he meant to speak, but then he ducked his head, coughing hard as the next crashing swell showered them both in spray.

Salt water ran down his cheeks when he looked up at her again. What did he see, but a silent dark silhouette? She must have appeared to him as a co-conspirator, come to hear his report before the official navy arrived. "Robicheaux refused," he told her in a hoarse voice so charged with fury it rose easily over the low roar of the surf. He coughed again, then looked up in the direction of the approaching helicopters. "Tell them that. He betrayed us. He refused to let us enter the code."

A hand grasped Ava's upper arm. She jerked her arm away, ready to dive back into the dark sea. But it was only Ivan. Sparks of reflected light glinted in the glass face of his mask. No way to speak without removing their respirators, and neither dared to do that. Instead, Ivan motioned with his head: *Come away.*

Together they slipped back into the cool dark anonymity of the night sea. Fins on, and then a sprint for the beach while she turned over in her mind Tyrone Ohta's furious testimony: *Robicheaux refused.*

She would never know why. Maybe, with the moment imminent and real, Kaden's conscience had finally overcome the toxic righteousness that had let him join Sigrún. Or maybe his own impending death, with Angel Dust blooming in his lungs, had opened his eyes to the gross horror of what he'd agreed to do.

Or maybe Kaden had changed his mind for her.

She peeled off her mask as she reached the shallows, salt water washing away her salty tears. A wave foamed toward her. She ducked under it, then waded ashore beneath the deafening racket of the navy helicopters. A glance back showed rescue swimmers already dropping into the water.

Ivan had come ashore. She rushed to join him beyond the reach of the waves. "Ivan! We need to warn the navy that sub is a biohazard zone."

"Word's gone out," he assured her. "They know."

chapter

26

HUKO HAD BEEN kinder to the island than anyone had expected—or maybe they really had been ready this time. The new and newly refurbished hotels, the dome houses, the solar farms, and the distributed electrical grid had all survived with minimal damage. The roads were a mess and the farm fields trashed, but they could be cleaned up and set right. More landslides had ravaged the valleys above Honolulu, but those were designated hazard zones anyway, and no one lived there anymore.

The navy began preparations to tow *Denali*, issuing a statement claiming an onboard emergency had forced the submarine to surface during the storm. Casualty figures were classified.

Ava made it back to her apartment near noon. She'd signed her lease agreement knowing the building was rated to only cat 2, so it wasn't a surprise to find the windows shattered and the interior a wreck. Still, it was strange to think that Hurricane Huko had gone through her dresser drawers, pulling each one out, upending it on the floor, and making off with all her electronic gear.

She wondered if the storm had ravaged her off-site backups too, but with no functional gear remaining to her, she couldn't check. Either way, there would have been nothing significant to find. Kaden had not shared his secrets with her.

Moving mechanically, almost overcome by the oppressive heat and the humidity, she gathered her sodden clothes and a few other surviving possessions. Then she crossed the street to Harbor Station, where she picked up a new phone from a still-operable vending machine.

The streetcars remained garaged, and taxis couldn't negotiate the debris-filled roads, but Ivan had let her check out a motorcycle. She rode it back to Waikīkī, returned it to the ready room, then walked around to the Pacific Heritage Sea Tower's public lobby. An exhausted-looking desk clerk, wearing an aloha shirt and a rumpled smile, booked her into a room, giving her an excellent rate now that most reservations had been canceled.

After calling her daughters and assuring them she was fine, Ava slept for fifteen hours, waking to the news that the president had reversed his position and refused to authorize the signing of the handover treaty—a peculiar change of heart. She had to believe that news of Sigrún's operation had finally reached him. Perhaps someone on his staff had taken him aside, explaining just how close his administration had come to self-inflicted disaster.

Of course, not signing had its cost. Relations with China would be fraught and filled with saber-rattling for years to come.

Abandoning the treaty also did not guarantee domestic peace. Hawai'i's people had seen their land, their lives, and the lives of their families offered up in exchange for debt relief. Hard to get over a betrayal like that. Hōkū Ala's activists would work to ensure that no one forgot—and demands for independence would surely accelerate. Ava sensed years of turmoil ahead. But maybe something better would follow?

She reported in early for work, needing the distraction. But Captain Isaiah Mahoi met her offer to help out with evening shift with narrow-eyed suspicion. "Eh, Ava. Things got a little rough, last time you took an early assignment. Maybe you should just work with dispatch for a couple of hours."

"I promise to stay out of trouble," she told him.

Eventually he sent her outside, where she worked with other officers, patrolling the strip's public areas, writing up damage reports, and working to replace broken security cameras. On the beach, a fleet of small bulldozers operated under lights to clear debris and rebuild the dunes. It wouldn't be long before the hotels started to fill again. They needed to be ready.

Two more days passed before an FBI agent knocked on the

door of her hotel room. Ava let her in, sure that she'd be out of a job soon, and that she faced years of legal issues. So be it. She wanted to tell what she knew anyway.

"But not in some secret court," Ava warned the agent. "I want a promise I'll be able to testify at a public hearing, without HADAFA filtering the reality of what I have to say."

Too much information was hidden away from the public eye, classified, for no legitimate reason. Sigrún had thrived in that culture of secrecy, a hidden infestation, evolving in dark corners and spreading unseen.

Ava said, "Let me do what I can to let in a little light."

Acknowledgments

After spending two years in the far-future working on the Inverted Frontier series, I wanted my next novel to be closer to home. *Pacific Storm* is the result.

I owe a huge thank you to my freelance editor Judith Tarr, who helped me to make this a better book, and to Sherwood Smith, who served as copy editor.

Thanks are also due to my beta readers, Dallas Nagata-White, Ilima Loomis, Ken Malphurs, and Ron Nagata. Ron went on to read the manuscript three times to make sure everything was just right, and Ken continued to patiently answer technical questions right up until the day I declared the novel "done." Thank you also to Gabby Hirata for her help with Chinese names. Any remaining errors and deficiencies are my own.

Last but never least, thank you to everyone who's taken the time to read this book, or others I've written. Your support and your encouragement are deeply appreciated.

Linda Nagata
October 2020

Made in the USA
Columbia, SC
12 October 2020

22657114R00159